WATCH YOUR MOUTH

ALSO BY DANIEL HANDLER

The Basic Eight

WATCH YOUR MOUTH

DANIEL HANDLER

THOMAS DUNNE BOOKS ■ ST. MARTIN'S PRESS ■ NEW YORK

The author would like to thank the following people: *Lisa Brown, Charlotte Sheedy, Melissa Jacobs, Ron Bernstein, Rebecca Handler, Louis and Sandra Handler, Joseph and Kit Reed, David and Barbara Brown, Gregg Sullivan and Susan Rich.*

Furthermore, the author would like to remind readers that *Watch Your Mouth* is a novel. The people contained in this book are fictional characters, and the things they do constitute a work of fiction. The author cannot imagine that anyone would think otherwise, but it takes all kinds.

THOMAS DUNNE BOOKS.
An imprint of St. Martin's Press.

Book design by Michelle McMillian

Library of Congress Cataloging-in-Publication Data

Handler, Daniel.
    Watch your mouth / Daniel Handler.
      p. cm.
    ISBN 0-312-20940-1
    1. Pittsburgh (Pa.)—Fiction. 2. College Students—Fiction. 3. Camp counselors—Fiction. 4. Jewish families—Fiction. I. Title.

PS3558.A4636 W38 2000
813'.54—dc21   00-029678

First Edition: July 2000

10 9 8 7 6 5 4 3 2 1

PART ONE

Brother Singulars, we are misplaced in a
generation that knows not Joseph. We flee
before the disapproval of our cousins, the
courageous condescension of our friends
who gallantly sometimes agree to walk the
streets with us, from all them who never any
way can understand why such ways and not
the others are so dear to us, we fly to the
kindly comfort of an older world accus-
tomed to take all manner of strange forms
into its bosom. . . .

—GERTRUDE STEIN,
The Making of Americans

THERE'S NEVER BEEN an opera about me, never in my entire life. Normally this wouldn't bother me. There hasn't been one about *you,* either, and besides, I'm still young. If my life were a play, this would be the last few minutes before the lights lowered and everything began. The audience would be milling around—the older couples in formal, non-funky suits with pearls hanging around the women's necks like drops of semen, and the younger people in black shirts and jeans because the formality of theater is an elitist tyrannical paradigm and lots of people in the clothes they wore to work because, frankly, by the time they got home and jumped into the shower and changed their clothes they'd either be late, which they *hate,* or they'd be on time but so stressed out that they couldn't really enjoy it, and frankly, if you're going to pay that much for tickets what's the use if you're not going to enjoy it, so what they do is just wear some slightly dressier work clothes to work and then go right to the theater, locking the briefcase in the trunk and sometimes even having time for a cocktail or something, but not for dinner because they hate wolfing down dinner and rushing to the theater, it's so stressful, they might as well go home and shower and change if they want to be stressed out before the show even *starts*.

This is some snatch of lobby-talk that Stan, the manager of the Pittsburgh Opera, overheard and never forgot. *And* never forgot to repeat. "*That's* our audience, Joseph," he said to me. "Just regular working folk. We have to create opera for them that's not just interesting but *fascinating, mesmerizing.* So that they transcend all the stress about whether to change or where to have dinner or parking or whatever, and really *hear* the music. That's what opera's *for*. Do you have any more of those candies?"

Because this *is*, you know, an opera. Fiction, like all operas: a lie, but a lie is sort of a myth, and a myth is sort of a truth. All summer long I was watching things happen with Cynthia Glass and her family that were melodramatic, heart-wrenching, and absurdly—*truly*—tragic. Dire consequences lurked around their house like the growl of cellos when the jealous fiancé, or the enraged father, or the Old Spirit of the Mountains descends on the lovers, flushed with horniness and the effort of singing over a fifty-piece orchestra *La Forza Dei Glasses. Le Nozze Di Incest. Cyn.* They *were* an opera and now the lights are lowering and here we are, reader or readers. No need to stress. An opera in book form is more convenient than the real thing, because you can eat when you want and wear whatever pleases you. Nothing, maybe. Read it alone in bed, the sheets lingering on your bare belly, your hips. Read it when no one's watching. Go ahead.

I know there are some operas that start right up, but this isn't one of them. Like Beethoven, whose only opera clears its throat with not one but four possible overtures, I've written a bunch of openings, all introducing the subject matters and what surrounds them. As somebody said in a book I've since lost, all behavior exists within a social and cultural context, so I hope these overtures will not exactly influence you, but tap you on the shoulder to get you looking in the right direction. Their purpose is similar to those hyphened taxonomies you can find clinging to the back of the title page like mold on a shower curtain, infecting your naked and vulnerable skin. You know the words I mean. I know that deep down you know what I'm talking about. Those Library of Congress things:

Pittsburgh, Pennsylvania—Fiction

Our story begins in Pittsburgh, Pennsylvania, where, the guidebooks would have it, "geography demanded a city." As if rich river-soaked land wanted nothing better than a bunch of greyed-out buildings dumped on it. The Ohio River is born where the Allegheny and the Monongahela meet in a wet intersection of sludgy vowels. As in all American cities, the areas are named after what was destroyed to put the houses there, and most of Pittsburgh is named after Indian things: tribes, land, activities. Cyn's neighborhood was between Shadyside, where all the trees had been trimmed to regulation width, and Squirrel Hill, where the only woodland creatures to be found were iron-cast and holding bagels in front of the upscale Jewish market. Johnny Appleseed is from Pittsburgh.

Say you spent an erotically scarring summer in Pittsburgh and later find yourself in an opera about it. If you want to appreciate an opera you read some background material, so you phone up the Pittsburgh Chamber of Commerce. The volunteers who answer the phone will be aghast at your interest. *Nobody wants to go there.* Nevertheless, they'll brush the dust off the full-color gloss and send you beckoning brochures.

The brochures refer to Pittsburgh as the Emerald City because it's surrounded by green hills. The city of Pittsburgh is crazy about color, having sprinkled the primaries all over the city in the form of Color-Coded Wayfinder signs. Like the curved stripes of the rainbow, the appropriate roads encircle the city, keeping you lost but at least monochromatic. Whenever I drove around trying to use the Wayfinders I could always, say, find all the Blue things I wanted but could never figure out how to skip to the next rung on the spectrum. But all this fascination with color is more than inappropriate; it's wrong. The color of Pittsburgh is a bitter black. Racially too. The great lumbering steel industry has left a dark powder on a brick that once photogenically matched the color of the people driven out of Duquesne Incline and Monongahela Heights.

It's a wonder, beneath all the smokestack sky, that the city can host "one of the nation's most spectacular collections of live birds," twittering away in the North Side. A regular field trip for campers at Camp Shalom, a Jewish day camp in the area. Also of note is the Benedrum Center for the Performing Arts, which seemed to me named onomatopoetically; as I drafted all this in the Center's library I could hear the Pittsburgh Opera Orchestra sounding it out: Be-ne-*drum,* Be-ne-*drum.* Across the street is a smaller music hall named for a ketchup company founded in Pittsburgh which celebrated an anniversary in the early '60s with a robot shaped like a ketchup bottle. The tri-rivered city would never see anything like it again until the third month of this tangled summer when an unearthly figure, cooked up in Mrs. Glass's basement laboratory, rose out of the Ohio and lumbered across the prestigious Old Jewish Cemetery. The brochure describes what goes on in August as "hot fun": "Grab your suit and sandals and head for the water. Summer in the Emerald City is hot fun. Make sure you take some loose cottons for the riverfront scene after dark, where there are plenty of deserted crannies for fucking Cyn. Average highs in the low 80s."

The trouble with marking poisonous medicines with a skull and crossbones is that cabinet-curious youngsters associate the symbol with pirates. This was the problem studied by a special committee at the Pittsburgh Children's Hospital, which is one of the sites of renown here in town. And of course the bridges. Cyn was considering an American History major, the seed planted, so to speak, by a high-school teacher obsessed with local history. Here George Washington rallied the troops, set up a fort demanded by geography. Two forts. Routed the British. The bridges were spun like strands of a web: Veteran's, Smith-field Street, Liberty, 16th, 9th, 6th, 7th, Duquesne, Pitt. Forts meant injuries and injuries meant hospitals, one of which drew up Mr. Yech, the new non-buccaneer warning of poison. Mr. Yech had few features but a big mouth which, it was clear, had just swallowed something that little kids did *not* want to swallow. As the frontier was tamed the Jews felt safe enough to settle

7

in the only city in America able to compose an internationally-recognized face of distaste. They needed somewhere to send their little Jews and Jewettes during the schoolless months and thus Camp Shalom was founded, and that's how Cyn and I ended up living in her parents' house in Pittsburgh, Pennsylvania during the summer before my senior year at Mather College. The curtain rises.

Laundry Rooms—love affairs begun in—Fiction

Our story begins with a clothes dryer. Cyn and I met in the laundry room just as she was discovering the Dryer of Eternity. Heedless of the coin slot, it kept spinning and spinning and dried everything, every time. That made it the direct opposite of all the other dryers. She was just peering into the empty, spinning machine when I rounded the corner. My chin was weighing down the pile of clothing in my laundry basket, making me feel sheepish and decapitated. She smiled and I told her about the Dryer of Eternity, and for the rest of our cycles we made small talk while around us the laundry room lurched in erotic rhythm. Inside the machines all of our clothing was getting wet and being tossed around.

The rest of it went like one of those pornographic magazines where people write in about their true experiences: *"Let me help you with that,"* I said, taking her wet clothes out of the machine and catching a glimpse of her heaving tits under her tight shirt. I accidentally brushed against her and her eyes widened as she felt the size of my bulge. "Only if I can help you with that," she said, dropping to her knees and unzipping me. She opened her mouth wide to accommodate my nine inches of man-meat as I lifted her T-shirt over her head and pinched her bullet-hard nipples. She tried *to swallow all my creamy love juice but I pumped out too much and she gagged, taking her mouth away and letting the rest of my cum spray all over her like pearls around an operagoer's neck. "We're not done," she panted, as she eased her shorts off and guided my fingers to her wet, gaping hole.*

Actually we went to dinner first, several dinners, after running into each other at parties about as accidentally as our lothario and his bulge-brushing. And don't you love how he can lift a T-shirt over the head of a woman giving him fellatio? Oral sex is a Möbius strip, porn boy. Truth of the matter is that in Locust, Pennsylvania, there is precious little territory to pioneer any sort of relationship. It's about as big as its buggy little namesake and because it's a college town the three restaurants are packed with everyone you know: "Hey! Are you two, um—?" It's not a good place for dating. For peace and quiet we went to each other's rooms—well, we both went to *one* of our rooms— and yes, it wasn't too long before Cyn eased her shorts off and guided my fingers to her wet, gaping hole.

Incessant. All year long. We'd miss classes. The dining hall would ring its last-chance bell while we probed each other across campus. We'd forget about people who were stopping by to return books until they knocked and we'd greet them, rumpled and impatient for them to leave. We got clumsy, bumping into end tables until the vase tipped and dumped the wilting flowers I'd bought at the Campus Center onto my bare back, the grimy greenish water onto her wriggling chest. We broke two lamps. We were falling in love like falling down drunk, like falling down stairs.

By midterms we didn't need to talk much, we understood each other so well. One afternoon while driving somewhere, I broke a long silence by admitting I'd never had sex in the back of an automobile; she pulled over and we went at it as the sweaty ghosts of her high-school lovers watched over us. Before she'd met me she'd barely ever had sex *not* in the back of an automobile, and it was the same automobile. She'd driven it to Locust, Pennsylvania, with duffels of clothes and graduation presents (unabridged dictionary, popcorn popper, coffee maker, unabridged dictionary) stacked in the backseat where she'd made them all come: the soccer-playing redhead, the pimply actor who got her in trouble with Dr. and Mrs. Glass for leaving cigarettes in her car and the tall one who played drums in a band and coaxed panting polyrhythms out of Cyn with stick-calluoused hands. It was like the car was some mad scientist invention that ran on bodily fluids instead of petroleum. She kept in touch with the actor, talking to him on the phone while I reached under the old shirt of mine she slept in. He was offering her a summer job at Camp Shalom. She accepted as she squirmed on the bed, covering the phone receiver to moan at me, and when he said he needed one more staff member she didn't have to look further than her own tongue and that's how Cyn and I ended up living in her parents' house in Pittsburgh, Pennsylvania, during the summer before my senior year at Mather College. The curtain rises.

Postal System, United States—mistakes—Fiction

Our story begins with a lost box. Each year, more than eighty trillion pieces of mail go through the United States Postal Service and more than fourteen percent of them are lost. Actually, I made up those statistics, but the person on the twenty-four-hour help line probably made up his, too. I could hear his pimples on the phone, pulsing like bubbles in lava as he told me all about my lost box in the tone of voice you use when some guy calls you about his lost package and you're getting off work in a half hour to go home and watch some rented porn.

I had an incomplete in a class it now seems too ridiculous to even mention. As the *Mather College Undergraduate Student Handbook* reads, "A grade of 'incomplete' can be designated for any credit class for a number of reasons. A major paper or exam hinging upon research that cannot be completed during the traditional boundaries of the semester would be suitable grounds, as would a true personal or medical emergency. Requesting an incomplete because of an overextravagance of sexual activity, Joseph, is really pushing it. Unless the completion of the course requires research to be done elsewhere, it is expected that a student will remain in the Locust area."

Well, *that* wasn't going to happen. In the summertime, any questions on the origin of Locust, Pennsylvania's name are resolved in a cloud of gnats. Plus, I had been offered a job in Pittsburgh. Cyn, who licked my stamps, kept in touch with an ex-boyfriend of hers, an actor. I had seen pictures; he was a pimply little thing who'd gotten Cyn in trouble for leaving his cigarettes in the family car after she'd get extravagant on him. Even after all those hand jobs, he was still looking for a stiff member. "Shut *up*, Joseph. I said a *staff* member." Two, in fact: Cyn and me. She was going to teach singing and I was going to run the Arts & Crafts Shack, spreading thick white glue out for children to play with. I couldn't possibly stay in Locust.

All this was fine with my laid-back professor, Ted Steel, a large, oversensitive man the likes of which make political conservatives rant and rave about the leftist dogma passing for academia nowadays. Although Mather was named for a Puritan, nobody read him there, and the permissive climate had torn the pedagogy apart like a hymen. Did you catch that odd phrase in the *Handbook,* the one that didn't belong? "The traditional bounds of the semester"? That's how Professor Steel talked. I let him think I was sleeping with my first man and he agreed to mark me "incomplete."

Cyn and I were taking her family car to Pittsburgh for the summer, but we couldn't fit everything in the trunk and we wanted to leave the backseat free because it was a six-hour drive with plenty of deserted side roads. Steel had signed off on special library privileges so I could write my final paper while exploring my gay identity in Pittsburgh. I wasn't sure what I was going to write my paper on, so I withdrew the maximum amount of books and shoved them into a big box at Mathermail, where every September wide-eyed freshmen retrieved heavy trunks filled with clothes and graduation presents (unabridged dictionary, popcorn popper, coffee maker, unabridged dictionary). Some sullen high-school part-timer, probably saving up for a car so *she* could tug orgasms out of pimply actors in relative privacy, took my money and said the box would arrive in Pittsburgh. It never did. Every so often I still get letters from Mather's Library informing me of approximately three hundred thousand dollars in overdue fines.

I called and called. I called everybody even remotely connected with the postal service. They all had pimples, lied about statistics, and couldn't locate my box, and that's how Cyn and I ended up living in her parents' house in Pittsburgh, Pennsylvania, during the summer before my senior year at Mather College. The curtain rises.

Wasps—circumstances as the result of attacks by—Fiction

Our story begins with wasps. Like the head of a grandmother, a grey and wrinkled nest was perched high in the corner of the Arts & Crafts Shack of Camp Shalom, a Jewish day camp in the Pittsburgh area. It was pretty much Shalom's inactive volcano— about eight years back somebody got stung but nobody else, and eight years back it was a kid nobody liked. So went the rumor.

But the Stock twins, Abby and Pinchas Stock, were readying the Arts & Crafts Shack for the onslaught of little Jews and Jewettes. They were scheduled to be counselors and were earning some extra money cleaning up the camp, a job which nobody but the Stock twins thought was anything but lounging around the grounds, taking a dip in the lake, and shooing gnats away from the nightly barbecue. The Stock twins took their job with a rabbinical seriousness. The Stock twins thought that they should clean up the camp, and when they saw what first looked like Grandma Stock, decapitated at last, they figured they'd better get that wasps' nest down before it hurt somebody.

For the camp-wide barbecues, the fat and friendly lesbians who worked as cooks used the mausoleum-sized brick barbecues by the side of the lake, but for counselors-only get-togethers there was a bright blue kettle on wheels. Abby Stock wheeled it over to the Shack while Pinchas found a stepladder and a broom with whiskers so dusty that the act of sweeping with it was a textbook example of dramatic irony. Having gleaned from somewhere that smoke was the thing that one did to wasps, the twins got a fire going in the bright blue kettle and threw some construction paper on the grill. A thin pillar of smoke—Pinchas, something of a Torah nerd, made a Moses

13

joke—wafted its way toward the nest whose wrinkles suddenly seemed to be wincing in distaste. The Stock twins thought about two handfuls of paper should do it. The Stock twins thought that the few wasps hummingbirding around the nest were probably the last couple of survivors. Pinchas went up the ladder.

Angry wasps clouded the air in strict arrow-shaped formations more like angry wasps in cartoons on television than you'd think. The arrow pointed first at Pinchas, who fell from the ladder and led the wasps to his partner in crime. Both of them were so covered in stings that their faces looked like seed cakes. Plus the falling ladder broke Abby's leg. The wasps made a quick lap around the Shack before returning to the nest, so that by the time the lounging counselors arrived on the scene it looked like pain had just *descended* on the Stock twins, out of nowhere.

Pittsburgh Bug-B-Gone, who rid Temple Ner Tamid ("Eternal Light") of the cockroach problem spoiling their kosher catering facilities, took care of the nest, but the problem of finding two more counselors at such short notice fell to the Head of Staff, a theater student who hadn't been accepted into any summer stock programs and so was spending the summer exiled in his hometown. Chastened, he was living in the sweaty bedroom of his youth and after dark would stroke himself remembering a girl from high school who would pull over halfway home from cast parties to bring him to a shuddering ovation in the backseat of her family's throbbing car. So when the Stock twins were peppered he didn't have to look further than his own sticky body. He was buzzing with panting reunion fantasies when he called Cyn, but he had to put his acting skills to use when he said of course she could bring her boyfriend Joseph, and that's how Cyn and I ended up living in her parents' house in Pittsburgh, Pennsylvania, during the summer before my senior year at Mather College. The curtain rises.

Golem—revenge through attacks by—legends concerning—Fiction

Our story begins with a golem, a figure in Jewish myth—sort of a Jewish lie, sort of a Jewish truth. Just as God, breathing into clay, created something that was in the shape of, but not as good as, Himself, man can breathe into clay and make something man-shaped but not man. Or in this case, not woman.

The trick, of course, is the ritual. The mythology of the golem sprung up in the sixteenth century in Worms, Germany, when a beleaguered rabbi, exhausted by the usual government evil, created a new ritual and with it a seven-foot-tall man made of clay. In many ways Pittsburgh is a perfect place for what was surely the first American golem, because although stories of the ritual differ, they usually say that river mud is the best flesh.

The sixteenth-century Worms fad in Jew-hating was a fairly common one in those days: the blood libel. Jews were accused of killing Christian babies and using their blood to make unleavened bread for Passover, a charge that's particularly laughable if you've ever had even a bite of dry, tasteless matzah. This is a reason why the Glass home is also a perfect locale for a golem revival, because Mrs. Glass cooked her delicious meals using mysterious ingredients obtained at dawn at the downtown market. Who knows what was in that sauce, or what creature previously owned those bulbous objects, rendered unreadable by carmelization?

According to the records, some Christians would kill their own babies, break into rabbis' homes and place the baby-bodies in the basement, returning the next morning with a mob. Now *that's* anti-semitism. Rabbis set up patrols to block this baby-planting, but all the Christians would have to do was toss the infant corpses directly into the rabbis' arms and return the next morning with a mob. The ghetto-hood watch wasn't working; the congregation wanted a better guardian.

The clay is laid out in the shape of a man and the creator is dressed in white. Candles are lit and the body is circled a number of times argued over extensively in horrifically dull texts on Jewish mysticism. The prayers are of course also in dispute, but my favorite is an alphabetical one sung by a hopelessly Gentile tenor in *Golem,* one of the productions that summer at the Pittsburgh Opera: "Ah, By Clay Destroy Evil Forces, Golem, Help Israel: Justice!" This brought the clay to an obedient, powerful and creepy life.

The fact it's the alphabet is worth noting. The golem, like so many aspects of Judaism, is inundated with the power of the Word. God's name is a secret—abbreviated "Ha Shem," or "The Name," most of the time. In the beginning, of course, was the Word. It's generally agreed that a short prayer, inscribed on a scroll of paper, should be placed in the golem's mouth; if he ever speaks, the Word of God tumbles out and the golem turns back into clay. Pretend *you're* an evil Christian, sneaking through the ghettos of Worms with a dead baby, when a seven-foot silent figure of clay steps out of the shadows. No way are you returning the next morning with a mob. That's the power of the Word. The name of the beleaguered rabbi was Rabbi Liva.

16

The name of the river from which the flesh was taken was the Moldau River. The name of the first golem was Joseph. The name of the story where all this is told is The Wondrous Tale That Was Widely Known As The Sorrows Of A Daughter.

Cyn had not the slightest interest in her religious heritage, but one time we were caught in a freak thunderstorm while walking around the campus cemetery, one of those picturesque old ones where people are always doing rubbings. We huddled underneath a tree, getting damp, then soaked, then horny: we did a rubbing. Cyn always preferred being on top and I always submitted, even when that meant my bare body pressed into mud and her hair and face dripping on me like a wet tree. Even when she shifted her position and moved her hands from the mud to my chest, leaving a thick handprint of clay on each shoulder, I didn't mind. As she constricted around me I felt like I was coming to life, obedient to her will. She stuck a clay-stained finger into my mouth and though the taste was bitter I was afraid to say anything and ruin it. The rain stopped but we didn't; I was afraid that somebody might see us, stepping out of the shadows on their way somewhere. But I didn't speak. I'd do anything for her.

And that's how Cyn and I ended up living in her parents' house in Pittsburgh, Pennsylvania, during the summer before my senior year at Mather. The curtain rises.

ACT I, SCENE ONE

The set for the first scene would probably win something in *Operagoer* magazine's Annual Audience Awards. In the foreground is an expensive garden, not quite in bloom but full of promise. There are a handful of enormous ceramic pots, large enough for a child's first bath, with small lime trees waving in the summer breeze like the hands of a spindly pianist, warming up. In fact the whole place is warming up: the flaccid hose, ready to spring into action if somebody pumps in water; bags of potting soil, swollen pregnant with earthy minerals and expensive dung; the prongs of polished tools, catching the glare of the sharply-angled lights installed for security reasons; a beckoning watering can and packets and packets and packets of seeds. In Pittsburgh, it's the heat *and* the humidity, so although the soil looks parched, the leaves are moist from the evening's condensation. If you touch them they feel like showered skin. The propsmistress accomplishes this look with a thin, clear paste—the same stuff they use to make those new-album posters stick to construction sites in seedier parts of town.

Cyn's neighborhood was a nicer one, and Cyn's street was a nicer street. Some English-majors-turned-urban-planners had named the streets after the headings in their syllabi; the Glass home was located in the middle of Byron Circle, a cul-de-sac inappropriately close to Hemingway Way. The neighbors all had each other's keys. The Glasses' house had stickers in the windows threatening an advanced burglar alarm system, but the stickers were all that were installed. Just about anybody could have walked into that house.

On summer days like this one, everyone washed their cars

while the radio played songs the fathers liked back in college. The rinsed foam swirled into the one drain that always clogged come October when the maples dropped Canadian propaganda over everything. Cyn's car is still dripping from her father's nostaglic scrub as the lights go up on a table tableau, framed perfectly by the garden window, up center. I am reasonably certain that even this far upstage all the singers can be heard. As the opera begins proper, Cyn Glass (*soprano*) is setting the table and singing of simpler times.

"We've had these dishes as long as I can remember," she said to me (*tenor*), swerving as I snuck up behind her to kiss her on the neck. I was holding silverware like a dozen roses, pointy ends up. She'd caught my reflection in the blue-rimmed plates. "Look how the overhead light reflects, behind your face. It's like you have a halo."

"Your angel," I cooed.

"My *fallen* angel," she said. "Look." A big crack ran down the entire plate like a smirk, and it threatened to laugh. "I'd better get another one."

"*I'm sure it'll hold,*" Mimi Glass (*soprano*) said pointedly, coming in with a pitcher of ice water. Mrs. Glass's first-act costume should be casual clothes that don't make her look fat, as she kept explaining to me whenever I saw her at home. She also had on an apron, heavily spaghetti-stained.

"It doesn't look like it," Cyn insisted, leaning against me affectionately and to shock her mother. Beneath her blue jeans lay her ass, warm and ready like something that'd been basking. Just three days ago we'd made love standing up for the first time to celebrate the end of finals. "Look, I can practically bend it, Mom."

19

"I'm sure it'll hold," Mrs. Glass said again. Then, peeking back into the kitchen, she hissed, "I can't believe you're talking this way, what with your father and everything. Of *course* it'll hold. Show a little consideration." She brought down the pitcher like a gavel and left the room, grumpy, with trombones.

"What was that?" I asked, while Cyn's eyes widened. She shook her head and traced the crack like she was teasing something. In my mouth there was something like an aftertaste, like maybe I should have stayed in Locust, wrote my paper, worked part-time for the Admissions office showing high-school students around the campus, but to be without Cyn's taste all summer long—"Did your father *make* these plates?"

"If he had," she said, "they'd *definitely* break." Another Act One trick; just before a revelation, the crowd comes in and the party starts with a full-out choral number. If the crowd would come in only a moment later all that tragedy could be avoided. Though in this case not really. Steven (*tenor*), Cyn's little scientific genius brother, brought in a platter of string beans, damp taut strands tossed with almonds. Mrs. Glass, now apronless but still grimacing slightly at Cyn, brought in a fleshy pink fish in a dark shroud of sauce, and Dr. Ben Glass (*baritone*) brought in his mother, Gramma (*contralto*).

We dug in. Mrs. Glass had driven across town in an inexplicable Sahara-ready Jeep the family owned, early in the morning while the filth of the rivers is still submerged in grey light and Cyn and I, back in Locust, indulged in soapy caresses, sharing a shower in the deserted dorm. "It'll be so good to be home," she moaned, while her mother took her tan sunglasses off her eyes and perched them on top of her head, the better to see the whole fish gaping on ice, laid out morgue-like on thick tables for all the wives to choose. She put hers in a clear bag while we toweled off, and by the time we hit the road, driving over the train tracks and spilling coffee on my jeans that Cyn could still taste on my legs come noon, Mrs. Glass had entered the Japanese Specialty Market where the imported rice wine was stacked neatly on shelves next to hand-calligraphed signs. She Jeeped back to Byron Circle and clopped primly past the hedges in her much-needed high-heeled shoes, the fish dangling from her wrist like a raw purse. The salmon soaked in sake all day long while Mrs. Glass mixed papier-mâché at the Pittsburgh Opera and Cyn and I sped past Amish farms and fast-food restaurants. By the time Mrs. Glass had put the finishing touches on the coffin and began work on *Die Juden* and Cyn and I reached the city limits, the fish had a thick, somewhat gelatinous skin to it, which was to harden to a flaky shell when Mrs. Glass popped it into the oven along with a special ginger-honey paste she'd put aside the night before. That evening, with firework French horns from the orchestra, the Glass family eats the meal ravenously and juicily, like we're gutting something.

"Quality food means quality time," Dr. Glass announced in a simple recitativo, a harpsichord strumming behind him. I could tell he'd said this all the time.

"Right, Dad," Steven said, spearing a bean.

"No, no," his father said. "I want to explain to Joseph why we're eating so well."

"Because it tastes good?" I asked. Cyn smiled and looked down at the cracked plate.

He smiled and touched his beard, a beneficent rabbi. "No," he said. "It's because a good meal makes everybody happy. Judaism is a religion which places great spiritual importance on

21

food—we fast to focus ourselves for atonement on Yom Kippur, we refrain from eating leavened bread as we celebrate attaining freedom during Passover and if we kept the strictest laws, we'd have a kosher kitchen, all the food becoming a ritual."

"We have a new rabbi," Mrs. Glass said, "who Ben really likes."

"Just so you don't think he always talks like this," said Steven.

"In the modern day, the evening meal is often the only time when the family can be together. The time should be *quality*. You know what Rabbi Tsouris calls it? *Family-making*."

Mrs. Glass, Steven and Cyn laughed at the same pitch as each other, as do the trumpets which along with the snare drum will be used throughout to indicate jollity. I pursed my lips into what I hoped was a non-mocking, attentive expression. Gramma spat out a bone.

"*Family-making?*" Cyn asked incredulously. "It sounds like—well—" Foreboding from quivering violas.

"Family-making," the good doctor said, smiling blandly, nodding sagely. "Anyway, if we have quality food, the meal can achieve spirituality. So I feel a personal commitment to having really delicious food, every night."

"Actually," Mrs. Glass said, "it's *me* who has the commitment to having delicious food. I'm the one who gets up in the early morning to go to that fish morgue."

"But it's *my* commitment," Dr. Glass said. It was the first time I saw this in Cyn's father: the implacable and irritating sure-footedness of those who are grandiose and wrong. "*You* may make the food, but it's *me* who really *commits* to having it be good."

Gramma coughed, wet and loud and startled me and I dropped my fork. She kept coughing; she hadn't said a word for all of dinner and now she was dominating the conversation. Dr. Glass moved like he'd been trained for such scenarios, which of course he had been, but all he did was stand behind her and unroll his sleeves. I thought for one moment he was going to reach into Gramma's mouth and pull out the troublesome bite, like veterinarians on public television who reach *into* the birthing cow, but he just stood there in medical readiness until she coughed it out by herself and it flew at the wall like a bug to a windshield. Cyn and I had killed so many bugs on the way to Pittsburgh that we'd run out of the blue soapy fluid that sprays from under the hood, and we had to stop and wipe the insects off the glass with the same sticky T-shirt we'd used to wipe sperm off our legs after our lunch in the back seat. Unsure whether laughter was appropriate, I looked down at my plate and for a moment I thought there was something wrong with my eyes: the salmon had split into two separate continents, with only my startled fork as a stainless steel Bering Strait. No. The plate was broken, smacked in half like a pair of breasts.

"Oh, gosh, I'm sorry," I stuttered. A high hornet buzz from a few violins. "I dropped my fork. I'm really sorry, I'll pay for it."

"Don't worry," Mrs. Glass said quietly. Under her bangs, long and straight as venetian blinds, her face had gone powder-pale. She licked her lips. She wasn't looking at me. Gramma was wiping her mouth with a napkin that matched everybody's. Steven was taking his napkin and dabbing at the glob on the wall which was stuck there in a neat spoonful. I couldn't understand why everything felt like a funeral until I tried to meet Cyn's eyes. She was looking at her father.

23

I'm a sucker for filling silence. Once I open my mouth there's no stopping me. "I'm very sorry. Of course I'll pay for the plate." Nobody said anything. Against the still-buzzing violins was only the sound of Steven's napkin against salmon against saliva against the wall. "It's weird that it broke that way, don't you think? There must have been some secret fault in the plate or something. You know, like when small earthquakes split big buildings. I read about this somewhere. Buildings that were supposed to be earthquake-proof, it turned out that a bunch of microscopic air pockets lined up in just the right way, by sheer coincidence, so even though the buildings were earthquake-proof it turned out that they couldn't protect themselves from earthquakes. Steven, you probably know more about this. Cyn said you were a science guy—do you know something about this? This wasn't even the plate that had the crack. What's that?"

That was the table shaking, rattling the serving spoons and making the unlit candles shake in their holders. I thought for a minute that the story I was telling was being fleshed out there in the dining room. But it was Dr. Glass. He looked like a volcano. His face was dark red and his hands were clenched into trembling fists and although it was probably just steam from the string beans it looked like smoke was coming out of his nostrils. It was making the table shake, that and the timpanis.

"*I'll—go—get—dessert—*" he stuttered in a terrible voice, and reached across the table toward me. I shrank back—it looked like he was going to throttle me—but he merely grabbed both halves of my split plate and carried them into the kitchen like Moses down from Sinai. A small river of sake-sauce began to widen on the tablecloth in front of me. Except for the color it looked like the stains on my sheets that had me eating dinner here in the first place. What in the world was going on?

"Did I say—" I swallowed as the Glass eyes swiveled like periscopes to my stained place at the table. "Did I—something wrong?"

Cyn smiled and half-shrugged. "You said *everything* wrong," she said. "It's O.K. You don't know and Dad knows you don't know."

"What—"

"Dad had a catastrophe recently at work," Steven said, bundling up Gramma's wad in his napkin like a party favor.

"It wasn't a *catastrophe*," Mrs. Glass said, thumping her water glass down and picking up some intact plates. "That's the whole problem. He keeps thinking it was a catastrophe. It was just—"

"A mistake?" Cyn said, raising her eyebrows.

"Well, it wasn't a success, let's just put it that way."

"My son is a *genius!*" Gramma croaked suddenly. Which is what she'd later do: croak suddenly. "Geniuses are never *wrong.*"

"Yes," Mrs. Glass said blankly. She held four dirty plates in a careful stack, towards her floppy breasts like she was nursing them. "Look, Cyn, *you* tell Joseph. Your father is still upset about it and if you're going to be here for the summer"—here she parted her lips to me in an impeccably puppeted smile— "he might as well know. The point is for our family to be together. You know, *family-making.*"

Cyn grimaced and brushed a strand of hair out of her mouth. "I wish you'd stop using that—"

"*Genius!*" Gramma said again. Her eyes hooded over and

from somewhere in my childhood I remembered that there was always a chance that Gramma was really a wolf in disguise.

Mrs. Glass exited. Steven poured Gramma some more water out of a pitcher made in Mexico and bought at the Mexican Specialty Market. Cyn leaned toward me and kissed me wetly on the mouth. Gramma snorted at us. Then, still kissing-distance, she told me in a lush, low voice about the Fall of Genius. Usually a tale of shame is introduced with lush low strings, violas or cellos in short loose bursts like something strumming.

"Three months ago my father finally got the funding to go ahead with the last phase of—well, this project. I told you he's a bone specialist, right? He's put together a lot of people's knees. Famous sports guys and everything. So he had this idea that he'd been testing for years—replacement bones made out of this new ceramic that they're building plane parts with. Dad read about it in one of those high-tech magazines. So he tested it with computer models and stuff, and then on some animals, although it was really impossible to tell how it would do with animals because of animal tissue. I don't know quite how." Offstage in the kitchen came the percussion of dropped silverware.

"How did he test it on animals?"

"What do you mean how? First they took rabbits and took out their real leg bones and put in these ceramic leg bones instead. They were supposed to be better than the metal and plastic deals that they use now. Then they tried it on chimps. It worked pretty well but Dad kept saying it was all irrelevant because animal tissue is different from human tissue. So they finally got the go-ahead—the money and the red tape or whatever. They tried it on this woman. She'd broken her leg in some

26

weird way when she fell off a ladder she was standing on to knock a wasps' nest off of her house. She was swinging the broom to knock it off and she fell. There were some complications, because the woman was stung so many times that they couldn't reset the bone properly—it turned out she was allergic so her whole body was swollen. Dad said it looked like she was wrapped in a sleeping bag."

"So he used the ceramics to cure *bee stings?*"

"*Wasps. No.* The wasps made her swell up so they couldn't set the bone properly, so by the time she swelled down the bone was all messed up. So Dad got the go-ahead—it wasn't just my Dad, by the way, but when it got screwed up everybody blamed him and the paper blamed him and so it might as well have been just my Dad—Dad got the go-ahead and they put this ceramic leg bone thing inside her leg and when she stood up the leg shattered. Instantly."

"Really?"

"Yes. It was awful. There was a big newspaper scandal and Dad was denounced everywhere."

"Wow."

"Stop that," she said. "*Really. Wow.* He's upset, is the point. And that stupid secret fault thing you were talking about was exactly the reason. I don't really get it, but the ceramic was developed in a way to compensate for any minute air pockets or something in the clay."

"Not *air pockets,*" Steven said in the tired air of somebody who has always done well in math. "They're—"

"Whatever they were, it was statisically improbable for these secret defects to line up in the right way to have the leg shatter, but—"

"*Impossible,*" Steven said. "Statisically *impossible,* not improbable."

"But it happened," Cyn said. "It can't be impossible."

"*Statistically* impossible," he said wearily.

"In any case, that's why he got upset," Cyn finished. She was still leaning toward me, her story breathing on my face, my neck, down my shirt. "So don't sweat it. The cracked plate just upset him."

"And it wasn't even the one that was cracked," Mrs. Glass said, stalking back into the room a little wildly. She picked up the butter plate and threw down dessert spoons like a witch doctor casting bones. "That's why it wasn't his fault, don't you know that? It's *exactly* like the plates!" She grabbed Cyn's empty plate and traced the crack through the traces of sake-sauce. "You see? Your plate wasn't cracked like this, Joseph, and *it's* the one that broke."

"That's exactly what Joseph was talking about," Steven said, giving me a half-smile of male camaraderie even though I was fucking his sister. "The crack didn't break the plate because the defects in the ceramic were not lined up correctly. That's why Joseph's plate broke even though he just dropped a fork on it. You could probably wham this one down on the table and nothing would happen to it."

"Really?" I said.

Steven took the plate from his mother and gave it to me. Gramma nodded sagely. My fingers were sticky. I looked at everybody and then whammed the plate down on the table, breaking the second plate of the evening.

"*What was that?*" Dr. Glass sounded positively cardiac from the kitchen.

"Oh," said Steven. Together we looked at the large pieces lying ruined on the table like uprooted sidewalk chunks. The plate had cracked right where the crack was, right where you'd think it would crack. Secret defects indeed. The son whisked the pieces away and the father emerged with a tray of strawberry-and-nougat parfaits.

During that summer, Mrs. Glass was mildly renowned at the Glasses' synagogue for making the best nougat in all the Sister-hood. Even the first night of my stay there she'd already perfected the recipe (the trick is omitting honey), so all the ceramic tensions were dissolved in spoons of moist stickiness and ripe wet berries. Everybody's mouths were wet and grinning, even Gramma's, and Dr. Glass relaxed and continued to talk at me. I nodded and scooped in berries; it was going to be a delicious summer. Jovial French horns or something.

"I'm really looking forward to working at Camp Shalom," I said. "And I really appreciate your letting me stay here."

"We wouldn't have it any other way," Mrs. Glass said, smiling. "It's good to see our daughter getting laid."

"What?"

"Usually she volunteers," Steven said. "She answered phones at a women's clinic last summer, and before that she candy striped at Dad's office."

Paid.

"Well, this summer *you're* not making any money," Cyn said.

"Steven is working at a very prestigious lab," Dr. Glass said. "Carnegie Mellon. Physics. We're very proud of him."

"I'm proud of him," Cyn said defensively. "I just wanted to point out that he's not making any money."

"He's made money previously." Dr. Glass licked the rest of his nougat off the spoon.

"Well, I'm glad this summer she's finally pulling her weight," I said. "I bet you guys were tired of covering her mortgage payments."

"*Ha!*" the doctor said.

"Well," Cyn said, "speaking of *tired,* I am. And Joseph and I have to make up the bed before we can even hit it. Can we be excused please?"

I promptly set down my spoon. "*Bed?*" Gramma said.

"Yes," Cyn said. "I know it's only eight-thirty, but Joseph and I had a long hard drive. Very hard. Very long. And we kept driving faster and faster and faster until we were through, and it was so hot."

"*Bed?*" Gramma said again. "You're sleeping in *one bed*?"

"Oh," Mrs. Glass said, "yes, we decided that, mother."

"*Together?*" Gramma shrieked.

"That's what they're doing at school," Mrs. Glass said. "It would be hypocritical—"

"It's the *summertime,*" Gramma said. I filled my mouth with nougat. "There isn't any school."

"It would be hypocritical to—"

"You don't even *know him*—" The violins swell; Gramma lifted her dessert spoon toward me like a gavel. "Well, *I* for one—"

"Mother," Mrs. Glass said patiently. "I talked it over with my daughter. And Ben. It simply doesn't make any sense to forbid them to share a bed, when they're just going to go back to school and—"

"*No!*" Gramma shouted. "*I won't have it!*"

"*Please,* let's not get to shouting about it. It's only the first night—"

"It's *against the law!*"

Steven giggled. "No it's not," he said.

"Well, it's against the *laws of nature!*"

"Please," Mrs. Glass said, smiling nervously at me. "Let's just enjoy our parfaits."

"*No,*" Gramma said, and here it comes: the old woman's curse. From such grumpy seniors do lovers die, castles crumble. It always happens at the wedding feast. "*If they sleep together under this roof they will not be forgiven. If they sleep together I call upon catastrophe to visit this house. If they sleep together,* this *will be my revenge.*" On *this* she held up her parfait glass like a goblet. The *parfait* will be her revenge? In some ways it made sense: a parfait is sweet. A parfait is a dish best served cold. The part with strawberries and ice cream didn't make any sense at all, but if anything's important in opera they always repeat it. "*If they sleep together,* this *will be my—*"

"O.K., Mrs. Glass," I said. "Everybody. I am very grateful to this family for taking me in this summer, and I don't want to intrude on anybody's hospitality. If it makes you feel better, I'll sleep in another room. I don't mean to upset anybody, and— well, besides, it will be good. I have an 'incomplete' from last semester, and I need to write a paper, so I'll probably be up late nights." I couldn't meet Cyn's eyes as I said this last one. "So it does make sense for me to sleep in another room. I mean, if you *have* another room. If it isn't intruding on anybody's hospitality to sleep *separately.*" I couldn't believe what I was saying. As if the idea of the summer was actually to work Arts & Crafts at Camp Shalom in Pittsburgh, Pennsylvania, of all places, rather than blanketing myself in Cyn's body. After sex we were usually so breathless we couldn't even summon up the energy to grab an inside-out T-shirt and wipe ourselves down; we'd usually just let ourselves drip-dry underneath the glare of cheap dormitory fluorescence. Now, during the hottest months of the year, I was agreeing to summon up the energy to leave the room. But I was raised right. And after the ceramic mishap during the main course I felt obliged to better my batting record.

Gramma's eyes—long, thin rectangles like cars from the 1950s—met mine, but she didn't say anything. She was still holding up the parfait; inside the glass, the remaining ice cream liquified and a strawberry toppled into the bottom layer of nougat.

"That's not necessary," Cyn's mother said to both of us. "I have made my decision, Mother, and I'll thank you to—"

"No no no," Gramma said, shaking her head. She stooped up and took a little sweater off the back of the chair. It was red with little black decorations, the Pittsburgh equivalent of a sweeping gypsy shawl. "I'm going home. I hope you two"—her arm sweeps were so vague I didn't know which set of lovers she meant—"do the sensible thing. The *right* thing. The *legal* thing."

"It *isn't* illegal, Gramma," Steven said. But Gramma was gone, scowling through the garden past the damp plants, quivering in fear of the curse. I haven't decided if this weighs down the opening scene too much, but a short ballet would be appropriate here: The Dance of the Terrified Plants. Faces emerge from the greenery, while offstage Gramma's cackles can still be heard, and the stagehands bang those metal sheets used to produce thunder. The dancers line up: flowers, trees, tomatoes, swaying and trembling. Through opera glasses you can see the ingenious way the dancers have been hiding in the foreground during this entire scene. The orchestra wails on, and untwining from the set are the thinnest, limberest dancers, who have been representing serpentine vines this whole time. The nuts and bolts would of course be left to the choreographer, but the music clearly indicates a broad outline. Shaking with fear, the plants group together and discuss the curse in hushed flora language. Gradually the swooning heat of the evening makes the discussion feverish; piccolos trill and the flowers swirl in small interlocking circles. The fever becomes desire; the music grows lush. While timpanis roll the pairing of plants grows less conversational and more reproductive. Flickering colored lights indicate flying spores. Despite the inherent asexuality the dancing becomes sensual, erotic, orgasmic. The plants fall back to their original places, quivering once more.

Meanwhile, Mrs. Glass and Cyn had left Dr. Glass and me with the dishes, because we didn't cook. Of course, Cyn and Steven hadn't cooked either, but I recognized the cleanup as a male-bonding stratagem and let it go; I was a guest. Cyn saw I was O.K. with it when she returned to grab her water glass and met my eyes. Picking up still more sauce-stained plates—how could any possibly be left, anyway?—I nodded at her, and hungrily watched her leave the room.

"Delicious, huh?" Dr. Glass said to me.

Watching her jeans was making me remember a sex texture: Cyn's denimed crotch rubbing up against my naked one, while her bare breasts brushed against my shirt which she hadn't yet unbuttoned, sort of a yin-yang of nudity and clothedness. Regretfully I returned to the dining room. "Yes," I said. "Salmon's always been one of my favorite—"

"I mean my daughter," he said.

What? His eyes were sly. Actually I couldn't see his eyes, but they could have been sly. In any case he was definitely sweeping crumbs off the table into one of his well-insured hands. I watched the spindles of bone or muscle or whatever-they-are moving underneath the skin of his fingers like the legs of a sleeper twitching beneath blankets. At any moment, an air pocket could materialize out of invisibility, and everything could crack. "Your daughter?" I said blankly. "Oh, yes. I'm sure she liked it, too."

"No, I mean *delicious*. My daughter. A good-looking woman. That's what we used to say when we saw a beautiful woman, back when I was at school. You know?"

I nodded. Mather College was in the throes of radical feminism but I kept my knee from jerking. I was trying to appreciate this family taking me in, and if I played my cards right the summer could spread its legs before me like a garden of earthly delights. "Delicious. I don't think I've heard that." And I'd rather not have it explained to me, thanks very much, Dr. Glass, sir.

"I think it came from calling a girl a dish. You know, *check out that dish!*" He turned to ogle an imaginary woman with exaggerated heartiness. Couldn't he just talk about basketball or something? "Then we began to get more detailed about the dishes, you know: spicy, delicious, whatever."

"I get it."

"And Cynthia's a delicious one."

Four bars of woodwinds before I answer. "Um,"

"Does it embarrass you that I say it like that?"

"Yes. I mean, *no,* not really. I don't know."

"I don't mean anything improper. I'm just proud of her."

"Yes."

"She's very pretty."

It struck me that maybe he was paying a compliment. "Well, thanks."

Dr. Glass laughed with a boom-boom of bass drum and trombone. "*You* should be thanking *me.*"

I blinked. "I just did."

He blinked, and then duplicated the laugh. "No, no, no. I mean, *I* should be saying thanks. After all, it's *my* genetic material that made her so delicious, right?"

Suddenly I could the see the Wayfinder sign that would lead me to some better topic of conversation. "Well, it could be heredity or environment, right?" A nice basic subject for doctor and student to rehash as we cleared the table.

"It doesn't matter. Either way I win."

"That's true. Well, nice going, sir."

"*Sir?* You're making me feel old." Dr. Glass took his handful of crumbs and dropped them into the bowl I was holding.

"Sorry. Nice going, Dr. Glass."

"Call me Ben." Ben leaned over to me and I saw suddenly the same curve in his lip as I saw in Cyn's whenever she leaned in to kiss me. I found myself wondering if the curves tasted the same, father and daughter.

"Nice going, Ben."

"Thanks," he said. "I'm just—I want to tell you something."

He tied an apron over his crotch and turned on the faucet. "Before you start living here, with us, for three months or however long it is."

Something about the way the bassoons were murmuring made me not want to hear it. "Do you want me to dry, or maybe I should shake the tablecloth out?"

Ben smiled sheepishly: *I don't mean to embarrass you.* "I don't mean to embarrass you. It's just that—I think mothers are more protective of their children immediately. I mean right *after.* Birth. Because they came out of their *bodies,* you know? I mean, of course I had a hand in it." He held up his hand; I pictured what *it* was. "It takes two, right?"

"Tablecloth?" I asked. "Shake it out?" Or hose you down, Ben?

"But I think the father feels more protective later, when she's grown up. When she's become a woman." Ben turned off the faucet and wiped his hands so there was a damp spot in the middle of his apron. "Look, Joseph," he said. "You seem like a very nice young man. Sheesh, now I'm making *myself* sound old. I mean you seem very nice. But I wanted to tell you—well, Cynthia is a very pretty girl. I look at her and I can see how you would look at her." He walked over and leaned into me again. If I just stood on half-tiptoe—"I don't mean it like that. You seem nice." Suddenly I realized what all this was about— a fatherly talk. He was nervous but protective. All this sex blather was just his way of eventually arriving at the same old girlfriend-father point: Don't you abuse my daughter. Many boyfriends were resentful of this kind of thing, but I understood it. I had the same feeling as I lay in bed with Cyn and felt the results of our sex evaporate, off to impregnate the air somewhere. The wetness on my leg—that had come from *me*. *Mine*. I could imagine how protective I'd feel if my fluid grew up, walked around, majored in something. Ben had obviously felt this way since he rolled out of Mrs. Glass's legs flush with fatherhood. Or maybe Mrs. Glass, like her daughter, preferred to be on top; I could picture her lowering herself onto him like a wet guillotine.

"What do you want to tell me, Ben?"

"I can see what you see: she's attractive."

The orchestra, in one big unison blast: BRUM!

"Cyn?" I asked. "You find Cyn attractive?"

"I don't *find* her attractive. I *know* she's attractive. She *is* attractive."

With each tense of the conjugation: BRUM! BRUM! BRUM! Obviously I was overtired. I reminded myself that Mrs. Glass had been glad Cyn was getting *paid*. Ben was probably saying *protective, objective, progressive, exhaustive*. Any of the words that rhyme, that over the sound of the faucet, wouldn't be *attractive*. Over the roar of rinse-water it could have been anything. But the faucet was *off*, those of you who couldn't find parking and are now guided into your seats by those pinpoint flashlights the ushers carry. The faucet was *off*. He said *attractive*. The opera was really starting up.

"Are you talking about incest?" I asked, but Ben just turned and smiled at me like I hadn't said anything.

This is the first entrance of one of the orchestral leitmotifs that will keep popping up as the plot-knot is tied tighter: The Unknown Dread. Lurking in the backing of the aria like a rapist hiding behind the fire escape, The Unknown Dread is usually sounded by some trombones: a simple, sinister tune, dark and low like fog on a swamp. The Unknown Dread, abbreviated in music criticism journals as "T.U.D.," will creep in and out of the orchestration whenever vague and hopefully-imagined trouble clouds the stage like hot water, filling pans that need to soak overnight.

"Funny you should say that," he said.

"A laugh riot," I said.

"No, it *is*. Somebody was just talking—but they didn't call it—what did they call it?"

"Um,"

"*Intergenerational sex!*" he said triumphantly. Hooray. "Somebody—actually, at the hospital, you won't believe his name. Like the book—well, it doesn't matter. He was saying that when there's a new member of the family—well, not of the family, no, but say a daughter's first—well, not first, of course, you and I both know that. But when a lover enters a family, it can make bare—what's the term? Lay bare? Lay something. Anyway, a father's—well, let's not speak in such general terms. My own feelings for my daughter is what I'm talking about. If you think of it as *intergenerational sex* you can think of it in its true terms—genetic interchange. What did he say? A force of nature. If I were attracted to Cynthia it would be for a reason— the continuation of the species, probably. Which makes sense if you think about it. You agreed that my genes have made some wonderful-looking children. Well, Cynthia has half of my genetic material. If she and I were to mate, the genetic pool for our children would be smaller. So the chances of producing more beautiful children would actually be greater. See? Intergenerational sex actually makes a lot of sense from a genetic perspective."

In my stomach, the salmon turned like a kicking fetus. I tasted my own sour breath, and nougat. He wasn't repeating something that somebody else had said: that was the oldest trick in the book, like calling a suicide hotline and pretending it's vicarious: *I have a friend who is thinking of killing himself. He's staring at a whole bottle of pills right now.* If you think something yourself, and it's something that would shock people, you pretend other people said it. "Having sex with your daughter," I said, "doesn't make any sense at all."

"Dad!" Steven's tenor is heard offstage.

"Of course, of course," he said dismissively. "Never mind. I see I've strayed here. You and Cyn will not sleep in the same room, is what I mean, because I have these feelings for her. They're natural. Having sex with your daughter doesn't make sense, of course not, not if you think of it as *having sex,* no. But even though it involves some of the same actions"—here he poked a finger—"it's not the same thing as having sex. There's an old saying: If I hit you on the head with a frying pan, would you call it cooking?" He picked up a frying pan and faced me.

"Dad!"

He blinked and dunked the frying pan into the sink. "I'm doing the dishes!" he called to Steven. "See what I mean, Joseph? But I've strayed. This isn't what I wanted to tell you at all. I wanted to—I just mean, Cynthia is—well, a *dish.* And she's as delicate as one. I mean a real one. To me. And I just want you to treat her—well, the way *I* would treat her. The way I *do* treat her. Do you understand what I'm saying?"

"Perfectly," I said in sort of a growl, and then barged right on. "Because I understand what can happen to a dish—or anything made of ceramics. Mrs. Glass was telling me. Sometimes all the flaws can line up in the same way, and disasters can happen." I swallowed. "Broken legs and such."

"*DAD!*"

"I'm *doing the dishes!*" he bellowed, looking fiercely at me. I looked right back at him. I was feeling pretty adhesive— *protective*—myself. The wetness on my leg wasn't the only thing in the bedroom that was mine. There was one dish he wasn't going to do. I looked at my hand, which was turning red from gripping Gramma's parfait glass. I put it down. My hand throbbed.

Steven came into the kitchen wearing only shorts. "I just wanted to *talk* to you about something," he said to his father sourly, and I watched the two of them. Steven's chest had only a small triangle of downy hair on it, very light tan and descending lazily to a point below the waist of his pants. I was a little surprised at the amount of hair, as Steven seemed so young, but I remembered my own body back in high school, remembered each eager patch of new hair, perky as crabgrass.

The Glass males began to argue over a compass of Ben's that Steven had just broken. Sort of a corny closing symbol, but it *is* an opera and I had no idea what direction the summer was going. I watched them bicker. Steven had the same curve in his lip, and the pattern of chest hair was probably genetic, too. That meant below his shirt the doctor probably had a thicker isosceles waiting for Cynthia to run her fingers through it. Picturing the two of them naked together made me grow trembling cold, even in the still-steaming kitchen. I felt a thin, nauseous ray of fear go through my torso, sharp and tiny like an icicle. A thorn of pain, a prick. Curtain.

ACT I, SCENE TWO

Later that night. A cymbal crash lingers over lush strings as the curtain rises to reveal the sweltering attic of the Glass home. Joseph has agreed to sleep there for the duration of the summer, one floor above the rest of the family in a small triangular guest room. It seems to Joseph that when heat rises in the Glass home, it rises into this room. It feels like a kiln. There's a double bed that dips down like a saggy diaper or a parenthesis. A small scuffed desk has been cleared for writing Joseph's paper, waiting for books travelling in a box which will never arrive, though of course I didn't know that yet. A small white bureau filled with empty drawers, a closet with the door half-open and wire hangers jingling from the lethargic breeze of the ceiling fan. Sometime tomorrow Joseph will unpack. Right now his duffels of clothing are on the floor, unzipped but unmolested. Which is more than we can say for the characters on the stage: Cyn and Joseph, naked on top of the bedsheets. The orchestra's pastoral strings are soft enough that the audience can hear our sweaty skin sticking and slapping as we go at it.

That night was an erotic milestone for me, one of those nights my mind would creep back to, years later and past curfew. It would play in the cramped porn theater in my mind at the slightest cue: when eating something that would run down my chin, when turbulence would make my airplane seat shake compulsively beneath my buttocks. I'd imagine it years later, alone in a dingy apartment, my days weighted by a lengthy recovery program. I'd imagine it months later, while Cyn and I were having sex that wasn't as good. I'd imagine it days later when one of my campers, having not reached the age of total self-consciousness, reached up the leg of her denim shorts, the better to scratch a tiny bleeding bug bite where my knuckles were resting now.

We were far away from one another, with our arms extended so that three of my fingers were inside her while her hand stretched to encircle me in a motion I always found breathtaking in its languid laziness. But not now—she was much shorter than me, so she could only grab my knee. The room was so hot that we were attempting maximum pleasure with minimum contact. Her inflamed sex was spread before me like one of those imported fruits you have to chop open to reach the edible part. Her fingers joined mine inside her, her chubby ring finger entwined with my index like sumo wrestlers. As her breathing got shorter and shorter her fingers contracted into a grappling hook; I faintly heard the crack of the skin on my knee breaking. I slipped on the sheets and fell face-first into her. We pulled our fingers out and I wrapped my hands around her like I was drinking soup. Once I open my mouth there's no stopping me. Her hands flailed to reach me and her moans turned to shrieks; to the audience I'm sure it looks for a minute like I'm killing her. Then she pushed herself away from me and sat up. I looked at her and she put two fingers in my mouth; one tasted like her sex and on the other one I could feel the thick, unwieldy taste of my own blood. It was running down my leg. It smeared a patch of burgundy on Cyn's dark skin when she pushed me to her and I opened the bedstand drawer for the required erotic catching mitt. After a brief and painful misthrust I was inside her. I was grateful to the family for taking me in this summer. Neither of us wanted to be underneath another body in this overheated attic so we stayed sitting up, Cyn's breasts swinging against mine like damp balloons every time we moved. Our mouths were hot, so kissing was uncomfortable, but we kept our mouths open and close to one another until our breathing found a sharp rhythm. She moved her hands from behind her back—I saw three of her fingernails had specks of blood beneath them from my knee—and around me, urging me on, and in. All the prepositions were in use: on, in, out, along, around, amongst, and as one of her fingers dipped lower and lower down the center of my back, through. Her finger was just barely inside me, like she was pushing a button. Which she might as well have been: we both lost complete control, pushing so fast it was more like shuddering, shuddering so completely it was more like a seizure, seizuring so hard that the orchestra has to extend its budget and hire some additional percussionists just for these ten measures or so.

My ears were still ringing when I finally wilted and the juice of our efforts flooded beneath us in a sudden wet stain. Tomorrow we'd feel the same thing in broad daylight during the Welcoming Water Balloon Fight at Camp Shalom. Just then we slithered apart, leaning against opposite bedposts like prizefighters mid-round. My whole crotch was waterlogged, as was Cyn's, although my blood had apparently evaporated during the excursion, or maybe just rubbed in, lotion-like. My knee stung. The sheets were a liquid mess. "Next time we have to do this in your room," I said. "I can't believe I have to sleep on all this."

"It'll feel good," Cyn said. Her leg was stretched out into the air making a faint giraffe-shadow on the wall. I watched it chew as she wiggled. "Plus, we can't do it in my bedroom. It's between my parents' and Steven's. They can hear everything. *You'll* be able to hear everything, too. My room is directly below this one."

"Who slept here?" I asked, looking around. "This feels like half a bedroom and half an attic."

"Well, it's *all* attic," Cyn said, "but it's been a bedroom too. My parents put my old bed in it when they redid my room, back in eighth grade. I slept up here while the workmen built those shelves and laid down carpet and everything. In fact"—here she slid over to me, draping her sweaty hair on my shoulder and both hands in my lap like a napkin—"in fact, it was here that I first heard my parents having sex."

"Really? Sleeping all those years in the next room and everything?"

"Well, I was in eighth grade, so maybe I never knew what I was hearing. Or never paid attention. I just remember sleeping in this room and hearing my parents directly below me, in *my* room. I think they were celebrating the new soft carpet or something." She stretched; the giraffe found a mate. "It was weird, figuring it out. It was about this time of year, so it was really hot."

It was indeed. I squinted at her shifting legs, feeling her float around me like the haze of humidity. The giraffes necked above us on the wall as her voice got hazy, her body got hazy, the whole room clouded over. "It was this sort of muted—*cushioned* thumping. And I was right above them. The sound was so *obvious* I felt like I was floating right above them. And then I just realized that thing you realize eventually—that your parents had sex and that's how you were born. I mean, when you think of your mom you don't think of her having sex. You know? At least, my *mom*. My *dad*, yes, for some reason I can picture him

44

having sex, but my mom just seems like my *mom*, maternal and everything. But I'm just telling you"—here the rhythm of the aria is broken, so this thematic phrase won't be missed even by the densest of ticketholders—"you can hear everything that goes on in my room from this room. The room is right on top of *my* room. The *bed* is right on top of *my* bed. That's all."

She stopped talking and we looked lazily at each other from across the bed, our come between us like a disputed lake. My body was warmed through at her sex talk; as the house creaked around us in the cooling air I could feel the summer evening's consummation of the entire house. My room was above hers, my bed above hers, and as the floorboards crackled it felt like our separate bedrooms were going to go at it with the same ferocity of their inhabitants. Cyn watched my interest pique with a wry smile before reaching over and touching the tip with her still-damp finger like she was seeing if the cookies were done. Shrugging she walked over to the closet. On her back I could see the picket fence of leaning against the headboard.

"See?" she said. "There are still some of my clothes here. Just the stuff I never wore." She pulled out something covered in plastic wrap, muted pink like a fetal mouse. "Gramma gave me this. It made me look like a scoop of strawberry ice cream."

"Good enough to eat?" I said.

"No," she said, putting it back. "More like very cold and fattening."

"But able to melt at any time."

"Shut *up*. And here's my bright green vest that was all the rage for ten minutes. And this dress with matching shawl that somebody brought me from Israel. Oh, look! My green flowered bat mitzvah dress! I looked like a shrub." She stepped into the closet and bent over like somebody waiting to be spanked. She bobbed her head back up, flamingo-like, wearing a bright orange ski cap. "What do you think of *this*?"

"Very nice," I said. "You look like a ski-bunny centerfold."

She grabbed it off her head and pulled out something else. "Oh, I *love* this one." I couldn't get a look at it because in a brief blur of color she tossed it off the hanger and onto her body, her arms sputtering for a moment as it went over her head like she had fallen into quicksand. Then she turned around and I saw her in it. I'm not going to describe the cut of the dress, or even the color which I still see on my eyelids whenever I'm tossing and turning, because I feel very strongly that a costume designer should be given as free a rein as possible in designing an excruciatingly sexual garment. It wasn't absurdly obvious like something black that raises curtains at the thigh, or some strict stripe at waist-level that offers the breasts like a pushy caterer. Off the body it would look like something respectable. It covered everything, but like wrapping paper you can't wait to tear off. You can imagine what it looks like. It looks like what you want. I know that deep down you know what I'm talking about.

I felt my lips drizzle with the juice of my gasp. "Wow. That— you look—why don't you ever wear that?"

She turned around slowly in it. "My father asked me not to."

The music changes. "What?"

"A few days after I bought it my father came upstairs to tuck me in and asked me never to wear it again."

"Your father came to—"

"Yeah, he did that for years, even when I was in high school. I miss it sometimes. He asked me not to wear it any more."

46

"Why? It's perfectly respectable." I looked at her again. "Sort of."

Cyn smiled. "Dad never cared much about respectability. He always said that caring too much about society's rules could lead to—what did he call it—*hypervigilance*. You know, always worrying about what's happening instead of actually doing something."

"Right," I said. But it didn't feel right.

"Yeah. So it wasn't the respectability. He said it would give him a heart attack. He was really uncomfortable about it. I can understand why; it's one of the few times I can remember him telling me specifically *not* to do something. But he said as a favor to him. Please stop wearing it. So I put it up here." She shut the closet door and with a start I saw that the outside of the door had a mirror on it. My own naked body, leaning against the footboard, swung into view. With Cyn standing by the door I could see both sides of the dress, all of her body offered up at once. I wanted to have sex with her. The foreboding music has dissolved back into the sensual themes of the scene's opening.

Cyn followed my gaze to the mirror and our eyes met in the reflection. "Yeah," she said. "It's a little creepy to see yourself when you are going to sleep."

"But that's not what *we* could use it for," I said, getting up and walking to her. I felt the footboard-brand on my back in geometric, sticky dents, and my erection toggled in front of me like I was taking something for a walk. She watched me in the mirror as I approached her, her face so close to the glass that her breath clouded both of our faces. Do you want to know what she looked like? Imagine her now, so you can be as turned on as I was. Aroused. Picture who you want—hips, mouth, hands, birthmarks, curves and skin and all the features you need to keep you here—because she was who *I* wanted. She was all the features I needed to keep me there. That's what she looked like, as the cloth of her dress purred against me. With my hands I parted her buttocks so that I could slide thick between them, the folds of the dress cradling me like a hammock. She put out one arm to steady herself against the mirror, wiping away the fog. Our eyes met again.

It's an important point in a romantic relationship when you can talk dirty, out loud. You've achieved a state at which you don't think your lover is going to repeat your sex whispers over coffee with friends and everyone will throw back their heads and laugh at you. Hopefully opera will achieve a state at which outright eroticism can be sung without giggles or scandal, because aside from encores in my mind this opera has only been performed once and it seems sort of a waste. We'll see. Watch.

My hand crept up her dress and one of us unzipped it, depending on where the costumer puts the zipper. The dress slid down her body catching for a second where we were pressed together. "Look," I said. "Watch." Both my hands crept around her shoulders in the mirror. Her eyes went from my eyes to my hands, where my fingers rested on her collarbones like I was feeling a pulse, which of course I was. "Watch my hands." Unsteadily she stepped out of the fallen dress. Her hand left the mirror and she put her hands on her own neck, nervous but watching my hands. I took each hand and travelled with them down her chest. "Watch *your* hands. *Our* hands. Watch your breasts." Our hands travelled to them together, me rubbing her rubbing herself. She swayed and I stepped to her, sliding against her back like a hungry chair. We moved lower. Watch us. "Watch your nipples. Watch your stomach." I couldn't see much of my own body in the mirror but I felt heated, fused into a column as flagrantly symbolic as the posts of the bed, yearning straight up toward the spinning blades of the fan. All the love we were having felt like *mine*, her body caressed by *me*. I could tell by Cyn's half-lidded eyes, glued on her own hands, that she felt the same way: it was all for ourselves, separate and sexy. I took her hands in mine and led her down, down. "Watch your hips. Watch your thighs." Our fingers curled together like a last-ditch grip on a building, the villain falling at the end of the movie. "Watch your—"

"Watch your *mouth*," Cyn said, smiling and disentangling. Shuttered in shadows as the fan kept turning, she strode confidently across the room. She turned to me, her mouth hanging open. "I couldn't stand up any longer," she said. "Come here."

"I plan to," I said, bounding over to stand by the bed.

"*Shut* your mouth," she said, and shut hers. Now I was swaying, my body bending in an arc like a fishing pole, having caught something. "Now I can't stand up any longer," I said, and staggered a knee onto the bed.

"On top," she said, and as usual lowered herself onto me like a wet guillotine after the ritual fumbling with the rubber device that probably won't make the opera. I moaned something. In the mirror it looked like Cyn was sitting alone, contemplating my severed, staring head, but the music is unmistakable: those curling waves of strings, up and down the fluttering scale, along with thunderous rolls of mallets travelling on upright, quivering cymbals. It's either sex or a storm at sea and we ain't on a boat.

49

Her arms spidered down the mattress to balance herself. "You know," she said, "it's a shame we're going to be together for the rest of our lives."

I couldn't answer for a couple of bobs. "It feels pretty good to *me*," I said.

She smiled. "Not *together*," she said, italicizing the word with some sort of torque. "*Together*." And here one of the spiders spun back up and clasped the breast that blocked her heart from view.

"Why?" I said. I reached one hand up and held it on hers, my hand over her hand over her breast and eventually over her heart. "I love you."

"Oh, Joseph, I love you, too," she said, toggling forward. *Exquisite*. "But I haven't slept with very many people."

"Oh," I said. It was if the red-haired actor stepped into the room. Could I meet him later?

"I want to have all the possible tricks for you," she said. "I wish I'd learned more before I met you."

"You're doing fine," I said. "Jesus, Cyn, we have incredible— wait!"

A stinging tweak of horns, there and gone.

"Great," I said again, and we smiled at one another. She leaned forward and dangled a breast into my mouth like Greeks dropping grapes. I munched, briefly. "Don't you think we teach *each other* enough?"

She tossed her hair; in the mirror it was like some brown bird fluttered by. "But that's like one of those schools that doesn't really have teachers, just supervisory adults and the kids learn from one another and it's all one happy family and blah blah blah."

We shifted together, like continental plates. Our breath grew hot and weird—earthquake weather. "What are we talking about?" I asked breathlessly.

She shivered away from me and fell back to the bed. The music should invert here, too; I'm not sure how. Still inserted I curled over like a beckoning finger, my legs climbing hers like trenched soldiers advancing. "No, no!" she cried sharply. *Retreat.* "On top!" Cyn gave me a sweaty grin and we resumed. "I just wish I *knew*," she said. "I wish I was *sure* I'd had sex with enough people."

"What do you mean?" I asked. Conversation was getting difficult to carry on as we carried on.

"I just—I've only learned about sex from other people who were learning about sex. I feel a little empty. I feel, I don't know, a void. The void of—I don't know, if it weren't so traumatic I think I should have learned about sex from somebody older, and experienced. Except that obviously that would be psychologically weird. That's why—no, stop that, listen to me—" She grabbed my hand from behind her and put it back on the bed firmly. "That's why in many ways learning about sex from my father would have been perfect."

Here it is again: T.U.D. The Unknown Dread, this time with trombones and bassoons as Joseph performs a brief soliloquy: *She can't possibly be saying what I hear her saying.* Chord. *What I hear her saying.* Chord. *It is not possible.* Chord. It's dead quiet except for the rustle of rude playbills.

"Sex with—"

"My dad. *One's* dad. I don't know."

"I think," I said, stiff and stiffly, "that one would feel an enormous sense of shame."

51

"Not shame," she corrected. "Probably *guilt*." She leaned back her head and looked down at me like a nude judge. She licked her lips and quoted something, I don't know what. " 'Guilt says I *made* a mistake, shame says I *am* a mistake. And I'm not a mistake.' "

"Not a mistake," I repeated, the same notes but a different register.

"Right," she smiled. "So I'd probably feel some *guilt,* the power of society telling me I made a mistake." At this point the music should say: *What?* "I mean, I know there's a big *thing* against it." She thrust herself against my trembling hips, pinning me to the bed. "But all behavior exists within a social and cultural context. Imagine if there wasn't a *thing*. It makes a lot of sense, educationally. Usually a girl and her father grow apart as a woman is developing sexually." She dangled one of her secondary sex characteristics into my mouth again, which was gaping open. "The mother is usually the one who teaches about periods, and the father doesn't know what to do. I think that's why he was so weird about the dress." She tossed her head back to the discarded dress, curled up near the mirror like shed skin. "It showed off my puberty. But if the father were traditionally responsible for teaching someone the ropes, so to speak"—here she grinned at me, in reference to a brief bondage experiment we'd tried back in bleary March—"then I could learn so much from somebody. And you would pass it on to your children. I mean, my father is an attractive man, fit, and—"

"You're talking like some male fantasy character in a dirty book," I said. I felt like I'd been caught reading it.

She shrugged and her whole body twisted in such a way that crossed the inevitable line. We both quickened with military precision and ferocity, like a field drum roll. Our faces grew furious and fell closer and closer to one another—we didn't want to fire until we saw the whites of our eyes. It occurred to me that all she'd said had maybe been nothing but talking dirty. Not a plan of action but some new toy to try, some way of taking the family stress after an invigorating year in the dorms and turning it into further fuel for our exploits. The idea of her telling me secrets to egg me on aroused me even as the secrets repelled me, and the *accelerando* of our our bodies drowned out T.U.D. and the unblinking mirror saw another splashdown. Cyn's exhausted flesh collapsed on top of me and I placed my hands behind her, pressing myself further in even as I retracted. I imagined the view from above, fluttered as the fan still spun, of my damp hands upon her like those of an exhausted castaway. The image of her body stirred me even more than the body itself, the idea of her being viewed, like this was all in front of an audience. She must have felt my resparking, because she raised up on one arm and one eyebrow, and shook her head.

"I *must* get to bed," she said, and hopped off me and the bed like her examination was over. She crossed the room and bent down to grab the robe she'd snuck up in. She picked it up by the scruff of its neck and regarded it for a moment before figuring out how to turn it right-side out—a perky oboe solo should do the trick. I myself felt wet, shaky, squinty. Fetal. In the usual bout of post-coital gloom I wondered bleakly how Cyn could be so casual. All our wailing and gnashing of teeth were measures and measures behind us, right now only the polite pastorals of the scene's opening accompany what we did. I stared at the room, gawky as a marionette; Cyn looked for her other sock with yawning patience. She was a loose woman. I had slipped in and out of her almost unnoticed, so clogged was her brain with the memories of listening to her parents and from the educational prospects of sleeping with her father. I remembered suddenly how her expert unbuckling when we finally succumbed in my dorm room, peeling away her own pants like the greedy unwrapping of birthday presents, had distressed me as well as hardened me, her refusal to even pretend that we were exploring new territory. How loosely had I slipped inside her, and now how loosely did I find myself in her family attic, embarking on a summer on the basis of so much fucking. She was a loose woman, and as she tied the cloth belt with a brisk strangling gesture I thought of what she'd told me about her father, what her father had told me about her, all the things I didn't know and wouldn't notice until I stepped on them like shards of glass on the beach. She was a loose woman, and as I considered all that lay untold between now and the last few gasps of August she felt like a loose cannon as well.

I could have spent the summer anywhere, called her on the phone in the evenings after grumpy days at some job. Thought of her discarded jeans before I slept at night, led myself to sweaty explosions in a sagging bed in some room creaking with unfamiliar noises. Then I wouldn't have heard the ones below me after Cyn had left the room and I was alone between the fan and her downstairs bed. The paternal knock on her door could have been the house settling, but all the muted gasps after that, whispered cadences creaking up from the house, had to be more than my dirty mind. My brain soiled as I strained to hear more, and obligingly the sound of the ceiling fan faded and I could hear low moans, familiar to my attic bed as the wind through the window. I pictured Cyn from above, fluttered as the ceiling fan I'd noticed when she showed me her room spun above them. My dirty mind could picture the doctor with his surgeon hands upon her like those of an exhausted castaway. I closed my eyes to hear better and the room turned to steam around me. I pictured myself floating through the vapory floor, down to her bedroom with the consummated carpeting and entering her body from behind. Would I be joining anyone there, like a guest? I couldn't trust the sounds of a house I'd never lived in, couldn't trust my body for an appropriate response as I shifted on the wet sheets and felt my own hands fumble down my hips. But the offstage aria, if indeed it's being sung, is lost to the audience's ear as the orchestra closes the act and leaves the dirty minds of the audience sputtering in the sudden surge of the house lights, on for intermission.

A BRIEF INTERMISSION

[The audience strolls out of the auditorium and chats about subjects tangentially related to the action.]

A typical day at Camp Shalom that summer went as follows: Cyn and I would leave the Glass home with the sticky stagger of people who are hot, tired and late. We'd be clutching identical plastic mugs emblazoned with Mather College's crest, Cyn's marked with a little red ribbon so we could tell them apart.

She drove us to Shalom in the same automobile that had bumped and ground our way to Pittsburgh, the same automobile in which Cyn had fondled our pimply employer, the engine rumbling beneath my denim shorts. We usually both wore denim shorts—the weather too hot for long pants and the campers too messy for sensitive cloth—and, at least at first, one of the two official Camp Shalom Counselor T-shirts we'd been issued. As the summer dragged on we grew lazier and lazier about rinsing the T-shirts every night and despite the occasional griping of the pimply actor the shirts appeared with less and less frequency, like the electronically rendered heartbeat of somebody dying in the hospital.

We never spoke, the whole way there, the whole summer long. We didn't need to. We never needed to. It was a mutual, unspoken agreement, like some family tradition that later requires extensive therapy. We didn't need to, but it meant that between Camp Shalom and the Glass dinner table the only private conversations that Cyn and I had were during or immediately following sex. The ride to camp would have been an ideal time for conversation, but never, the whole way there, the whole summer long. It was usually a twenty-two-minute drive, meaning that we could leave Byron Circle at a quarter to eight and only be seven minutes late. We'd slink into the Mandatory Staff Meeting and the pimply actor would glare at us, less for tardiness than the way we'd come in. In a mutual, unspoken agreement we'd always enter the meeting smiling or even laughing at one another as if we'd been chatting blissfully the whole commute instead of waiting for our coffee to cool and listening to the grating radio announcer update us on our tardiness. The hit song that summer was "Bing Bing Bing," which according to the chorus, is the sound my heart makes when I see you babe.

It was also the sound of the gong which divided up the Camp Shalom Day into Hello, Peace and Goodbye. The gong wasn't a gong proper but three empty cans of government surplus peanut butter glued together to make a large hollow column and suspended from the Mitzvah Tree. Each summer the Arts & Crafts students repainted it. Mitzvah means "blessing" in Hebrew and even the campers with no religious education at all knew that "Shalom" could mean hello, goodbye and peace, depending on when you said it. "Like if you said it when someone was leaving," the Camp Director said in her pert little voice, "it would mean 'goodbye.' " And if you stood around the flagpoles in the morning and sang the national anthems of America and then Israel, it would mean Hello, the first third of Camp Shalom's day. The Camp Director would make some announcements. Then there would be an All-Camp Activity which I remember only from the brief blurry snapshots of All-Camp Activities in the Camp Shalom brochure: A water-balloon fight, leaving everyone's bodies soaked and the grounds littered with small rubber fragments of blue and white, the colors of the Israeli flag. Capture-the-flag, using one ragged blue panel and one ragged white panel that I had cut at the Arts & Crafts Shack. Cyn and I breathlessly pressed together during All-Camp Hide and Seek, my orgasm rivering into her cupped hand as one of the Rosen twins checked the nurse's office, but not, thank God, its closet. A tinny hora from portable speakers, with us romping around the flagpole. Something in the pool.

The Camp Director would declare winners and losers and the kids would all scamper to the Morning Activity, the second scene in the Hello Act. Based on some checked-off preferences mailed in by Mom, the kids could learn new Hebrew songs from Cyn, rehearse vaguely Jewish skits under the direction of the pimply boy, glue things in the shack I managed, play a variety of sports rechristened with Hebrew names, get wet under the sunglassed silence of the lifeguard, or, until it was discovered that what they were doing was pairing off to tongue each other in the semi-seclusion of the Theodore Herzl Grove, go on Nature Walks. Bing bing bing and it was time for Peace: a kosher lunch.

The Goodbye gong marked the afternoon activities, and by the end of Goodbye everybody was cranky, so the two-thirty closing ritual at the flagpole never had the soft-focus magic of the brochure. The cranky audience had to listen to a brief presentation from one cranky group of activiteers. Cyn's kids would sing. While the pimply director stood in front and mouthed the script, we'd see a vaguely Jewish skit. The lifeguard would break his silence and present the day's Most-Improved Swimming Medal to some blue-lipped boy who would take the certificate in his proud little puckered hands. And, before Nature was shut down until further notice, a blushing couple would hold out a leaf they'd probably pressed between their heaving Camp Shalom T-shirts.

My own presentations were a mixed success. Pieces of cloth, decorated with dried macaroni, beads and glitter, the better to cover bread for Shabbat, were an ideal project, but it honestly hadn't occurred to me that papier-mâché candleholders were a bad idea until every last one of them caught fire and burned down to their wire-hanger frame in the Goodbye presentation. Assigning each Hello child a pair of animals and getting the whole Goodbye group to collaborate on an ark was an inspiration, but construction-paper mock Torahs drew angry phone calls from Orthodox parents pointing out that The Word is properly written on lambskin. After finding inspiration in events best left undescribed until Act III Scene Two, I trooped the shackers down to Red Sea Creek to scoop mud into big plastic vats which originally held ice cream donated from Scoberg's Scoops for make-your-own sundaes. They bitched as we lugged them back up the hill, but everybody revelled in the filthy enchantment of dumping the mud onto a big plank and forming it into a giant seated figure. The little Katz kid donated two marbles for his gaping eyes; his leering face was scraped out of the muck with popsicle sticks. We covered our golem with a sheet and the lifeguard helped us slither him over to the flagpole where he dried, a mystery, all day long. For once nobody was cranky for the final ceremony, but in all the excitement I forgot a key rule of golem-making: it's the Word of God, not the clay, that makes a golem a golem. Mud, when it dries in an atheist context, is just dirt. What looked mighty when wet was as flimsy as construction paper. The friction of the unveiling broke his left leg. It crashed and dusted on impact. The sheet raked him over; his face fell like a bad cake. In a final insult, his right eye rolled right out, hit a small rock and broke into jagged halves, the Katz kid's best shooter. By the time his whole body was unsheeted he didn't look like a golem. He didn't look like a statue. He looked like a pile of shit. Four of the eight-year-olds cried.

I almost redeemed myself with the God's Eyes, almost. Put the sticks together to make an X (*Not* a cross; this is Camp Shalom). Weave the yarn around them in concentric, sloppy squares. Switch colors. Tie the ends. Around and around and around. The results are somewhere between spiderwebs and quilt squares; when the tidier girls made them in dozens of colors with splindly tassels on the corners they looked like the confettied photographs in biology textbooks of tiny creatures supposedly found in every pond. As inexplicable as finding one-self in Pittsburgh for the summer, God's Eyes became a fad. First adorning the roof drains of the Arts & Crafts Shack, then the Camp Director's Office, then the dining hall, then the other shacks and the infirmary and the changing rooms at the pool and then every available overhanging, with miniature versions appearing on kids' keychains and belt loops and ears and then given as friendship tokens, romantic tokens and Nature Walk tokens, the God's Eyes surveyed the whole camp within a few days of their debut. Kids would sneak away from swimming to raid the diminishing yarn reserves of the Shack. Missing kids would return as the gong rang, breathless from their excursions, grass stains on their untucked shirts, clutching exchanged tal-ismans of their lust, damp from their sweaty palms. The very act of unravelling yarn became foreplay for the pre-teens. Cyn gave me one as a joke after she mounted me in the changing room during lunchtime, the damp room swirling around us with the ghosts of who knows how many bashful boys hiding their circumcised erections behind the blue and white Camp Shalom towels, how many chlorinated orgasms achieved in the trembling privacy of the stalls, wiped off hairless chests with toilet paper, rinsed in the pool as soon as the protrusions sub-sided? God knows. They saw everything, things I couldn't have seen myself, and they told me I must have been wrong. All summer long, blinking in the breezes, we were watched over by the handmade surveillance of God's Eyes.

ACT II, SCENE ONE

A pre-curtain woodwind interlude establishes the three weeks between the first we know of Dr. Glass fucking his daughter beneath the attic floor of Joseph's borrowed room and the eye-piercing blaze when the footlights hit the dagger Mrs. Glass is holding. If the director blocks it carefully, the soprano should be able to catch the light at every angle of her arc, sweeping the audience in pure glare like something arriving from another planet.

But it's just a prop. After the first week of camp, instead of riding home with Cyn I had been walking over to the Benedrum Center for the Performing Arts to finish off my incomplete in their library. Of course it was still early in the summer, and my box of books from Mather College still hadn't arrived, so there really wasn't much work for me to do, but when Mrs. Glass suggested it Cyn agreed so readily that I said O.K. Intellectually I knew that between working together and living together Cyn and I needed some time apart, but I didn't want to. Still, the Benedrum Center for the Performing Arts had a library which could at least give me an idea for the paper until my books arrived, and when I got bored I could stroll down to the Props Studio where Mrs. Glass made the necessary objects for the summer season. It was a fine way to spend my late afternoons, there in the crowded company of plastic ivy, plaster vases, sofas with trompe l'oeil velvet brushed onto them. Meanwhile, the good doctor would return to Byron Circle about the same time, his practice faltering after the ceramic bone disaster, and Cyn said she wanted to spend some quality time. Alone. With him.

"Nice dagger," I said, and Mrs. Glass turned and smiled at

me. She put her finger on the tip of it and it bent droopily. The audience sighs in relief; it's rubber.

"How are you, Joseph?" she asked, taking her finger off the dagger so it bobbed like a freed penis. "How are the Shalomers? How is your paper going?"

"The campers—Hello, Goodbye, Peace," I said, sitting down behind a row of white wig heads. "The paper—Going, Going, Gone."

She turned down the radio to hear me better. Out of the speaker the summer's biggest hit was revving up—"Bing Bing Bing." The sound my heart makes when I see you babe. "You're done with the paper?"

"I haven't started," I said. "I call the postal people *every morning* and they can't help me."

"I know what that's like," Mrs. Glass said. She thrust the dagger to her own scarcely-sagging breast, took it away, thrust it again, gave a satisfied nod and put it in a box filled with daggers. "I called the clay people today for the umpteenth time and they just keep saying, 'it's on its way, it's on its way.'" The clay people, apparently, talk in high screechy voices; that section of the dialog is at the top of most sopranos' ranges.

I nodded miserably. Mrs. Glass was cutting shiny foil for another dagger. "By the time the books come there won't be any time to write my paper."

"Then you have to write your paper without those books," Mrs. Glass said firmly. She disapproved of my incomplete.

"Yes, Mrs. Glass," I said mock-meekly.

Mrs. Glass smiled. "I thought you were going to call me Mimi," Mimi said. "I'm sorry to snap at you. I'm just stressed that the season's approaching so quickly. There's only something like twelve days before we open, and all the clay hasn't even arrived for—"

"I know," I said. "The summer's going really fast. It seems like last night when I had my first dinner here and Dr. Glass told me he lusted after your daughter." Or, I got to meet Cyn's grandmother. Or, we had that delicious salmon-and-sake thing. Or something.

"Just wait until you get older," she said, creasing the tip of the blade. Next she opened a small jar of clear sticky glue, to keep everything in place and make it shine. "Your whole life will just *race* by. I can't believe my daughter's already the age I was when Ben and I were—well, when *I* was in my first year at college, Ben and I met and immediately—well, I can't believe she's bringing somebody home already, you know? Nothing against you, of course. I just can't believe—Ben and I weren't married yet, but both of us were free thinkers, and—you know? It just *races* by."

"Um,"

"I just can't—I can't believe. I mean, *little Cynthia!* I was *her age* when Ben and I"—she gestured circularly with the half-finished dagger—"and now *that little baby* is *bringing boys home*—I just can't believe you guys are having sex already! I mean, if Cynthia were my age—Cynthia *is* my age—she'd be having sex with Ben! Her father! I mean—"

"I know what you mean," I said. On the wall, mapped out in masking tape, were the outlines of tools that had been taken down.

"I'm sorry," Mimi said, wiping the wet dagger with her fingers like she was smoothing a feather. "It's just on my mind. Cynthia is already in college, and even Steven is getting bigger and bigger.

When he was born he was completely hairless, Joseph. You should have seen it. Ben always said that it was a wonder, because I'm so hairy." She shook her hair and held up the dagger to the light. Though the orchestration to this point should be as bewildering as the aria itself, here when the new dagger glints everything should stop. Absolutely.

"You don't seem that hairy to me," I said, believing this to be the polite response.

"You haven't seen all of me," she said, sweeping her arm down her front as if describing an apron. "*All over,* I'm telling you. But Steven came out of my body like a Ping-Pong ball. You know? I remember holding him in my hands and his head was like those white peaches that show up at the Farmer's Market for maybe three weeks tops. I forget what they're called."

"I know what you mean," I said, eager to skip past the table-tennis part of the conversation. "They're like albino peaches but they're not. Or something."

"Right," she said, stabbing the dagger into herself again, checking the tip again, starting another dagger. "His head was fuzzy like that. It was so fuzzy and warm, fuzzy and warm like the belly of a bird. I wanted him so safe, when he was hairless like that. I felt the same thing when Cyn came out of me—fierce and tender love, this book called it." She took one long-nailed hand off the raw dagger and reached over to a book that lay next to her purse. She scratched her sticky hands on the jacket, briefly, like she was typing a single word. I couldn't see the title. "Fierce and tender love. He just felt so vulnerable. I wanted him safe in the world."

I thought of the big brick house on Byron Circle, squatting on its foundation, its windows stickered with warnings of an elaborate alarm system. And every morning Mimi drove him from the house—I mean, gave him a ride to work to the prestigious lab before heading to the Benedrum Center for the Performing Arts. I wondered if he and Mimi talked, if the car gave the same erotic bedspring rattle as it lumbered over Pittsburgh's bridges and streets, carrying Steven from his solid house to a hermetically sealed room. "He seems pretty safe to me," I said.

"Well, *now,*" she said, shrugging the dagger like *now* was a movie she didn't care for. "Now he's all grown up. He was such a *serious* boy. I remember one day he got worried because he stepped on a crack in the asphalt at his school—that was one of the reasons we ended up putting the kids in private school, because the public school grounds weren't kept up that well— anyway, he stepped on a crack and he was terrified all day long because he thought he'd broken my back. You know: 'Step on a crack, break your mother's back.' But all those days are gone."

"He doesn't step on cracks any more?"

Mimi smiled, stabbed, started another. How many daggers did they need, anyway? "It's just that—do you mind if I tell you something? It might be a little embarrassing."

I wondered if Mimi could see in my head the mortifying sex circus she'd already shown to me—an image of my girlfriend's mother, hairy legs spread, expelling Ping-Pong-ball children like some machine designed for batting practice. Or if she, one floor below me, felt chilly shame pressing upon her like a steamroller as she heard the noises I kept hearing, the whispers, the creaks of the carved wooden bedframe Mimi had undoubtedly found in an out-of-town antique store and brought into the city slowly in the far right lane with hazard lights clicking in relentless rhythm, the moans covered by sweaty palms. I'd been in perpetual embarrassment for weeks now and I haven't decided yet how an orchestra can best convey this. "Go ahead."

"Well," Mimi said eagerly, "a few days ago I was airing out the house. You know it's not good just to have the air conditioning going all the time. So I opened the window at the end of the hall, you know, the one above that little wrought-iron table I showed you?"

So far this was as far removed from mortification as the Glasses got. Anti-embarrassment. Non-mortification. "Yes. Little claw feet."

"Right. Well, whenever I open the window in that hallway it always opens one of the doors. Some air pressure, or wind rushing thing. This time it made the bathroom door open. Steven's bathroom. And he was just stepping out of the shower."

I examined the little outlines of masking tape. A hammer? A chisel? What fit? "Oh."

"I mean literally stepping out. He didn't see me. He was stepping over the side of the bathtub, you know? And I could see *everything*. He was reaching for a towel." Mimi stepped into the middle of the room and pantomimed it for me and all the blank wig heads. First one leg and then the other stepped out of the invisible tub, arcing like fired missiles. I could see what it looked like to watch him, and when she reached for a towel the crotch of her paste-stained jeans was spread flat in front of my eyes like a stretched canvas and I knew what she was talking about. If I could just reach over and turn the radio way up, I could hear the biggest hit of the summer instead of—

"I could see *everything*. My little hairless boy. Well, not any more. He had this small triangle of downy hair on his chest that went down to—like, I don't know, like a landing strip." The timpani comes in first, thrumming out the rhythm of the now-familiar theme: T.U.D. The Unknown Dread is here in the Props Studio, the cellos, the violas, the bassoons sneaking into the air over the radio and into my ears and the ears of all the Styrofoam heads. "I could see *everything*. My boy has grown up. Little Steven has grown up. I just keep thinking about it. His body has come to fruition." Her voice here should throb with vibrato, each quiver moist with expectation like a mouth watering. "I just keep thinking about it and thinking about it. His body, stepping out of the shower like that. I'm attracted to him."

The orchestra, in one big unison blast: BRUM!

"Mrs. Glass, you're kidding."

Mrs. Glass turned to face me, her eyes and mouth all sharp angles. Tense as a wire trap, she looked like a line drawing of herself. An outline. She wasn't kidding. Her mouth pulled up at the sides into a geometric smile. "I thought you were going to call me Mimi."

"Mimi you're kidding," I said flatly.

"No. I mean, just think about it. Sleeping with one's son—if one is attracted to him, of course—actually makes a lot of sense."

"Incest?" I asked, amazed at my non-amazement. It was like the fourth newscast of a military maneuver or a just-discovered ten-year famine. The first time is horrific, of course, but by the fourth night they're using the same footage over and over again and by now the crisis has a title: Standoff at the Border. Starvation in the Desert. Incest in Pittsburgh. With the "Bing Bing Bing" soundtrack the catastrophe was even cushioned in commercial sponsorship. I could watch this, if there's nothing else on. I could tune in.

"Well, not *incest*. Not if you think of it as incest. I mean, all behavior exists within a social and cultural context. I mean, think about it: children are born of sex. My son came out of my vagina. He nursed at my breasts. Why shouldn't he suckle again, at puberty? It would be fulfilling a different need, that's true, but it would be filling a need nonetheless. I mean, the taboo against in—the taboo against a child sleeping with a parent and vice versa—the taboo against—"

I stepped in like a co-host. "Intergenerational sex?"

"Yes! That's great! *Intergenerational sex!* I love it! The taboo against intergenerational sex is really interrupting the natural flow of sexual energy between a mother and her child. The book I'm reading has something that really stuck with me."

Mrs. Glass—*Mimi*—turned off the radio and picked up her book. She flipped through it as I got a look at the spine: *When You Can't Be Friends with Your Mother*. "Here it is," she said, and read out loud: " 'The greatest paradox within the relationship between child and parent is that children's beliefs about parents come from the parents.' " She paused for me to take this in.

"You think that suggests incest?" I asked.

"Well, not *directly*. But I think it implies it. If I teach my son that I shouldn't sleep with him, I'm teaching him that the sexual urge isn't a natural one, because I'm teaching him that it is unnatural to have sex with the person who had sex to bring him into the world. You see what I mean? *When You Can't Be Friends with Your Mother*. When I can't be friends with my son— and he's been so moody, so *adolescent* lately—maybe I can be something else."

"That's—" I said, and dragged my hands up my face like I was removing makeup. "That's wrong," I said finally.

"Is it?" she said. "Think about it. Particularly sleeping with one's *son*. The mother-son relationship, for thousands of years, has always been a problem. This book points it out perfectly—is it just a coincidence that the word 'daughter' is one letter removed from the word 'laughter,' and the word 'son' is one letter removed from the word 'sob'?"

"But those are just *words*," I said. " 'Daughter' and 'son' could have been *any* words."

"Could they have?" Mimi asked. "Here, read the book and then we can talk more about it if you'd like." She held out the book to me.

"I'm pretty busy," I said. "I don't really have time to read anything except for my paper."

"Write your paper on this," she suggested quietly, and reached her arm out farther. She was holding *When You Can't Be Friends with Your Mother* by the corner, and it sagged out of her hand like something about to spill. With a chime of resolution from the woodwinds, Joseph uprights the book.

I put it safely in my hand, opened the cover and read the chapter headings as Mimi returned to her work. "Mother as Degrader." "Mother as Critic." "Mother as Martyr." "Mother as Champion." "This sounds like a cast list," I said.

"You can't show him a cast list!" boomed the voice of a fat man (*baritone*) with stringy hair who walked into the Props Studio and shut the door behind him. On the back of the door was a poster I hadn't noticed in these three weeks: KNOW YOUR ENEMY in black block letters, over a sneering line drawing of an old man's face with a large puffy nose and narrow slitted eyes. Soon they'd be all over town.

"Stan," Mimi said with the patience of somebody who has a stupid boss, "I'm not showing him the cast list. I'm showing him a book I'm reading."

"The daggers done?" he asked.

"Yes," she said. "They're in the dagger box."

"Chains?"

"In the chain box."

"Fists?"

"The clay hasn't arrived yet."

"You ordered *more clay*?"

"Yes, but it hasn't come yet."

"Why in the world would you order more clay? Last week you ordered more clay and the week before *that* you ordered more clay. You must be careful with the clay, Mimi. We've gone over budget already and clay costs money."

"Not until they deliver it," she said. She cleared her throat. "Remember, Stan, when you hired me you said I would have all the budgetary support I needed. You want clay fists, I need clay and lots of it. I don't have to remind you about what happened last summer, do I?"

"No," Stan said quickly. He patted his coat pockets until his hand crinkled against something inside. With a smile of recognition he pulled out a bag of individually wrapped carmels, unwrapped one and threw it into his mouth. "I'm just concerned about the budget, is all."

"This season is going to be a *smash*," she said.

"What happened last season?" I said, gathering I was never to be introduced.

"Who are you?" said Stan sternly. Until now.

"Stan, this is my daughter's boyfriend, Joseph. Joseph, this is Stan, the General Director for the summer season."

"Glad to meet you," I said, holding out my hand. For a second Stan looked at my hand and clutched the bag of caramels closer to his body. Then he realized I wanted to shake, not take, and he shook.

"What happened last season?" I asked again, eager to keep him here rather than remaining alone with the Mother as Lover.

The aria begins simply enough. "Well," Stan said simply, "last season was the first summer opera season in Pittsburgh. We had a very small budget. We still do. All of Benedrum does. Pittsburgh is a dying city and there's no money for the arts. They call this town the Emerald City, but the color of Pittsburgh is a bitter black. The great lumbering steel industry has left a dark powder on a brick that once photogenically matched the color of the people driven out of Duquesne incline and Monogahela Heights." Bassoons bulge with bitterness.

"But what happened last summer?"

"Last summer we put on Faussy's *The Marble Statue,* which has, of course, a big statue in the middle of it. The middle of the stage, I mean. During all four acts. We were supposed to borrow one from Denver Opera but we were outbid at the last minute by a Miami *Aïda.*"

"Atlanta," Mimi said.

"*Miami,* Mimi," Stan insisted. "You didn't work here."

"In any case, the props department had to build a statue and they kept complaining that they didn't have the budget. This was before Mimi worked here."

"This is why Mimi works here," Mimi said.

"They built the statue but they didn't have any clay so they used papier-mâché, and they what-you-call-it, they did that thing to it to make it look like marble."

"Marbelizing," Mimi and I said in unison, but at major thirds.

"Marbeling, right. But it didn't shine, and you know the aria that the Prince sings, *Your eyes shine like the statue in the square.* It had to shine. So they put shellac on it." He looked at me significantly.

The violins fill a pregnant pause with an eight-bar cadence before Joseph replies, "So?"

"*So?*" Mimi says incredulously. "*So,* you can't put shellac over marbelized papier-mâché. At least, not over whatever structure they had. It won't hold."

"So it didn't hold?"

Stan shook his head. "Worse than that. It gave way when Mathilde was clinging to it in the finale. You know, *Statue, give me your strength?*"

"I don't know the opera."

Stan looked a little huffy. "Well, it's very famous. Not that this town will ever do it again. 'Statue, give me your strength!' WHAM! The leg of the statue broke right in two, and the whole thing came apart and fell on Lucretia Allenza, who was singing Mathilde that summer. And she's not a small woman."

"She's fat," Mimi said.

Stan looked uncomfortable; he unpeeled another caramel. "I wouldn't say *fat.*"

"You wouldn't?" Mimi said. "She's a *professional soprano,* Stan. She's as big as a house."

"The press had a field day," Stan said. "I always thought it wasn't coincidence that backlash is shellac spelled backwards."

72

"It's not," I said.

"Yes it is," Stan said. Another caramel. "Think about it."

I thought about it. C-A-L—"It's not."

"Oh. Well, I don't mean backwards. I mean, one of those scrambled word things, where you switch all the letters around and it makes it backlash. Acronyms?"

"Anagrams," Mimi and I said, with the same lilting melody of "marbelizing."

"Right."

"I don't think it's an anagram, either," I said, the letters swimming in my head like alphabet soup. And it isn't. Even years later I try it, and the best I can get out of "shellac" is "she call," which she doesn't.

"In any case," Stan said, "that's why Diva Allenza isn't singing with the Pittsburgh Opera anytime soon, and that's why we have a new propsmistress and a slightly larger budget. But even so the clay is overburdening us. I mean, why do you require so much clay, Mimi? The expense, the expense! Clay is always expensive, Mimi! Because clay comes from the earth, and there is a limited supply! Clay is the source of all life, Mimi! God breathed into the clay of the earth to create man—now you dare to order shipment after shipment of clay to create props! Unless you are hoarding the clay yourself for some nefarious purpose! Confess, propsmistress! Confess!" There, on the "fess" of that last "Confess!" is a high E flat—solid and strident like the French horns that back it up.

"Sheesh," Mimi said. "I'll try to be more careful, Stan, but you know we want to make opera that people will remember."

"That's true," Stan said. "I mean, once I heard some people talking in the lobby during intermission. They were talking about how they always attend the opera in the same clothes they wore to work that day, because by the time they go home and jump in the shower and change their clothes they'd either be late or they'd be on time but so stressed out they couldn't really enjoy it. And frankly, if people are going to pay that much for tickets what's the use if they're not really going to enjoy it. So what these people did is they wore slightly dressier work clothes to work and went right to the theater, locking the briefcase in the trunk and sometimes even having time for a cocktail or something, but not dinner because they hated, these people, to wolf down dinner and rush to the theater. It's so stressful. They might as well go home and shower and change if they want to be stressed out before the show even starts. That's what they said, what's-your-name—"

"Joseph."

"—and I never forgot it. And I never forgot to *repeat* it. Because *that's* our audience. *That's* our audience, Joseph. Just regular working folk. We have to create opera for them that's not just interesting but *fascinating, mesmerizing*. So that they transcend all the stress about whether to change or where to have dinner or parking or whatever, and really *hear* the music. That's what opera's *for*. Do you have any more of those candies?"

"What candies?"

"Weren't you holding a little box of candies?"

"No," I said, holding up *When You Can't Be Friends with Your Mother*. "It's a book that Mrs. Glass—"

"*Who?*" Mimi said sharply.

"It's a book that *Mimi* is lending me," I said. I handed it to him. "Sorry it's not candies."

"It's O.K.," he said. He looked at the spine. "Not your fault.

When You Can't Be Friends with Your Mother, huh? If you can't be friends, what can you be? Eh?" He elbowed me and leaned in so I could see his caramel-coated teeth. From a dirty mouth comes a dirty joke.

"Please, Stan," Mimi said. "Your tight-budgeted propsmistress has to get to work."

"Anyway," Stan said, "all I am trying to tell you, Joseph, is that we are really trying for maximum drama this summer."

"I know the feeling," I said.

"That's why we're making a whole box of daggers. When Abigail stabs Pinchas at the end of *Die Juden,* we are having her stab him furiously and repeatedly. We don't care if the dagger crumbles after each performance, so long as Pinchas dies a horrible death. That's why we are paying for a whole box of daggers. We want Pinchas to die as violently as possible."

"As well he should," Mimi said firmly as T.U.D. returns. "If I ever found out that my husband was sleeping with somebody else, I'd probably kill him and then go mad. The more violent the better, as far as I'm concerned."

If this were a novel, the presence of Cassius the dog, kept in the back room on the days when Mimi would jog with the dog around some of the prettier lakeside territory, would have had to be established by now. You couldn't just have him howl and mention, in the same paragraph, that sometimes Mimi brought her big black labrador Cassius to work with her and kept him in the back room. But this isn't a novel. This is an opera, where motivation can strike at any moment. One love letter and an engagement ring is thrown back at the tenor. One thrown ring and a woman can throw herself down the stairs. One thrown woman and war can break out and the gardener can reveal himself to be Zeus, in disguise. Or a woman, disguised as Zeus. Or somebody who came just a little too late to tell the woman not to throw herself down the stairs because he didn't read the love letter after all. Or he did. Or when a dire prediction is made, a dog can howl offstage chilling the bones and lowering the curtain for a few minutes while the frantic stagehands carry the Props Studio away and lower the walls of the Carnegie Mellon Physics Department cafeteria. This is an opera, and you don't need to know why the dog is there—you don't need to know *that* the dog is there—you just need to know that when it howls it means that the remaining two and a half acts aren't going to be happy.

ACT II, SCENE TWO

A simple chord from the oboes spotlights me and my boredom as I wait in the Carnegie Mellon Physics Department cafeteria. Steven was fifteen minutes late. I'd already ordered a lemonade but wasn't yet bored enough to read *When You Can't Be Friends with Your Mother,* which I'd been dragging with me unopened for almost a week now. I was hot, hot and bored. I'd borrowed Cyn's sputtering car, while she spent quality time with her father, to drive around the curves of the Color-Coded Wayfinder Signs with the windows down, until the university finally appeared in the horizon. Outside it was some triple digit of degrees and the cafeteria was windowless. It was three o'clock—*three-fifteen,* Steven was fifteen minutes late—so the lunch crowd, presumably, had returned to its experiments. The room was swathed in occasional coolness by a large rotating fan like those searchlights in prison break movies, that swing and swing and finally find the felon with his homemade knife at the throat of the warden's daughter. Don't shoot, boys—he's not bluffing. Every time the fan hit my face it chilled my sweat and dimmed the radio. "Bing Bing Bing," the sound my heart makes when I see you babe, turned to a dull white noise every ten bars or so. The orchestra, of course, doesn't duplicate this. It just keeps playing.

Steven finally arrived in a long white lab coat. Underneath, I hope, he was wearing shorts, but he looked like a flasher. I remembered seeing him without his shirt that first night I arrived on the set, and thanks to Mimi's description I could picture the rest.

"Hi," he said. "Thanks for coming. Sorry I'm late. We had a problem with the gold."

"The gold what?" I asked.

"Just gold," he said, smiling faintly like somebody who's working on experiments you can't possibly understand. "We're working with gold. Let me just grab some food and we can talk."

"Sure, sure," I said, trying to sound careless. I couldn't imagine why Steven wanted me to come here. I looked down at my sweaty tumbler and saw through the swirling rind and sugar to the dull gloss of the wood of the table. It felt like a set.

Steven brought his plastic food to the table and sat down across from me. He didn't say anything so I didn't say anything either, just kept sipping. The radio kept playing and the searchlight kept spinning. I was wishing this prisoner could escape. I couldn't imagine why he'd wanted me to meet him for a late lunch, even when I said I couldn't make it until after Goodbye. All summer long I hadn't spoken more than a dozen words to Steven directly and that was on purpose. Steven, at a distance,

77

was a little desert island in Cyn's wild sea of a family, the one who wasn't interested in intergenerational sex but in whatever he had suddenly started babbling about in front of me now. Steven's only aria is accompanied by a small, sputtering brass ensemble.

". . . and we strip the wire with a pair of pliers, just an ordinary pair of pliers, we just rip it down the wire and, of course, the very tip of the wire, the very very tip, is just one molecule in width. One measly molecule wide. So we take the laser I was talking about before, and Cyn—"

"Cyn's here?"

"She is?" Steven's head followed the arc of the fan around the room, a smile of surprise smeared on his mouth along with egg grease. "She's not here. What was I—oh. No. *Since* the tip is only one molecule wide, the laser bounces off that one molecule and hits the gold. From the way it hits the gold, we read with this"—he stuttered for a term that a Mather liberal arts student could understand—"special meter thing. We can tell from the way it reflects off the wire's one molecule, off the gold—we can tell *exactly* what the gold is shaped like. I mean, on a molecular level."

Cyn's roommate had been a puckered little chemical girl whose only redeeming quality was her constant lab work, keeping her away at all hours so that it wasn't *too* often that Cyn and I would make love just three feet from her snoring, pimply face, holding our hands over each other's mouths to absorb our moans into our skin. I knew how to make small talk with science types. "So this whole new meter thing you're building is based on ripping up a wire with pliers?"

"Well, that's how we get the wire to have a one-molecule width."

"But after you rip it, it could be *any* width."

"Not the very tip."

"Yes the very tip," I insisted. "I mean, it could be two molecules, side by side."

He smirked. "Yes, actually it could. But that's one of the founding fallacies of physics in the first place. Entropy is increasing. You know what that means?"

"Yes."

He explained it anyway. "It means that systems are breaking down quicker and quicker through the power of chance. Reactions between disparate parts occur at faster and faster rates, and the way they change their surroundings forces us to abandon our previous assumptions at an astounding rate." Metaphors in operas are always corny, *always*. "We've already experienced a problem with using gold, because they've just discovered a new type of gold. S-gold."

"S-gold?"

"Yeah. They put—because—well, I won't explain it all, but because it's a different kind, sort of a different molecular—well, let's say it's a different *species* of gold. So we're calling it S-gold for now. It's—it's pretty interesting." His voice trailed off suddenly and he dropped the subject. I watched his fork prod at a flat little stack of garnish: half an orange slice, a piece of parsley and an inflamed nipple. As his fork pierced the nipple my eyes filled with memory like an allergic reaction. One of my fingers was poised over Cyn's nipple, the nail sinking into it like a trick we taught our campers, months later, to make their mosquito bites stop itching momentarily. I could see her sex contracting in expectation while my own stretched toward her like a hungover arm, under the covers, toward the cursed, necessary bleating of the alarm clock. I poised myself over her—not our usual position—and moved my fingers from her breast to the bedcovers, for balance. With a sharp vocal—like a burst of brass when the forbidden lovers are discovered, later, in Act III Scene One—she grabbed my wrist like I was taking candy without asking, and returned it to her breast while I wobbled unsteadily between her legs. She met my eyes as she took my weight, and with a lurch she grabbed my other hand, and, looking at me from sharp bright slits, wrapped my sweaty fist around myself. She wanted to come this way, without me inside her, while she watched me stroke myself just inches from her poised sex. Teetering, wronghanded, frustrated and loud, I did it. This was the beginning of about a month's hot interest in masturbation. For weeks afterward we would lie next to one another and stare at the blank tiles of the dormitory ceiling while in the periphery we could see the lustful and selfish movements of our own fingers between our own legs. "Keep your hands," Cyn would pant, a horny cop, "where I can see them." Starting in sensual silence and closing with desperate, heaving gasps, we'd make ourselves come without touching one another except for the trembling *thunk* of our hip bones as they shivered against one another, like silverware in a drawer in a kitchen in a house in an earthquake. But it was never as good as the first time. For all the unpeeling we did in the weeks that followed, we never completely recollected the raw afternoon where she collapsed under the throb of her swollen nipple while I stroked myself, kept stroking myself. Even after I came I kept stroking myself, wanting to give her more and more until my veins ached, strewing more of my ejaculate like pearls upon the forestry of her sex.

"I guess I should stop beating around the bush," Steven said. The cleaved maraschino cherry of the evocative garnish paused for a minute on his tongue before disappearing down his windpipe, past that small triangle of downy hair, very light tan and descending lazily to a point, that I'd seen the first night I'd arrived in this humid and heaving city. It was hard to concentrate in here.

"Go ahead."

He sighed and dropped his fork to the plate in resignation. What could this be, that he wanted from me? Some sort of pseudo-fatherly advice, some locker room talk? He was past, way past, the age of worrying about hairy palms or going blind. Pittsburgh had an aggressive program that made condoms more available at school than exam answers, so he wasn't going to slip me a twenty and wait outside the drugstore while I debated whether his teenaged paramour—some geeky science girl at the lab? a high school flame whose parents hadn't dragged her to Europe or something?—would prefer something Ribbed for Her Pleasure. "It's about girls," he said finally.

"What can I help you with?"

"Well," he said. "When you—how did you—O.K., you and my sister are—"

Bing Bing Bing is the sound my heart makes when I see you babe. Bing Bing Bing don't you know that we really got it made. When you walked into my life, I felt my heart sing. Everywhere I go I hear Bing Bing Bing.

"Yes?" I said finally.

"How did you approach my sister?"

"What do you mean?"

"When you first—well, when you began thinking romantically—do you know what I'm saying?"

"You're saying how did I make my first move on your Cyn?"

"No," he said quickly. "I don't know. I mean, how can you tell when someone is interested in you? There's this person. I wish I could get inside her—"

"Would this be your first time?" I asked.

"What?" Steven's head followed the arc of the fan around the room. "What? What was I—oh. No. I wish I could get inside her *mind*, just to know if she's interested. Because it's sort of a delicate situation. I mean, if it turns out Cynthia isn't interested, then—"

"Cyn?"

"What? Well, I didn't want to tell you who she is, but yes."

"What?" The castaway, adrift in the wild sea of Cyn's family, approaches an island only to find that it's the slick back of a terrible sea serpent.

"Her name is Cynthia."

"Like your sister Cynthia?"

"Well, sure." He blinked, laser-quick. "I mean, let's pretend it's my sister, because it's as good a situation—a *hypothetical* situation—as any. I mean, it would be a delicate situation if I wanted to approach my sister, because if she wasn't interested it would be awkward, you know? *That's* my situation. *That's* what I'm talking about. Hypothetically, of course."

"Hypothetically? Hypothetically let's say you want my advice on how to approach your sister?"

"Well, Cynthia—let's just talk about this situation for now."

I struggled to find some facet of this conversation I could face, and talk to. "That would be incest."

"There's a better word for it," Steven said, licking his lips. "My father and I were just talking—what was the word?"

"Never mind," I said. I couldn't believe how easily *I know what you're talking about* could come from my mouth. "Forget the word."

"It's on the tip of my tongue," he said.

"Forget the word. Forget your *tongue*, Steven. Surely you can understand that it's difficult to discuss this situation. Whoever you have a crush on, it's not going to be like incest."

"Well, not if you think of it like that: *Incest*. But all behavior exists within a social and cultural context. I mean, it's like what I told you about entropy. Systems are breaking down quicker and quicker through the power of chance. Reactions between disparate parts occur at faster and faster rates, and the way they change their surroundings forces us to abandon our previous assumptions at an astounding rate."

"You said that already." Though the second time around he sings it differently.

"Yes, I know, but this time I mean it in reference to—I wish I could think of the phrase my father used."

I sighed, scarcely audible over the growing T.U.D. "Intergenerational sex."

He snapped his fingers. "That's *it!*" he said. "If you think of intergenerational sex within the context of entropy, it doesn't seem horrible but the natural consequences of scientific progress. I mean, it's like what happened with the gold. Entropy is increasing, resulting in that S-gold I told you about. Think of an S-family. S-father. S-mother. S-sister. S-dog, even."

"Interspecies sex?"

"Well, not in my case," Steven grinned. "But that probably isn't so far off, entropically speaking. But within the family—why not? It was individual molecules reacting within the element of gold that produced S-gold—why not a family whose molecules would react with one another, and produce an S-family?"

"That's about the worst science I ever heard," I said, attempting to sound lighthearted. The flutes try the same thing.

He frowned, and I could see in the cross wrinkles around his mouth a genetic history. The same frown when the doctor-father—the S-father, maybe—was reminded of the ceramic leg, buried in that poor girl, snapping in two. "So you're not going to help me with Cynthia?"

"We are speaking hypothetically, right?"

Steven blinked. "Sure," he said.

"I mean, you really have a crush on *somebody else* named Cynthia, who isn't your family member but in some other difficult situation, some other social and cultural context, right?"

"Well, sort of," he said. "It's like that book you're reading there. *When You Can't Be Friends with Your Mother*. If you can't be friends, maybe—"

"Mimi gave me this book," I said, pulling my hands away from it like it might have rabies. "She was saying something similar about it."

"My mother Mimi?"

"Yes."

"She lets you call her that?"

"She *asked* me to call her that. What's wrong with that? Cyn and I are—"

"It's just strange. She's always hated her name. She hates to hear it. She's always regretted being named something even a little unusual. She says it's easier to go through life with the simplest, most invisible thing that people can call you. She always said she hoped I'd forgive her for naming me something unusual."

"Steven isn't unusual," I said.

"It's *Stephen*," he said. "With a P-H."

"Stephen?"

Stephen smiled. "As in phony."

The horizon shifted, in front of my eyes, like a set being lifted to reveal a bare stage where anything can happen next. I knew nothing. I'd been living in a house for more than half a summer and around me the molecules were shifting to an S-house, an S-half of an S-summer. My assumptions were no longer viable. I was as far from knowing what was going on as the soon-to-be-rejected suitor in one of Mozart's little marriage operas, lollygagging around with gay little vocalizations before the entrance of the fickle woman. I muttered something and left Stephen at the table, stumbled into the bathroom where the last chords of the act reverberate in the tiny, stained tiles. "Your're stupid," said a graffito in the last stall, and I didn't have any idea whether the misspelling was an accident or on purpose, some scientific joke. Maybe everything was a scientific joke. Maybe everything was my dirty mind, stained like old porcelain and held in my panicked, sweaty hands, encased in my thick skull. As in the changing rooms back at Camp Shalom I felt the ghosts of masturbation around me, the sudden erections of high-school boys throwing their lab coats open and their shorts down to beat around the bush, their S-sisters moaning in the meters of their minds. But I didn't know if that was *real*. It could be hypothetical. It could be nothing, nothing but my own dirty mind and the erection I found, born of it, when my hands stopped clutching my brain and moved lower. *Your're stupid,* I thought to myself, panting from panic and imagination, my hands moving to lower my shorts, dipping and sagging over my skin like a slow curtain.

A BRIEF INTERMISSION

[The audience strolls out of the auditorium and chats about subjects tangentially related to the action.]

The Board of Directors raised eyebrows to the rafters that spring when they announced that the Pittsburgh Summer Opera Season would consist entirely of anti-semitic operas. The Benedrum Center for the Performing Arts, it was said at the press conference held the first day Cyn and I sixty-nined, was the first American opera company to host such a season, perhaps the first opera company in the entire non-fascist world.

This assertion wasn't strictly true. Just before I embarked upon this terrifying and sexy summer, a senior at Mather College was pounding out a thesis for his degree in anthropology which studied a small high-minded group of bigots who stopped patronizing the opera, ballet and symphony in Jackson, Mississippi, because they felt the aesthetic morals were getting soft on Communism, Catholicism and interracial marriage. This was back in maybe 1950. Withdrawing all donations, these fine upstanding folk formed the Concerned League of Art and Nature and it doesn't take a Talmudic scholar to figure out that's

C-L-A-N. Clan like Ku Klux except with a C because these folks thought it was more subtle that way. They also thought it was more subtle to put on one season of original operas, music and theatrical presentations with titles like *Symphony of the Nigger Problem* and *The Interbreeding Daughter.* They put them on in a church with costumes sewn by the wives/sopranos.

The Mather senior, like all Mather seniors, was given a special carrel in Wigglesworth Library—everyone called it The Wig— in which to analyze this sour little sip from the melting pot. Every night he'd go to the carrel and work on the thesis for a couple of hours, then let his printer spew the draft as he went out, leaned against the brass statue of Michael Wigglesworth and smoked cigarettes with other thesisers. When there were two more butts at the feet of the Puritan he'd go back and proof-read. Then he'd type his mistakes back into the little screens that made the corridor of carrels an eerie aquarium blue. And *then,* before he left, he'd rip the draft in half and stack the little half-sheets of paper next to the pay phones, so people could jot down numbers on the back of "Cornel East said in his *Matters of Race* [check this!] that the Klan's interest in gaining credibility through the annals of high culture is an interesting contrast to more earthy forms of self-recognition in urban black communities, such as [find out what that album is that Andrew listens to]."

If you were breathing heavily in the little telephone cubicle, if you were exhaling in strict time, if you were panting on the phone, these little draft fragments would curl up and skim around like leaves in a breeze. The blank side would flicker with the typed side. You wouldn't think that you could read it, there as it flickered. You wouldn't think enough of it could catch your eye, and you wouldn't think there was room for it in your head, because most of your brain would be consumed by the voice on the phone. Cyn was telling me everything she would do to me if I came to her room right then, instead of writing my paper. She thought I was in the main lobby of The Wig, where a row of pay phones was always busy; she thought she was exciting me somewhere where I had to play it cool. I let her think that, let her excite herself exciting me. But I didn't have to play it cool. The aquarium was closed—the anthros must have been out smoking near the statue of Michael Wigglesworth in front of the library—so I could listen to her with my legs spread, touching myself through a pair of denim shorts I'd wear constantly when Cyn and I worked together at Camp Shalom in Pittsburgh a month later. I could listen to her as the half-sheets of someone's thesis draft, thoughtfully stacked for jotting down phone numbers, curled and drifted with my own sharp breath. It was occuring to me, as my breath grew sharper, that I could go to my flaky professor Ted Steele and get an incomplete. I wouldn't have to write the paper until later, so right now I could walk across the heaving late-May lawns of Mather and have Cyn make good on her promises. You wouldn't think that you could think all this and still read a few stray paragraphs of an anthropology thesis with any comprehension, or that you'd forget all about it as you hung up the phone, already incomplete, and lurched across campus with your erection tugging at you impatiently.

But you would be wrong, because I remembered it. By July the city was papered in advertisements showing a caricatured Jewish face—an old man with a large puffy nose and narrow slitted eyes—captioned KNOW YOUR ENEMY. When Stan told me that Pittsburgh was the first American opera company to host such a season a bell inside my head went bing, bing, bing. I remembered something about Jackson, something about an interbreeding daughter. But I didn't say anything, because it wouldn't hold any water. Nobody remembers something they read on the back of a half-sheet of scrap paper while having phone sex in a library named after one of America's earliest poets, Michael Wigglesworth. It sounds like you're making it up. It sounds like you spent too much time at the Benedrum Center for the Performing Arts and the season's opera plots seeped into your dirty mind, particularly when the operas are things like *Die Juden,* where the Aryan daughter is seduced by Pinchas, a dashing Jewish boy, marries him despite her father's pleas, suspects him of having another lover and in Act IV discovers him in the arms of his yenta-soprano mother and stabs him repeatedly, killing him as violently as possible. Everybody dies. Or like *Rachel and the Rabbi,* where the conniving Rabbi Ben convinces Rachel to refuse the handsome tenor suitor, not because he's Christian but because Ben wants her for himself. You could make something up out of that. Your dirty mind could make something true. Or like *Alma,* where the daughter of the Grand Inquisitor is kidnapped by not one but *two* rabbis only to be rescued by the Spanish Army, angry, cross-wielding and singing in Italian. The opera company put them on, of course, for irony. Not like Jackson at all. They put them on so people would be aware that anti-semitic operas were in fact composed as late as 1965 (the experimental *Lox!,* performed on a smaller stage). They didn't put them on because they were *true.* They didn't put them on because these stories were *true* stories, not at all. If you thought they were true, then there was probably something wrong with *you,* not with the lovely family who took you in all summer long, the generous doctor, the propsmistress who let you call her by her first name even though you were still in college and she didn't even like her first name, the brother who didn't want to discuss anything like *that,* but wanted to discuss something else, something perfectly innocent, or maybe never invited you to lunch at all. You could have made that up, too—as if the Physics Department would have its own special cafeteria, as if they'd make scientific geniuses eat in a windowless room at the height of summer. You couldn't tell anybody these stories—they'd think you were making them up. *The Golem* was the flagship of the summer season, and everybody knows *that's* not a true story—a good Christian woman who marries a Jew in an act of self-hatred, changing everything about herself, changing her *name* to suit him, while meanwhile he is secretly building a horrible monster. Spurned by Christian society—"We spurn you!" the choral number goes—she struggles to escape her husband's clutches with the help of a sympathetic priest. Enraged, the husband arouses his long-awaited golem as the leitmotif noted in criticism as "The Unknown Dread," abbreviated T.U.D., reaches a thunderous volume. A towering figure of clay destroys the soprano whom the Jew calls "The Loose Woman"—everybody knows that's not a true story. Everybody knows a story couldn't end that way no matter how dirty your mind is, and not to dismiss the subject as easily as all that but the audience must get back to its seats for the third act.

ACT III, SCENE ONE

It's exhausting to think about, but if you drive around a neighborhood—try it yourself, but first put some decent clothes on so nobody will think you're a child molester looking for the one child in America who hasn't been told never to get into a stranger's car, and best of luck to you—in every house there's a family of people remembering clearly and obsessively what the other people have said and forgotten. You'll show a finger-painting to your father, and he'll say, "That's nice. Go wash up for dinner," and your hopes of becoming an artist will join your daily grime in the drain, despite the hundreds of other finger-paintings he's celebrated in minute detail, magneted to the galley of the refrigerator. Your mother will let something carelessly slide about your sister which will become a Doric column in your mind, the central piece in the Temple of Sibling Opinion. "I hate olives," your brother will say once, and you'll never give him any even though he loves them, he just hated *that* one. "My daughter is attractive," somebody will say, and they won't mean it one-tenth as much as you do. There in the dining room behind the fancy-paned glass and those stickers touting an advanced burglar alarm system, families are investigative reporters. They write down their favorite things and quote them, out of context, all childhood long and through all the dinner parties of adulthood: at college gatherings with cheap red wine and stir-fries, over the exquisite grilled fish of early marriage, then with the carpools all I had time to do was throw together this casserole, hope you like it, and mixed into the pureed peas of the home where you sit on the porch and stare moodily at the shuffleboard courts. Drive around the neighborhood, you

dirty old man—Frost Road, Hemingway Way, Byron Circle—
and see the houses quivering as the wrong words stick. The
fire-tools shiver in their little jars. The lid of the wooden box
from Indonesia rattles at the corners. The plastic slipcover on
the flowered couch crackles as Rabbi Tsouris (*basso profundo*)
settles on it. I'm sorry: *cue music,* it should have been going
already.

He and I were alone in the house. Stephen was still at the lab
and Cyn, I guessed, was spending quality time with her father.
I was supposed to be working on my paper at the Benedrum
Center for the Performing Arts Library—Stan had even given
me special dispensation to check out the books there, if I
wanted—but I didn't like being even that close to the Props
Studio where Mimi waited with veiled comments and studded
leather belts. I'd taken the bus to the gates of the Glass neighborhood and walked up Frost Road, left at Hemingway Way
and then down Byron Circle with my sweaty palms plunged
into the pockets of my denim shorts where my key was hiding
like a kidnapper in wait. It was a windy day. I was halfway up
the brick steps when I spotted a stranger waiting patiently by
the front door of what turned out to be, when I let us both in
with my own key, an empty house. He said he was Rabbi
Tsouris, although Tsouris is Yiddish for *trouble* so that couldn't
have been right. He said he had an appointment with Mimi, and
that could have been right, so I led him into the living room,
where I'd never been in the two months I'd been here. As the
curtain rises to the Rabbi sitting down on the slipcover, I thought
that maybe nobody ever sat in this living room, that even after
all this time—just last night I'd offered Stephen a hated olive—

92

there were rules in this family I hadn't even heard of.

"So how are you, Rabbi?" I asked.

He crackled in his chair. "*I'm* fine," he said, and the italics were lost on me—didn't *I* look well?—just as their musical equivalent, a sinister murmur of woodwinds to signify approaching illness, will be lost on all but the most careful of listeners, or those who have read the verbose essays in the glossy playbills—"listen for the sinister murmur of woodwinds to signify approaching illness, a hallmark of the subtle decoration in Handler's work."

"Glad to hear it," I said. "I'm sure if you have an appointment with Mimi she'll be along any minute. They're really working her to the bone over at Benedrum."

He frowned like I'd made a bad joke. "I'm sure—*Mrs. Glass*—will be along, as you say. She shouldn't be working so hard, particularly now."

I tried to remember what Stan had said. "Well, people want—Mimi's boss told me that he wanted to make this season *mesmerizing*." I was enjoying watching the Rabbi's face pucker every time I called a grown-up by its first name. Outside it was a windy day.

"Mesmerizing I'm sure it will be," Tsouris said. "Though I can't say I'll be seeing any of the productions."

"You don't approve of the season?" I asked.

Tsouris smiled at me. "You make it sound like I'm opposed to summer. But *no,* I don't really approve of the anti-semitic operas. There was a real outcry from some of the more conservative rabbis in town, but I didn't join that. I don't want to see it banned. But I disapprove, yes."

93

"Why? Don't you think it—I mean, don't you see? It's supposed to be *ironic*."

The Rabbi sighed. "You young people and *irony*. You think if you dress something up and wink at it, it's all right. I suppose every generation tries to think it's doing something for the first time, and your way is to, I don't know, *garnish* it. Put it sarcastically."

"But don't you think it makes a serious point, to do it that way? I mean, to present these operas in—"

"To show it condones it," he said gruffly, shifting on the sofa and showing me a pale, crackly stripe of skin between his pants leg and his sock. What was he condoning, with that lizard-belly skin? "There's a Talmudic saying: 'We do not see the world as it is, we see the world as we are.' The Benedrum Board is revealing itself to be—well, *entrenched* in anti-semitism. If they really wanted to do something ironic, why don't they do—I don't know—*lousy* operas?"

"Because—"

"Because people wouldn't *go*, that's why. They want to make something *mesmerizing*. And what's *mesmerizing* to those schmucks?" The Yiddish rolled off his Pittsburgh tongue like a bandage off a scab. "Anti-semitism. It's not ironic at all, not really."

"Then why didn't you join the other rabbis and sign the petition, or whatever?"

"Letter to the editor," the Rabbi said, waving his hand like it didn't matter, or he was blessing me. Outside it was a windy day. "Because I didn't feel like it was my place to do that. If the Benedrum people want to do such a thing, who am I to stop them? It's not like I'm some great moral authority."

"You're a *rabbi*," I said.

There's always parts in operas where some random, outdated ideology that nobody cares about blunders in, like a sudden gust of wind that blows open bedroom doors. "That's no reason to judge. I mean, rabbis are beholden to a certain Gospel. But most Jews drift around different Gospels. They don't just let Judaism run their lives. There's lots of different Gospels out there. The Gospel of Work, and the Gospel of Relaxation. The Gospel of Power. The Gospel of Fun, of Enjoyment, of Relaxation. I said that one I think. There's the Gospel of Self. More and more, people are finding themselves following a variety of Gospels. They're Bi-Gospel. They're Tri-Gospel. Pan-Gospel. It's not my place to tell people what to do. That's why I'm here today. Mrs. Glass has called upon me in her time of need, but to listen, not to judge. I may disapprove of her actions, as strongly as I disapprove of the operas, but I'm not going to judge. It's my job to be now here, not nowhere."

"What?"

"Now here, not nowhere. You've never heard of this?"

I blinked. The audience fidgets, waiting for more sex, or a stabbing or something. Be patient, please. Stop crinkling the playbills; outside, I believe I have mentioned, it was a windy day. "Now here?"

"Now here and nowhere are the same word. You know, they're made of the same letters. It all depends on how you look at it. God is *nowhere*. God is *now here*. You understand? It's in the Talmud."

"I thought the Talmud was in Hebrew."

"The *idea* is in the Talmud. It was modernized by somebody. It's a modern idea—that's why I'll be using it today, to help

95

Mimi. She thinks, in her state, that nothing's left. She thinks she's *nowhere*. But there's no reason to give up hope. She can be *now here*. It's all in how she looks at it. I'll be trying to offer her my own Gospel. I'll be trying to offer her God—but not a judgmental God. Not the kind of God who would track her down and punish her this way. I'm offering her God as therapist, a God that can help her. She needs to find courage. And the real *irony* is"—he looked at me significantly—"she should just look around her. The heroines of operas are always triumphing over adversity—*real* operas, anyway, not the schmutz they're passing off this summer." He paused. "Look at *Medea*. Now *there's* a brave woman. She knew she was *now here*. At the end of *that* opera—have you seen it?"

"No."

"At the end, they ask her, Medea, what is left? Everything is destroyed, everything is gone. And you know what Medea says? She says, 'What is left? There is me.' *There's* a woman for you. 'What do you mean what's left? Everything is left. *I* am left.' *There's* an opera they should show the world."

"Doesn't Medea kill her children?" I asked.

"Yes," croaked somebody behind us, and there was Mimi, slung in the doorway of the living room like something hanging to dry. She had a smudge of clay on her face from the Props Studio and she looked tired. How long had she been there, on stage? Her costume will have to match the drapes or something, so she can emerge gradually and no one will notice her until that one word, low in her range: *Yes.*

Rabbi Tsouris stood up. "Mimi," he said, and glided over to her. He took her arm like an old movie, and settled her down on a slipcovered chair. Mimi let these things happen to her like they were part of an examination. "Yes, Medea killed her children," she said meanwhile, looking at me.

"Will you excuse us?" the Rabbi asked me stiffly, and Mimi began to tremble. Her skin made little shivering crackles on the slipcover and I stepped backwards out of the living room.

It's difficult to construct a soliloquy when I'm narrating this to begin with. A further soliloquy, a meta-soliloquy maybe. Rabbi Tsouris and Mimi begin mouthing things to one another, while the lighting focuses on Joseph, lurking by the curtains that match Mimi's costume: *Ah! Mimi looks terrible. And why is she home in the middle of the day? Why did she have an appointment with the rabbi? Does she suspect that Cyn and Ben are sleeping together during these afternoons of quality time? Ah, quality time—the very concept sounds suspect! Ah, Jewish house of intrigue and misery! Ah, my tainted Cyn! My lovely flower gone rancid in Mimi's twisted and evil kitchen! My precious porcelain figurine shattered like ceramic bone in the operating room of her father! Reduced to a one-molecule width by the lecherous laser of her brother! Oh, my turbulent head, blowing like the wind outside, because outside it is a windy day, signified by the roll of the timpani!*

And roll it does, a tempest of T.U.D., as Joseph stumbles past the curtains like he's drunk poison, careening in billiard angles from one wall of the hallway to the next. Mimi and Tsouris freeze in a tableau of conference so we know we're supposed to keep looking at Joseph and because, obviously, I wasn't there to listen in on them. I was there in the hallway, though, when the signal is given to the stagehand. He's slightly overweight and has a pen in his mouth because he's not allowed to smoke on the set. Since "it's exhausting to think about, but if you drive around a neighborhood . . ." he's been standing with his hand on the doorknob of Stephen's bedroom, listening through headphones for the signal to pull it open as the wind rises and makes good on its foreshadowing. Outside, I hope you know by now, it was a windy day, and that window was open, the one above the little wrought-iron table with little claw feet. You will remember that wind, because of some air pressure or wind rushing thing, opens doors and exposes nudity.

It will require, I suppose, a brave tenor, though with tricky enough lighting you could have a body double, with the real Stephen moaning the high A-flat behind a scrim, while Cyn's hand reaches for the erection of some guy they get from wherever they get naked people for art classes. In some *Salome*s it's downright embarrassing, when the typically-shaped operatic soprano removes the seventh veil and we wonder why Herod lusts after his niece-turned-stepdaughter when there are so many healthy, more slender objects available in his stable. But opera is sort of a myth, and a myth is sort of a truth, and truly, Stephen's body was delectably formed. Even in horror you can find lust, and such was mine that I understood the mother (still tableaued across stage) who didn't want to be *friends*. Damp, Stephen was framed in the doorway like a gift, his eyes glassy with eagerness, his arms hovering in mid-reach, aching with the paralysis of a readiness afraid to show itself too keenly and spoil everything. I'm sure even our pen-chomping stagehand, hiding behind the door with the doorknob poking him, leans to look at Stephen's body, and pokes back.

Having been cooked up by Mimi, it should be no surprise Stephen looked so delicious. His shoulders were delectable, the knobs of his shoulder blades rising like drumsticks of perfectly-roasted chicken. His legs were trembling like a watched pot, and the landing-strip triangle of downy hair cleaved the cutting board of his chest like those perfectly sheared scars down a loaf of fine bread. And *no,* we won't call it a baguette, that's too French and large. Stephen's whole family is short; Cyn, in fifth grade, was nicknamed Shrimp. Stephen's shrimp was curled, like a real one, and damp from the pupil of the shrimp's one eager eye to the bouquet of coral around its base, damp with late-teen musk as familiar and crave-inducing as garlic butter.

Dinner was ready. Cyn's hand was half-clenched like she was picking up a fork, while Stephen was the most eager of waiters, not the ones who scowl "Who had the scampi?" but croon, whisper, whimper, "Please. Please." And the rest moans. A-flat, over a chord of violins thin as a bedsheet. Behind Stephen, everything was familiar, although I'd only seen his bedroom during a brief tour the day of my arrival. I didn't have to see any more of Cyn, just the forearm, just the foreplay. The blankets and sheets had been thrown to the bottom of the bed, hanging on to the mattress in a frozen grimace of rippled corners, leaving the playing field bare for unencumbered gymnastics. The pillows were scrunched at the other end, cowering against the wall; I remembered how many times my thrusts had scooted Cyn and me to the very top of the bed, her spidery hand grabbing a pillow and stuffing it behind her head to stop the knocking on her skull. I saw Stephen's underwear and pants, fallen in concentric puddles near his arched bare feet. I didn't have to see Cyn to know she had pulled them down. I didn't have to see her face because I knew what she looked like when she was hungry; it was the same expression I could sense each night when her father scooted her to *her* wall, when she left me alone in the attic. I didn't have to see any more than her spidery hand. I had seen enough.

The last A-flat melts right into the most tempestous T.U.D. yet, topped only by the finale in Act IV, Scene Two. The timpani rolls again and our headphoned stagehand shuts the door as the body double is brought a robe to dull the chill, and shoes so he won't step on some stray set-building nail as he walks to the dressing room.

Mimi saw me re-enter the living room, and her whole body snapped like she'd been in tableau during my absence, or had been talking about something she didn't want me to hear. She changed the subject as briskly as changing beddings, casting a new thin layer of whiteness over the stains of whatever had been going on.

"But how do you make one, really?" she asked Rabbi Tsouris.

Tsouris sighed with the trombones. "I didn't come here to talk about golems," he said. "You know I'm not taking sides on the summer season, Mrs.—"

"*Mimi,*" she almost snarled, "*Mimi. Please.* Can't you *please* tell me? It's important."

"I really came here to talk about your illness. I want you to know, Mimi, that God—"

"Is a therapist, I know," she said. Her hand was as spidery as her daughter's, now that I looked at it. "I *know* that. But if you really want to make me feel better—*I want to know.*"

"O.K.," he said carefully, shifting and squeaking on the slip-cover. "Well, it's a myth, of course, so the actual process is debated." Mimi shrugged impatiently, almost a tic. "But it's generally agreed that you need mud from a river, you know: river clay. And the creator is a rabbi."

"Does it have to be a rabbi?" Mimi asked sharply.

"It's a *myth,*" Rabbi Tsouris said.

"Isn't a myth a sort of truth?"

"Mimi, I don't think we should be talking about this. Obviously you're upset. You're ill, and—Joseph, would you excuse us?"

"Don't change the subject!" Mimi snarled. Her spidery hand flickered out to me again. I sat down instantly like she'd cast a spell. Stephen's buttocks (I didn't mention those, did I? Ripe, magnificent.) were probably squirming on the sheets now, bucking towards Cyn's hungry mouth, but mine were stiff on an uncomfortable chair in the corner. *"Tell me."*

"I guess it doesn't have to be a rabbi," the rabbi said. "It could be anyone. It's a *myth,* Mimi. We have to talk about what's *really* happening right now." The wind blew outside and I wondered what other doors had opened, had shut. What was *really* happening, here? "But if only to satisfy your curiosity, I'll tell you, briefly. The rabbi would use river clay and lay it out in the shape of a man. He'd dress entirely in white—"

"The golem?"

"No, no, the rabbi. The golem, I guess, was naked. I mean, he was made of *clay,* so I guess we could call it naked."

"And?" The coffee table trembled, and so did I, and probably Stephen, and Cyn, and the cellos.

"And, there's not much else. He lights the candle, as I remember, and circles the body and does some sort of a chant. Mimi, I don't know why you're asking me about this, frankly—there's

a golem ceremony in one of the operas, isn't there? *Golem?* Some sort of—"

"*Alphabetical* chant?" Mimi asked. "Isn't it *alphabetical?*"

"You know," the Rabbi said, and stood up. His legs shook slightly. Mimi looked at him like he was going to boil over. "You know," he said again, "we shouldn't be talking about this. You're very upset, Mimi, and you need your rest at a time like this."

"*Alphabetical?*" she asked again. "Just *tell* me. In the opera, it's alphabetical, it's something like 'Ah, By Clay Destroy Evil Forces, Golem, Help, Justice!' Wait, there's no I there, what begins with I?"

"*I don't know,*" the rabbi said, and started towards the door. "You're very upset, Mimi, and I came here to offer you—I didn't come here to talk about Jewish myths, for God's sake. You can't seek comfort in myths, Mimi. You have to seek comfort from your troubles with truth, with God. And I'm not offering you a judgmental God. You think God is *nowhere.* But he can be *now here.* I'm offering you God as Therapist—"

"I don't want a therapist," she said. "I want a golem."

"We'll talk later," Tsouris said, in a voice that said: "You're crazy." He opened the front door. Outside the air prowled down Frost Road, Hemingway Way and Byron Circle like a stranger in a car. I stood up and walked to the doorway and watched his spidery hands as they buttoned his blazer. They were as spidery as Mimi's, as spidery as Cyn's; everybody's hands were spidery. Everybody's hands looked alike; from the wrists to the fingerprints we were all identical. Mimi took a few steps towards him, and he raised both hands defensively, halfway between benediction and shoving somebody off a cliff. "Will you make sure she gets some rest, Joseph?" he said to me. "I'll talk to her later." He turned to leave, *now here,* but soon *nowhere.* Behind me the wind blew some door shut—a sudden snare drum from the back of the orchestra. "You need some rest, Mimi," he said, all God as Therapist. "Go to bed." And as the rabbi turned to me I realized it didn't have to be Therapist. It could be The Rapist. It could be God as The Rapist.

"Take her to bed," he said to me, and it all depended on how you looked at it.

ACT III, SCENE TWO

The Glass home, in the dead of night. An early scene in *Alma* takes place in a graveyard in the dead of night. We know it's the dead of night because we hear three tones of a church bell: "Bing! Bing! Bing!" The tolling takes its toll; just three notes from Christ's sanctuary and the rabbis clutch their heads in agony and support themselves on headstones Mimi has fashioned out of plaster. But the Glass home didn't have any church bells, or even a grandfather clock with its pendulum tongue hanging low and loose like impotence. It was a doorbell, ringing three times at three in the morning, that woke me up.

I sat up instantly, so the entire audience could see my face. I threw the covers off me, leaving them to hang onto the mattress in a frozen grimace of rippled corners, as they had earlier in the evening when Cyn's spidery hands had guided my mouth to her sex, still tainted, I swear, with the taste of her brother. She came quickly, and left quickly. I'd heard her enter her bedroom, followed no doubt by her silent father, and thought I caught a full-out moan just as the wind rose outside, covering the sound of Mimi entering Stephen's room. Then I'd dozed until—I looked at my bedstand clock—three in the morning. Who could be ringing?

The doorbell rang again, four bings. I didn't hear anyone's feet pattering on the Pakistani rug lining the entry hall; "Let it ring," I could hear Cyn moan to the doctor, as she used to moan when the dorm phone rang, back at Mather. Well, *I* couldn't.

My own robe was wrapped around my stereo to keep out the damp of the Mather Summer Storage Spaces, but Ben had lent me one of his. I picked it up from where it was draped over my empty desk and tied it around my body. It occurred to me that it might be my box of books, arriving finally in some three A.M. emergency delivery so now I could write my paper on something other than opera and Cyn's family.

I didn't have any slippers. Each of my footsteps was a bare, comfortable slap, covering all the gasping behind the bedroom doors. As I turned and slapped past the little wrought-iron table with claw feet, the window above it latched closed, the doorbell rang again, calling me like Pavlov. Ben's rough cloth jostled against me as I neared the door, but as I reached for the chain lock something moved out of the shadows.

I jumped back and knocked into a decorative ceramic pitcher from Mexico, which fell from its wicker perch to break into three large pieces on the floor, snapping like bone. The dog, of course, *the dog.* Cassius had nobody to fuck either, and so had slapped to the door himself and waited, black against black, for somebody to answer it. He'd been *nowhere,* and *now here,* like God. "Nice God," I said, all three A.M. dyslexia. Who could it be?

It was a block of clay, tall and dark like the cabinet of oak in which the TV sat back in the Glass den. Somebody had hoisted it on one of those wheeled carts—dollies?—and placed it on the front porch, a big geometric slab, a raw Stonehenge. It didn't answer my question. Cassius stepped in front of me and sniffed it, and then jerked back as a white hand curled around it like a spider.

"Sorry," the hand (*countertenor*) screeched, and if there'd been another Mexican pitcher out on the porch I would have broken it. The hand led a whole pale body in overalls out from behind the block. "I didn't mean to startle you," he said. Have you ever heard a countertenor? A man who can sing in a soprano range without surgery? It sounds like the squealing of brakes. "Mrs G. said I could deliver this any time."

You recognize this part, of course, the jaw-droppingly obvious suspicion. The Chief of Police promises Tosca that her true love won't be executed, after all. The bullfighter says he loves Carmen no matter what. The maid announces the arrival of a man in a dark coat; *"A dark coat?"* the husband cries, at high E, but the wife just sits and keeps sewing. "If I dance for you," Salome says, "I can have *anything I want?"* and the audience sits and fidgets, daydreams about a late supper, thinks *Don't be such a sucker. Get out while you still can, you stupid, stupid tenor.*

And I guess I could have, too; bounded past the clay monolith and down the color-coded thoroughfares to a bus station, a train station, an airport. I didn't move, of course; it's a *four-act* opera, and the hero is suspicious but keeps right on going. I nodded dumbly at this pale figure, and stepped aside; he tilted the dolly and rolled in what must have been thirty, forty pounds of clay. He stopped just as the wheels reached the biggest piece of pitcher. "She said it goes to the basement, but I don't do that," he said. "She can do that herself." He reached deep into a pocket in the overalls—I watched his hand crawl around his stomach like surgery—and came out with a small clipboard, a pen dangling from a fuzzy white string. "You gotta sign for it. Right there."

Cassius sniffed at it, and I stared, in the light of nearby lampposts, at an "X" with a straight line. I remembered the argument I'd heard with Mimi and Stan, down in the Props Studio: Mimi was ordering too much clay. I didn't want to be responsible for any Benedrum wrath, not while my books still hadn't arrived and I was using their library *gratis*. I started to hand it back to him, unsigned, but his pale hands wouldn't unclasp and take it. I looked him in the eye, this three A.M. countertenor, this mysterious visitor lugging clay in like a coffin, this augur of doom, this symbol. "Sign," he said, applying the brakes again, and rather than see him any more, rather than hear him, I grabbed the pen and scrawled "Mimi" next to the X, found myself bowing back as he bowed to me and put the clipboard back in his body. As I shut the door I heard him shuffle off. Cassius was snuffling at the clay, but it was so dark and deep I couldn't imagine it smelling like anything. I reached out and touched it, like those cavemen in the movie who touch a big black marble slab and change history forever. It was damp, damp and big, immobile and permanent as death, something that looked like it had always been standing in the Glass entryway.

I reached down and picked up the pitcher pieces. I could make out dim drawings of animals which had been marching in a line around the rim. I was holding a bear, flanked by the first half of a cow and the last half of a fish. Did they even have bears in Mexico? Maybe this was a dream, this big slab sitting in the entry way of the Glasses' like a warning. Maybe the radio was on in my room, and "Bing Bing Bing" had doorbelled its way into my slumber. I locked eyes with the cow head and considered.

The attic had no radio. BRUM: T.U.D. This wasn't a dream-within-the-opera, this was just the opera. I put the remnants of the herd on the wicker table with the dim hope that somebody would think it had just *broken,* like Ben's failed bones. In return I'd do a good deed. I angled my bare foot against the cold metal rim of the dolly, if that's what it's called, and leaned the clay toward my rickety body. The slab and I did a brief, sloppy two-step as I adjusted to its weight. When I reached the door to the basement steps, Cassius pulled out the dog-acting stops for the sake of ambience and whimpered, trembled and refused to go any further. There's that obvious suspicion again, the operatic equivalent of ignoring a gunshot you hear in the next room. When is it ever, ever a car backfiring?

My own spidery hand batted at the wall for the light switch, and for a few seconds I thought the slab, the dolly and I were all going to tumble to the basement floor and go the way of the pitcher. But the light flickered on and we began our descent, although with the slab leading the way I couldn't see anything, really, until I reached the bottom of the stairs. *Had I known the sheer horror which awaited me I never would have gone further than that door.*

It was spread out on an enormous table which was covered in a sheer white sheet. The light shone on it in almost fanatical brightness; I could see every crack, every smear, every knuckle and vein. Next to the table was a small utility cart with a stack of books and one of those fancy tins for olive oil. She'd used up all the oil, apparently, and had sawed off the top with something

107

to store all her tools. There were some rubber spatulas, and little shovels and some knives, and a few wiry implements I'd never seen before. I'd never seen any of it before, really. I looked at the top book in the stack: *Ritual* was all I could make out in the title, the rest smeared by clay, but at the bottom, in a slender little marketing font, was "by the author of *When You Can't Be Friends with Your Mother.*" And then I had to look at it again, even though I knew what it looked like and knew what it was. I knew what it was. At first it didn't look like clay. At first, because it was so strange, I thought it was me; my reflection in some mirror being stored in the basement. But it wasn't me: it was lying down. It wasn't made of skin. It was dark brown, like the clay I'd dragged down here, and for a second it looked like liver, like some horrible hors d'oeuvre platter for cannibals. *Who am I, chopped liver?* my brain babbled, but it wasn't me.

You know what it was. If it'd had a head, it would have been maybe nine, ten feet tall; I knew that the block of clay I held had a head in it, waiting to emerge. I read somewhere that Michelangelo said that to carve a woman out of marble, all you had to do was remove all the parts of the marble that didn't look like a woman. Mimi's tools were rinsed. They were eager and dry. They would find everything that didn't look like the head of the golem she was building in her basement.

It was a man, at least I'm pretty sure it was a man. The genitals were a mere smooth lump, like on those plastic fashion dolls, but the hands were big, the shoulders enormous, the nails on the fingers were rounded and carved out carefully. Despite being uncovered, and despite the heat of the lights, it hadn't dried. The golem looked damp. The wrists and ankles had visible veins, slivered into life by one of those wiry things in the oil tin. The bottoms of the feet had rough patches of crust, like someone who walks around barefoot all the time. It was excellent work. Nothing was dusting away on the golem; on the contrary, he looked in his prime. He looked ready, except for the head. He was almost ready.

The cold damp of the basement slid through me, up through my bare feet, as I circled the sheeted table. It didn't look like a person, even a headless one; it was too big, and it looked too much like clay. It looked like what it was, so large and sudden that it made a three A.M. delivery of clay look as boring as mail. It looked like a golem, a golem still in process, and there was no reason a golem should be in the Glass basement and I didn't want to be there either. I was afraid to touch it, it looked so good. I could smear it, wreck it, or perhaps—or perhaps feel a pulse, a small ripple of muddy blood in the vein of dark clay. I didn't want to look at the blank space of sheet just above the neck. I didn't want to picture a face on it, any face, a face that could inhale and bring oxygen into the carefully-constructed lungs I was positive were in the cavernous chest, a face that would finish it, a face that could open its eyes. I walked backwards up the stairs, my cold feet shuffling rough friction on the chilly steps, both hands shaking for the bannister. When I reached the top of the stairs I couldn't even turn the lights off and be alone in the dark with it, even for the mere moment before I opened the door, tripped over the dog in the darkness, shrieked and threw the door shut. *Let the light stay on,* Joseph sings, *let it stay on all night, I will not return there. Let it banish the shadows from my soul and from this evil place.*

I turned the corner and nearly ran into the golem. I shouted one hoarse syllable and slipped to the ground as it towered over me, wrapped in its sheet. It was only when he reached down to me that I saw it was Mimi, her dark hair beheading her in the dim light. Her nightgown did look like a sheet, but as she stumbled over my stumble, I saw it wasn't nearly as big: her arms were bare, her legs were bare, and as she floundered for a second on the floor, the hem shifted and I saw the curve of one of her buttocks. My own legs were splayed wide, with my robe nearly undone from my fall; she must have seen everything of me as she grabbed my knee in her panic and raised up to a kneeling position. Her nails dug into my knee as she found balance with one hand and hiked her nightgown down with the other. I retied my robe and looked up to meet her face. I expected to find her smiling sheepishly but her mouth was nearly invisible in the dark. What I could see were her eyes, wild sparks in front of the window that blew open doors.

"*What?*" I hissed, instead of *sorry*. Mimi inhaled loudly and I looked at her face again. She might have been crying. "*What?*" I said again; the only reason a mother is up crying in the middle of the night is when someone has to go to the hospital.

"*Don't you hear it?*" she whispered. "*Don't you—*can't *you hear it? Isn't that why you came down here?*"

"*What?*" I said again, and she stood up. Above me, I couldn't see anything but the sheet again; her nightgown ended in a dark hole, like something unfinished.

"*Don't you hear it?*" she hissed again, and in one gust my hopes that I'd been imagining everything, everything, like an elaborate sick opera staged in my head, crumbled like something knocked to the floor. Because I heard it, of course I heard it. I'd been hearing it every night, from a floor above.

Standing next to Mimi listening to it felt like she was watching me have sex with her daughter. The muffled moans could be no one but Cyn, and the rhythmic creaking of the wooden floors could be nothing but sex with her. It wasn't the wind. It had never been the wind. Dr. Ben Glass was sleeping with Cynthia Glass as sure as that cold clay golem waited downstairs. Mimi and I stood at Cyn's door, almost pressed up against it in our concentration. Mimi sniffled again, and as she leaned against me I felt her tremble behind her nightgown. She whimpered, but I don't think she was crying. Her trembling was furious, keyed-up, the friction of her body shaking against mine was more electric than sad. I leaned into her like an instinct, although from the audience it could just look like I was listening closer to the sound of my lover with her father. Mimi murmured something, and then gasped. The gasp was because of my other instinct. Beneath my garment, like a half-finished secret, I was coming to life, and I felt her gasp against the thin triangle of my exposed skin, at the neck of the loosening robe. But I don't know what the murmur was. In the rustle of our draping and undraping clothing, as the lowering curtain likewise rustles over a thin and deep bed of cellos, I made myself miss the murmur. I told myself that it wasn't really my family, and so her murmur didn't apply to me, not at all. A real son or daughter had to hang on every word a mother said, but that wasn't me. I could ignore what I wanted and concentrate only on the sensation of her breath, Cyn's distant moans and the creaking of the wooden floor. I told myself those were the only sounds in the house. I told myself that it wasn't really my family, and so I didn't have to hear the word she murmured against my skin. It wasn't me. *Motherfucker*. Curtain.

[The audience strolls out of the auditorium and chats about subjects tangentially related to the action.]

Why didn't he leave, why didn't he just leave? That's the trouble with modern operas, with modern settings: the audience asks modern questions. You wouldn't think of telling Madame Butterly to wise up *vis-a-vis* Pinkerton's return, or asking Otello to rethink his hankie-as-proof-of-adultery schemata, or telling all those women in winged helmets to sit down together and think up a way to break the *Ring Cycle*. Oedipus, how about you find out more about this girl before you make your move?

No. The bounty of Cyn's body is becoming a stronger motif than the T.U.D., but let it; it *was*. In all likelihood the soprano they get for Cyn won't have the same skin that enveloped me and kept me in unwavering place like a bone. Each night, the restless damp of her skin, sweat-tinged with summer, would turn my own restless damp into my own restless damp. Cyn would tuck me in as my penis still quivered, and would lean close to allow me to taste each nipple before she padded downstairs to her father. I couldn't leave that, that tucking in, those breasts dangling like bait: it was a booby trap. I couldn't leave, not with her sex in front of my eyes, the flush of her climax against my throat, around my fingers, through the blankets of the bed she no longer lingered in. I couldn't part with the parting of her legs, couldn't pack my things as she unpacked me, one sticky night bending me over the desk and flicking her tongue between my buttocks until I spent a salty sob on the blotter where my paper was supposed to be written. The next

112

morning the stain was still there, left there each morning by the set decorator for continuity's sake, along with the one in the hallway, following the close of Act III.

It stayed the summer. It stayed through each afternoon after the Goodbye session, when I would go to the Benedrum Center for the Performing Arts Library, preferring to listen to the neighboring rumble of the orchestra rehearsals than whatever other rumbles I would hear if I went to Byron Circle. Cyn went home. Most days, Mimi wouldn't be in the Props Studio, though occasionally I'd stop by and find her for a silent ride home in her Sahara-ready Jeep, the backseat crowded with shopping bags of supper. I stayed for each dinner, the juicy fishes and chicken with grill-lines marching down the breasts. Mimi would unpack the bags and marinate something, not for that evening's dinner but for the next, or the next, and I stayed for all of them. She made roasted asparagus that stood straight up out of some sort of cornmeal mattress and I stayed to dip each tip in the hand-picked blackberry salsa before wrapping my tongue around it. I stayed to flick my fork between the two potatoes roasted to a stinging blush to find the sticky sob of river-fished caviar between them. You can't start something so difficult and exoskel-etal as lobster claws cooked inside a pomegranate and not finish it, or *I* can't; once I open my mouth, there's no stopping me.

Every year, whether the whole family is sleeping with one another or not, Jewish law requires a meal as loaded and struc-tured as those late-summer dinners: the Passover Seder. In the Seder rulebook there are four descriptions of children and how to tell them why they should stay and finish the meal.

The wise child says, "What are the testimonies, the statutes

113

and the laws which the Lord, our God, has commanded you?" The wicked one says, "What is this service to you?" "He says 'to you,' " the Haggadah rages, "but not to him! By thus excluding himself from the community he has denied that which is fundamental." The simple child says simply, "What is this?" but I *knew.* I had the surety of wind blowing a door open, of sheets pulled back for a bare playing field, of a spidery hand on a sure and hungry course. These children weren't me. I was much worse. I was the child who does not know how to inquire, the fourth act in the Passover Child opera. I was at the feast because I didn't know how to inquire. What you're supposed to say to that child is, "With a strong hand the Lord took us out of Egypt, from the house of bondage," that's really what it says, smirky prose even in a non-incestuous home. But that's not what anybody said to me, and so there I was, undelivered. Like a box stopped en-route I was trapped in the house of bondage, a lost kid, a kid who doesn't know how to inquire.

And you in the audience are the same, you of the *why doesn't he leave?* clique. Otherwise why are you finishing your coffee, wide-eyed in your rush? You've been to the opera before, or you haven't but strong hands have taught you how to behave. You stay for the whole thing. You keep quiet, and don't move, and let the opera play itself out. Even if the plot is full of holes, the action full of unanswered questions, even if you've entered the action yourself by entering the mother herself, you gulp the rest of it down when you hear the oboe rehearsing one phrase over and over: T.U.D., T.U.D., T.U.D. Soon the conductor will stand in the narrow spotlight and give the downbeat, and you don't want to be on a bus, on a plane, or just walking out of the color-coded city limits. You don't want to be anywhere but here. You want to sit quietly in your seat as the last act unfolds, as certain and random as the letters of the alphabet: Ah, By Clay Destroy Evil Forces, Golem, Help Israel: Justice. You don't know how to inquire, but if you sit tight, if you stay perfectly still and leave the continuity unbreached, you might find out.

ACT IV, SCENE ONE

As if skipping ahead nearly a month and changing the scene to a hospital room isn't disorienting enough, there's a backstage technical difficulty and the dry ice machine kicks in as the curtain goes up. The fog is not supposed to appear until the following, and final, scene in the cemetery, but there's nothing those headphoned henchmen can do about it: it billows all over the complicated metallic bed, all the clear plastic vines of IV tubes, the get-well flowers, until the scene looks imaginary, or like something that doesn't, that couldn't exist: there is no intensive care ward in heaven.

The strings are hushed and polite: visiting-hour strings. Strings that won't wake the patient, or the woman keeping watch. But the singer can't take her cue—the downbeat is lost in churning fog. In a second, the conductor makes a decision and waves his baton dismissively like he's killing a bug. The orchestra wavers off; the timpanist, posed for the sudden loom of T.U.D., lowers his sticks, shrugs and taps his drum boredly. The snare player whispers something to him and he smiles, as the fog surges over the rim of the stage and gives him a powdered wig. The conductor, still in the spotlight but with nothing to do, feels he must say something and turns to the audience. "I'm sorry," he says, and everybody laughs, too loudly. He grins sheepishly at the concertmistress, who hates him, incidentally, and says it again: "I'm sorry. We'll begin again in a minute." Act IV, Scene One, the machine fixed. If you please.

ACT IV, SCENE ONE

The music begins first, just the strings, hushed and polite: visiting-hour strings. The curtain rises to reveal a blindingly white, and perhaps still hazy, hospital room. Mimi is sleeping in the complicated metallic bed, surrounded by the clear plastic vines of IV tubes and get-well flowers flowering away in vases emblazoned with the snowflakes of faux-cut crystal. Beside her, Gramma sits dozing in a chair. Remember Gramma? The gypsy always returns at the end to reap the benefits of cursing. For more than two acts she's had to wait backstage in full makeup, poor dear, just to flop herself in this chair and feign sleep. As the strings continue, their visit guided along by some polite timpani footfalls, you can see the contralto's shoulders heaving with breath, either with post-allergic wheeze or from some sleepy overacting.

The footfalls are literal; an Orderly (*tenor*) enters, the only black man in the production. It's wonderful how modern composers are incorporating the entire spectrum of The American Experience into their work, instead of just the elitist white culture: there he is, the Orderly. He enters the room with a tray of inscrutable slabs of breakfast and places it on a small table. With a beatific smile so charming on Orderlies he gazes at the heaving Gramma and, like clearing steam from a window to see out, rustles at her arm to wake her. The timpani rustles along with him, but not Gramma. He rustles again but she doesn't wake.

116

Still standing far from her body so the audience can see what he's doing, the Orderly reaches out to her neck like he's spotted something to wipe off. But, as the rustle becomes a roll, it doesn't take a repeat of T.U.D. for us to realize that Gramma has already been wiped off. She's been wiped out; Gramma— the T.U.D. arrives anyway—is dead. "She's dead!" he sings anyway, and as some supernumeraries come and fetch her still-heaving body away the Orderly launches into an aria which will be immortalized forever as the aria black tenors use for auditions. Mimi sleeps on.

It, the aria, details the irony of Gramma dying while on death watch, and that, as an Orderly, he knows all about watching. As an Orderly, he spends his time ostensibly watching out for others, but really, like Gramma, he's dying inside. As some canned jazz-riffs begin to shuffle behind him, the Orderly expands his death watch metaphor to incorporate black people, who sit and watch on the fringes of society but who are dying inside. The audience, white as a hospital, is equally moved by the tenor sax solo—played by the only black man in the orchestra—and their own guilt. "But who will watch me?" he sings at the climactic close, and it's a good question—many people will not be watching him. Their eyes will be on Gramma as she is carried off, looking to see if the contralto has indeed stopped breathing.

And it really happened that way, that day. Cyn and I drove to the hospital directly from Camp Shalom, having received special dispensation from the pimply actor to skip the Goodbye ceremony for the rest of the summer—or, as he said, "for the rest of the summer, or, until, until Mrs. Glass, I hope everything will be O.K." We parked in the lot. We trudged beneath the

117

hot, wet sky to the Osteopathy Ward, the very site of Dr. Glass's—Ben's—broken-bone shame. It was a revenge better than anything Mimi could have cooked up in the basement: she had something wrong with her bones.

When the doctor spotted Mimi's Jeep, parked off the road just next to the shore of the Ohio River, directly across from the Old Jewish Cemetery where she'll be buried in the next scene, he must have thought she was the victim of some violent crime, but the unconscious woman lying face-down in the muck wasn't dead. She'd been driving home, Mimi explained later, when the aching in her bones that she'd been feeling for months, and never told anybody about because she didn't want to bother them and she'd thought it was probably just all the long hours at the Props Studio, suddenly overwhelmed her and she had to pull over. Good thing the doctor had come along when he had, otherwise who knows who would have preyed upon the helpless Mimi, there at five in the morning on the shores on the Ohio River.

Why she'd been driving at five in the morning, away from Squirrel Hill rather than towards it, was explained as vaguely as the specific nature of Mimi's disease. In fact the whole scenario seemed vague, as if shrouded in thick dry ice. The doctor (*tenor*) who had come upon Mimi, for example, was rife with curiosities. For one thing, his name was Dr. Zhivago. For another, he was a bone expert—he'd been one of the panel which had upbraided Ben during the Ceramic Bone Fiasco. So not only was he the one who rushed Mimi here to the hospital but was now exclusively supervising her care, even shipping in special nurses (and Orderlies! Notice the Orderlies! The entire American Experience is here!) to work under him.

Dr. Zhivago was as gaunt and thin as a ghost story, with beady little flickering eyes that made him seem like he was always taking notes. He was. He jotted them down on a clipboard as he hovered over Mimi and we hovered over him. He would not, just would not tell us exactly what was wrong with Mimi, who looked fine except for a constant wince of pain taped onto her face like a piece of paper you'd use to remind yourself of something: LOCK THE BACK DOOR. DENTIST TOMORROW. MY BONES HURT. "It's cancerous," Dr. Zhivago said, "but not quite cancer." We'd have these conversations in the hallways, with nurses and orderlies padding by, their footfalls like tympani. "It's in the core of the bone. She cannot even bend her knees. Unfortunately, her leg bones have broken in several places, but we can't go in and set them otherwise it might set off a chain reaction."

Stephen, who did nothing all day but study chain reactions, would ask for details, but Dr. Zhivago didn't give him any. "Could we have some more details?" Stephen would ask, and Dr. Zhivago would say, "No." Gramma was usually sitting watch at her daughter-in-law's bed, and Ben was always sitting on a bench a ways down the hallway, out of earshot and glaring at Zhivago. Aside from the tension which already existed between the two osteopaths, there was another wrench in the works: Mimi wasn't speaking to her husband. She hadn't spoken to him since That Night, and had scarcely spoken to Cyn. Zhivago passed on the message to Ben that not only did his wife not want him to treat her, but not to visit her. Cyn was clearly torn, but soon ended up spending these late afternoons and evenings on the bench next to him, so it was just Stephen and me standing across from a renowned bone expert who had just happened to be happening by the banks of the Ohio River at five in the morning.

"I just don't understand it," Stephen said, running a spidery hand through his summer-bleached hair, all shaggy from months at the lab. "What was my mother doing there? Where was she going? Where were *you* going? What is this? What's happening?" Zhivago would write something down in his clipboard and frown. "You shouldn't be talking so much to me," he would say. "You should be talking to your mother. She's in a lot of pain. She cannot even bend her knees." Then Stephen would look at me, like I knew something more than I was telling. And I did, too: I answered Zhivago's phone call saying that Mimi had been found by the banks of the Ohio River—a phone call that, bing bing bing, jostled people out of all sorts of bedrooms, all the wrong ones, their faces smeared with the puckered and smug look of the recently laid. Stephen and Cyn and Ben—in the dim hallway I couldn't even tell who had come out of what room—hovered by the phone as I stood in Ben's robe and relayed the news. There was a lot of slapstick room-switching again, as everybody rushed to get dressed for the hospital drive: nobody knew where to go. I did, though. I knew where to go. I went right down to the basement and flicked on the light while Cassius sniffed at the brushes, dripping and rinsed. The room was clean. The golem was gone. I couldn't remember what Rabbi Tsouris had said about golem-raising— did you have to do it by a river, or did you just need river mud?—so I didn't say anything to Stephen. He'd ask more questions, and look at Dr. Zhivago, and then at Cyn and Ben on the bench, her hand on his knee in tender comfort, and then at me, and his shoulders would sag with resignation, like a body found dead in a chair.

It was, that afternoon, just another twitchy orchestration, like the oboe which accompanies Zhivago's announcement note-by-note. Cyn and I were stalking silently down the curiously dark hallway when the doctor suddenly stepped out of Mimi's room and stood there in silent silhouette like a movie monster. Cyn broke her silence and shrieked, a little bit. "I'm sorry," Dr. Zhivago said. Behind him we could see Stephen standing by the bed and stroking Mimi's hand.

"It's O.K.," Cyn said. "You just startled me."

"No," Zhivago said, and put his clipboard behind his back. "I mean, I have some bad news. Your grandmother is dead."

Cyn blinked, and frowning, chewed on a nail. Her face reddened like she'd been slapped, or kissed a long, long time. "You can't even—" she sputtered to him. "You can't get them straight. It's my *mother*, you—"

"No," Zhivago said again. I watched Stephen lean in to kiss Mimi, watched her hand close around his like an anenome. "Your mother is doing better today, actually. It *is* your grandmother. I mean, it *was*. She *was*—your grandmother is dead. We found her this morning. She died in her sleep." Stephen and Mimi's entwined hands moved up the bedsheets slowly as he murmured something to her I couldn't hear. Zhivago stepped back and blocked my view; had the hands moved down to the metal railing, or up, to Mimi's breasts? "She was watching over your mother and died in her sleep. I'm very sorry."

"My—*grandmother?*" Cyn, too, was trying to look over Zhivago's shoulder. It's difficult to twist your body that way, and sing the rather complicated scale to which *"grandmother?"* is set. "My—somebody just *found* her, just like that? My *grandmother?*"

"Your mother is fine," he said. Now I could only see a bit of Stephen, just his skinny legs, bare beneath his shorts, and his dangling feet. In decades back, couples were allowed to be alone as long as the chaperone, peering from a discreet distance, could see everyone's feet on the floor. Now I saw one of Stephen's legs raise like he was mounting a horse, and Zhivago, following my eyes, shut the door softly. "Mrs. Glass is fine," he said. "It's your grandmother who is dead." There were all sorts of bedside manners going on here, and none of them were good. All behavior exists within a social and cultural context, but what explained this, this ghost story doctor, this mounting son?

"My *grandmother?*" Cyn said again. She looked at me like she couldn't quite place me. "My *grandmother?*"

"What happened to your grandmother?" Ben said behind us, and we all jumped. He was looking at Cyn and me with the elaborate care of not looking at somebody else. Dr. Zhivago coughed and put his hand on Ben's shoulder.

"Mimi is dead," he said.

Ben looked from the hand on his shoulder, to Zhivago's eyes, and back, several times, hand-eyes, hand-eyes, hand-eyes. "What?" he whispered.

"I thought you said she was fine," I said, pointing to the closed door.

"Gramma—Gramma's name—she's *also* Mimi," Cyn said, and then, with a trill of cellos, shuddered.

"What?" Ben said again. "My mother—"

"She was watching over Mimi," Zhivago said. "We found her this morning. Just—in her sleep."

Ben shook his hand away. "What?"

Cyn reached out to her father's shoulder. Her face was so calm, so sober and professional it looked like she was offering him a position. I mean a *job*. "Your mother is dead," she said.

"*My* mother?" he said. "Not *your*—"

"Mom's all right," she said.

"Well, not really all right," Zhivago said.

"It's Gramma. She died in her sleep," Cyn said.

Ben blinked, didn't get it, blinked, got it. "Oh," he said, and his shoulder sagged like someone had let go of the strings. "*Oh,*" he said, louder. Cyn put a hand on his shoulder and he shook it off. His eyes were fixed on Zhivago.

"No," Dr. Zhivago said. "You can't see her."

"She's my *mother!*" he shouted.

"Oh," he said. "You can see *her*. She's downstairs. We took her downstairs. You can't see your wife."

"What's *going on?*"

"Your wife," Zhivago said, "is leaving you. Whether she recovers or not."

"What?"

"Your wife," Zhivago said, and this time he shrugged, almost. The cellos shrug, too, a low, noncommital growl. "Your wife is leaving you. I'm sorry to be the one to tell you."

There was a pause—the conductor, arms raised, looks like he's about to sneeze—and then *blast!*, the trumpets scream in as Ben leapt at the doctor with a roar. Cyn grabbed him by the waist, but his arms kept going, clenched and roaring. Zhivago

123

stepped aside in one clean lurch, and then grabbed Ben's wrists. The clipboard clattered to the Orderly-shined floor.

"*What?*" Ben screamed. "*What? What? What?*"

"I'm going to have to ask you to leave," Zhivago said. "I'm sorry—"

"*What? What?*"

"Um, Cynthia, could you—" Dr. Zhivago moved Ben's wrists to my girlfriend, offering them. "Could you take your father—"

"Ben," she said, and then, glancing at me, changed it. "Dad," she said. "Come on." Ben was rumbling like a volcano; the timpanist, by now, is getting blisters, and the golem hasn't even shown up.

"*What?*" he screamed again, and Cyn burst into tears. Zhivago dropped Ben's arms, and Ben dropped his own arms, and Cyn let go of her father and I stepped toward Cyn to put my arms around her. *This,* I thought: *this* I could offer her, shelter from tears, me and nobody else. But Ben hugged her, too, awkwardly covering my arms as well until we must have looked like an orgy, with Zhivago standing sternly over us. I let go, and stepped back, and the two Glasses walked, entangled and crying, down the hallway leaving me alone with the chaperone.

Zhivago coughed. I leaned down and picked up the clipboard from where it fell, and when I glanced at it I saw it was a prop. For the audience, this will not be such a surprise, but we in the hospital expect the real thing from doctors. On the top page— and on the other pages, as I flipped through them—there was nothing but squiggles, semblances of writing that when viewed from a distance, could look like notes. Up close I could tell he hadn't written anything down, never, the whole time he was taking notes. On each page were little wavy lines, just a little sketch of the surface of the sea. It was a prop. It was fake. "What is—" I said. I was the child unable to inquire. "This is *nothing*. What's—"

Zhivago put an arm of clear threat around me, a thug hug: *How's the family?* "Joseph," he said to me, "I think you should go home."

"I—"

"I mean *home*, Joseph. You don't belong here. This is a family time. The *Glass* family."

"These notes," I said, handing them to him, "are blank."

"Look around you, Joseph," he continued smoothly. "A woman is dying. Another woman is dead. Just go home, Joseph. This isn't your family."

I tried again. "Why aren't you taking any notes?"

He looked at me sharply and snatched the clipboard from my hands. He glanced at it and took his arm from around me. "You shouldn't be concerning yourself with Mimi," he said.

"Those aren't notes!" I said, and Mimi's door opened and Stephen, flushed and rumpled, stepped out of the room.

"My handwriting," Zhivago said stiffly, smiling at Stephen, "is illegible. Like all doctors'. We're doing all we can, let me assure you."

"Is she going to be O.K.?" Stephen asked Zhivago hoarsely.

"We're doing all we can," he said again.

"I can't live without her," Stephen said simply, and leaned up against the wall. Half his shirt was untucked. "I'm not—I can't sleep. I can't eat. I'm not eating without her." This, at least, was true; with Mimi in the hospital all of us were just heating stuff up and then retiring immediately to our bedrooms. Cyn didn't even come up to the attic any more, though she didn't go to sleep; I lay awake all night listening to all the bedroom doors open and close like chattering teeth. "Is she—"

"We're doing," Zhivago said, "all we can."

"Where's Gramma?" he said.

"Your father has arrived," he said, gesturing down the hallway. "Find your father, Stephen." Stephen put a finger in his mouth like he'd cut it, and walked down the hallway, the noise of his sandals bouncing off the walls. "Frank," I heard Mimi call weakly from her room. *"Frank."* After lurking behind the door during this whole scene we finally hear from the dying woman. "Frank."

"Just a minute," Zhivago—*Frank,* I guess—called to her. He put a hand on the doorjamb and looked at me. "You see?" he said, gesturing to Stephen, still wandering down the hall like a freezing orphan. "You shouldn't be here. This doesn't really concern you, Joseph. This woman—this mother—is very sick. She's in horrible pain. She can't even bend her *knees,* Joseph." Mimi called him again. "This—this isn't about you."

"I love her," I said, trying one more time.

He almost rolled his eyes. "*Everybody* loves her," he said, gesturing into the room.

"Cynthia," I said. "I love Cynthia." I hadn't said that for so long I felt like it wasn't much of an explanation, like it wasn't enough, or wasn't true. Something slipped into my hand like a secret note was passed me; when I looked down Cyn was standing next to me, her little palm inside mine. Zhivago opened his mouth, closed it, walked through Mimi's door, and closed it.

"Joseph," she said. Her voice was sad, and unaccompanied. I haven't talked of it enough, but this is a love story, you know. A love opera. It just has a sad ending. Maybe because it was a hospital, I looked at Cyn and for one clear moment, didn't see an inch of her body. I bent towards her and felt in that instant something patient and vulnerable, some internal rhythm behind all this orchestration, and the rushing of my blood.

"I love you," I said again, but here the orchestra kicks back in: T.U.D.

"Joseph, I—"

"Look," I said. "Let's leave. Let's get out of here. Both of us. Together or something."

"I can't," she said.

"Yes," I said. "You know? We could go back to Mather. Or drive off somewhere, like a movie."

"I can't," she said. It wasn't a movie.

"You *can*," I said.

"I don't want to," she said simply, and let my hand go. I looked at her fingers; everything was stained. I saw Cyn's spidery hand and remembered what it had clutched, what she had done. I took a step backwards and closed my eyes.

"This family," I said. "This family has done terrible things to you, Cyn. This isn't right."

"They aren't happening to *me*," she said. She pointed at the hospital wall like I hadn't seen something that was plastered there. "They're just *happening*."

"No," I said.

"I have to stay here," she said. "This is my mother."

"I *know*," I hissed, stunned at the fury in my throat. Everything was hot. "I *know* what you've done, Cyn."

She just looked at me: that's all she did. Just *looked* at me, blank and wrong. An eyebrow went up like a periscope. "You *know*—"

127

"That little—*that little table*," I said. I blinked, burned. "That *little table*, Cyn. The window over it makes the wind blow. It opened the door of Stephen's room."

"*What are you talking about?*" she screamed. She put her hands to her ears. "*What are you talking about?*"

"I *saw!* I *know!*"

"*No!*" she screamed. Her face was red, or maybe everything was: my eyes, looking at everything and turning it all red. Cyn was crying. "I don't—I can't hear this. I don't know what you're talking about, but *you can't go crazy!* This isn't—*this isn't you! This isn't about you!*"

"*I saw it!*"

"*What are you talking about?*" she screamed. "*Get out of here! My mother—*"

"Your mother *knows*," I spat, and shuddered. The room rumbled around me with the brass, and the percussion and all this drama. "She's—your mother *knows*, Cyn. She was *listening!* She's—"

"*She's dying!*" Cyn screamed, and Dr. Zhivago opened the door. Behind his sharp-angled body I could see Mimi, sitting up on the complicated metallic bed. I saw her pale hospital face, framed with her unwashed hospital hair and plastered with that hospital grimace of pain. And something else. I stalked past Zhivago and right up to Mimi to make sure I hadn't missed it. She followed my eyes and then, dropping the grimace for a smile, leaned up to me to speak. I heard Zhivago stomping toward me, and Cyn crying in the hallway; she didn't have much time.

"*They won't—*" she croaked, and frowned.

"What—*What are you talking about?*" Cyn screamed at me,

and I felt Zhivago's hand on my arm. Mimi looked at me and shrugged.

"They won't what?" I asked. *"What?"*

"What are you talking about?" Cyn screamed again, and I realized maybe she wasn't screaming at me.

"I want you out of here," Zhivago said, pulling at me.

"They won't what?" I asked, and Zhivago stopped. The orchestra waits.

"They won't," she said finally, and smiled like a skull, "believe you."

"Out," Zhivago said, reanimated. He dragged me toward the door. I looked right at Mimi. I wouldn't forget what I saw.

"It's unbelievable!" she shouted, and from her throat she spat a loud cackle. *"It's unbelievable!"*

I couldn't look at Cyn as Zhivago pushed me into the hallway. I didn't want to see where she had gone as the door slammed: into the room, or after me, or into the arms of somebody else. Mimi was right: *unbelievable,* all this sordid incest, the monster in the basement, all the lies and bedroom sneaking and significant looks over meals, all this illness and looming death, all blossoming like horrid tulips from a filthy mind. *Mine.* I stumbled out of the Osteopathy Ward and vomited into a little thicket of greying plants somebody had stuck in the middle of the parking lot, some vague and fruitless decoration. It didn't belong there. I heaved again, and put my face into my hands like I was removing stage makeup. How can you see this? The curtain has fallen, that's how, and the three men finish the scene at the edge of the stage.

I took my hands away and looked up at the hot, wet sky, beating down at me like I was hung out to dry. My chest was beating with breath. I sounded like I was sobbing. But as I looked around the scraggly lot it wasn't me; it was Stephen, not five feet from me, crouched against the smooth cement of the hospital wall and sobbing. He turned and faced me, but I wouldn't speak to him. Now that they were out of sight, Mimi could get up out of bed and shake hands with Zhivago over a scene well played, but I needed to stay silent and out of sight. If I spoke, I thought I'd crumble, like a golem is supposed to if it ever opens it mouth, if you know what I mean. And you *do:* I know that deep down, you know what I'm talking about. Stephen walked closer and closer to me but I didn't say anything, didn't even nod. If I opened my mouth, I knew I'd crumble with the knowledge of what I saw there in Mimi's hospital room, which as the audience fidgets is taken apart as Mimi and Zhivago walk out a back way, to await their curtain calls.

"What—what happened?" Stephen asked me. "Did anything—is she—what happened?" The words rattled in my mouth like a bite of something, but I didn't answer. Stephen looked at me, and then past me and his face went dark. A shadow fell over us as Ben approached, but I barely noticed. As Ben and his son glared at one another, I sat right down in the parking lot and tried to sort it out: *unbelievable.* Mimi collapsing by the side of the river, having slipped from the house in the middle of the night, carrying—*unbelievable*—a clay man she had constructed in the basement. And then, sitting up in the complicated metallic bed, her pale hospital face framed with her unwashed hospital hair, that hospital grimace of pain and something else, something which nobody would believe. What, this summer, had I made up, pieced together like something in Arts & Crafts?

Ben sat down next to me, our legs sloping straight off the curb, downhill. We were all downhill from here. Stephen was stalking off, even further downstage. Ben sighed and turned to meet my eyes but I didn't say anything. I couldn't say it. I knew what I had seen, and I couldn't say it. There, stored in my mouth, were all the words of what I had seen but I had to keep them there. The hospital room was all dismantled, the cemetery almost constructed for the final scene, and I couldn't say anything. I knew what the words were—*Mimi, sitting up on the complicated metallic bed, her pale hospital face framed with her unwashed hospital hair and plastered with that hospital grimace of pain, and her legs, bent at the knee, angled up towards her chin like she was stretching them.* I looked at Ben's legs, and my own, and felt the words clearly behind my teeth: *Bent at the knee. Bent at the knee.* But I didn't say anything. The opera was ending, and like all opera endings the bodies were going to pile up. If I didn't speak, if I sat quietly like a child unable to inquire, mine wouldn't be one of them. If I watched my mouth maybe I'd live.

"Can I tell you something?" Ben asked me, quietly, finally, but I put my hands over my face again, like a curtain.

ACT IV, SCENE TWO

Before the curtain rises, the chorus finally sings. Fans of the composer will call it an act of genius to save a chorus until the final scene, but the choristers will call it a gold mine; while the main characters have to show up early for makeup and costumes, the chorus gets to wander in sometime around the second act and stand backstage in sweats for their big scene. None of those powdered wigs for the grand chorus-party in *La*

Traviata, or the black dust of stage-grimy Jews in *Die Juden.* It's an easy gig, a Perfect Crime: You go in, you go out, nobody gets hurt.

The text is from the prayer book that Rabbi Tsouris read at the grave—so polite! So earnest! The muted green cover, and that respectful, respectful font: *In Contemplation of Death,* the heading reads, but the rest is set for unaccompanied, four-part offstage chorus. *The Name, Creator of the Universe and all that lives, I pray for healing and continued life yet I know that we are all mortal. If only my hands were clean and my heart pure! Alas, I have committed many wrongs and left so much undone! And yet I also know the good I did and the good I tried to do. May that goodness impart eternal meaning to my life. Blessed is The Name, Ruler of the Universe, the righteous Judge.*

"The Name" is undoubtedly Tsouris's favorite little quirk, rather than "Lord" or "King" or "He" which might alienate the congregation, drive them away. But as the audience peers through the fog—*now* the dry ice—to the cemetery, we see that nearly *everyone* has been driven away. The Memorial Service was fairly packed, but due as much to the rain-threatening clouds that gnarled overhead as tradition, Mimi's coffin is lowering, as the curtain rises, to a gravesite attended by precious few, although it reads like a crowd: her husband, her lover, her son and her daughter; her husband's lover, her son's lover, her daughter's lover, her daughter's other lover and the Rabbi, reading a prayer in gender-altered English translation.

It was clearly going to rain, as clear as a rolling cymbal and a shimmering viola vibrato. Beside us the Ohio River was swollen with muddy water, an engorged vein of dirty, dirty fluid. I knew the feeling. For the past several days since we had arrived at the hospital to find Zhivago waiting for us next to an empty, complicated metallic bed, my own bed in the attic had become complicated and metallic. It went without saying—as did nearly everything in the Glasses' almost-mute house—that Cyn didn't come up, so I sat up alone for most of the night, just listening. The orchestration was dense: the muted pizzicato padding of sneaky feet, the piercing glissandos of the wind, the snare-drum *slams* of bedroom doors. Beds creaked like xylophones while the rain hammered like brass. Over at Camp Shalom, the August rain was keeping all the kids indoors, making them sweaty and loud and horny. My head and body throbbed along with them all day, and at night, alone in the attic, I couldn't tell if the pounding was internal or external, whether it was my own dirty mind, dreaming of unbelievable things, or the ripe house closing around me like one of those humid flowers from Act I Scene One, that garden ballet back when everyone was alive and Cyn was moist only for me.

And it *was* unbelievable; Mimi is right. *Was* right: Nobody would believe me. In the attic I'd try to sort out all the scenes: the plate breaking in Act I Scene One; Cyn's finger inside me in the following scene that night; *When You Can't Be Friends with Your Mother* in the Props Studio at the start of Act II; Stephen's sweaty advice-seeking lunch in the Physics Lab cafeteria at the close of it and then the spidery hand stroking the moans out of his eager throat; Mimi's hot gasp against her husband's loosening robe as it fell from my body, Mimi's bent knees before her death. When had things *just happened,* as Cyn said, and when had I composed them, set them to the creaky music of this house? If "Dr. Zhivago" was unbelievable, what about the golem in the basement, or a whole season of anti-semitic operas, or Ben sampling his delicious daughter after she'd sneak down from our wet bed? Eventually, all this mulling over would make the whole summer one sticky blur of sex, and I would no longer know who I was thinking of, me with Cyn, or me with Mimi, or Mimi with Stephen or anyone with anyone. I'd part my own knees and compose an ending, as wet and final as a cloudburst at a funeral.

Nobody, only the sky, broke down as the first few shovels of dirt fell on the coffin some poor propsmistress had to sweat over for days, just for a few seconds of stage time. The sky just *shattered,* the water breaking over us like something was about to be born from all this water and mud and grief. The orchestra—if there had been one at the funeral, which of course there hadn't—roars, too, the timpanist going for broke in these final moments of Act IV. Because everything, here, is ending: The Glass family, having warped itself down to the fragile bones, would now claim one more life in its tragedy, and the sudden rain provides a perfect background, a nice and scary context for the monster's arrival. Because all behavior, don't you know, exists within a social and cultural context, and the Glasses all began running around the cemetery within a social and cultural context of *rain.* It was *raining.*

When the rain descended upon us, we were in a perfectly devised tableau (besides two supernumeraries, there to fill in the grave, who scurry off at the first sign of trouble): Rabbi Tsouris in the middle, the engorged river fluttering behind his dark black robe; Ben and Stephen stage left, staring at their feet, the better to see their skullcaps; and Cyn and I stage right, with her arm linked through mine formally and with such tender inappropriateness that I wanted to push her into one of the cemetery's patches of mud. But the rain did it for me. When the sky broke, Cyn's nails scratched into my wrist like a suicide attempt and when I turned to look at her it was as if the ground had swallowed her up; her small body was wrapped in a black dress wrapped in mud. Rain ran off my face, through my eyes; I wiped them again and saw that Cyn had almost fallen. The thunder roared like trombones, if there had been trombones there at the Old Jewish Cemetery. The thunder almost drowned out a scream.

"What happened—what?" I said to Cyn, looking around, and then I had to say it louder. "*What?*"

"What?" Cyn asked me. Her voice was raw like she hadn't spoken since the hospital, which was practically true. She was trembling and holding a hand out. "It's just *rain*," she snarled. "*Nothing.* It's *raining.*" She gave me a look of disgust and held her hand out farther. I reached for her but heard the scream again.

It was the Rabbi. Stephen and Ben both had their mouths open, holding their coats together in a tense wet hug and making their muddy way towards us in a monster-movie walk. But Tsouris was the one screaming. He had turned around, his black robe billowing behind him, but even over the trombones—*thunder*—I could tell that he was the one screaming, screaming and pointing to the wet mass of river raging in front of him. The muddy water was curling with the force of the cloudburst, emerging over the bank like the tip of a cape, or a dark and murky sunrise, or like the arm of something, hoisting itself out of the Ohio.

The Rabbi screamed again, but the sound was cut off by a splash—Tsouris had gone flying into the river like a rag doll.

135

There was a spray of mud and another roll of thunder and for a moment I couldn't sort anything out. If Tsouris *hadn't* fallen in, why was there such a scream, such a splash? But if he had, who was standing on the bank, covered in mud and shaking its fists?

Not who. Not a person. *What.* It was finished; sometime in the middle of prop-building and bone-aching, Mimi had fashioned a head out of that blank block of clay which had arrived at three in the morning like a nightmare. With Cyn yelling something at me, and the thunder rolling and Stephen coughing and Ben shouting something, the golem's silence was even scarier than its bulging fists and the way its mute and quivering body seemed to rise up out of the river bank, like it'd been there all along just waiting for someone to make it up. Before I could fully register its presence it had already reached out and grabbed Ben by the flying wet hem of his jacket and yanked him to the ground. His face hit the mud and with a gurgle he slid right into Mimi's grave.

Stephen had reached me; his face was pale and mud-splattered. "They said it would rain!" he shouted to me. "They *said!*" I looked at him, smearing the rain away from my eyes. He hadn't seen it, maybe, or couldn't talk about it, maybe, or maybe there was nothing to see. But I could see *everything:* the still-sputtering river, the puddles on the ground pouring into one another, and Ben's hands on the rim of the grave as he tried to hoist himself out. Behind him was Tsouris, who had some-how found dry land; he was kneeling on the ground, shaking the mud off his arms. I ran to help Ben; I don't know why. Maybe if I hadn't helped him—but I didn't help him, not really. When I reached the mouth of the grave I reached out a hand for him to grab, but my palms were so muddy that he just slipped back down, landing on Mimi's coffin with a *thump*. *If only my hands were clean and my heart pure! Alas, I have committed many wrongs and left so much undone!*

I turned around. Stephen was yelling. The golem had reached them and Cyn was now down on the ground, with the golem kneeling over her with its fists raised, like a timpanist over his dark, loud drum. I ran toward her, each foot slapping the wet ground like a spank. Stephen was looking at me and screaming, over and over, like I was a monster, like the monster was me. Which shouldn't have surprised me, but it did. Covered in rain and liver-colored grime, I must have looked like a monster, but it surprised me anyway, and I hesitated. I stopped for just a second, and looked behind me where the Rabbi was helping Ben out of the grave. I stopped just for a second, and in that moment everything was lost.

The golem's fists came down, one at Cyn's neck and the other inside her mouth. Her scream became a wet gurgle, and even over the noise I could hear something snap. Bone probably. Stephen screamed, his voice cracking to the highest register, as if puberty had been blurred along with his mud-scarred features. As I looked at him, the monster did, too, and stepped toward him as he screamed louder, wider. Now I was kneeling over Cyn, my arms out wild in the air. Her eyes were closed and her head was turned funny sidewise, with her chin on her shoulder like she'd rather break her neck than look at me. Her legs were bent like they couldn't be, just snapped sudden and sharp like they couldn't be bothered to find the knee, just had to bend over, and break. Where was she, the Cyn who had brought me here? Where was the daughter who had brought me into this family, into this whole drama, this opera? There was nothing here to explain this. Anything that could be behind all this misery was impossible to believe, or even to see; the rain grew, pelting down on me even harder, and I couldn't tell if the golem had reached Stephen or if he had just fallen into the mud. There was nothing to believe here. The librettist, or God, or golem, was nowhere.

Or *now here,* depending on how you look at it. I looked behind me and Ben was screaming, shaking his arms at me like a drummer, but the Rabbi was saying something, something definite but inaudible as the thunder rolled. But when the sound passed I caught a few words of Hebrew, some traditional Jewish incantation I wouldn't have thought Tsouris could get through without stumbling. And he didn't: with a wet slap he fell to the gushing earth, but raised himself up on his elbows and kept shouting *something,* just as the earth hit *me.*

I was knocked to the ground, and when I blinked back the mud I saw the clay figure standing silently over me. It was unbelievable, literally, something I could not believe, something I was unable to inquire about. The golem raised its arms just as the Rabbi completed whatever he was saying, and another burst of rain poured down on the figure. Its arms, towering over me like something unreachable, wavered and then stopped in the onslaught. The golem *shifted,* its legs moving like they shouldn't, and in a few seconds it was unrecognizable in the river. Ben reached me and pulled me up, still shouting, looking past me at his daughter, his lover, his son's lover and my girlfriend, all of them splayed out and dead on the ground. Stephen grabbed my other arm, his face all rage and earth. They were shouting at me. The Rabbi reached us and, with a cry, knelt by Cyn and started something all over again. The golem was nothing, or was gone; it was just the rain and the rest of this family.

I spat some gob of the golem's fist out of my mouth and looked up at the late-summer downpour. There was so much sound I couldn't sort anything out, couldn't bear any of it. I opened my mouth in a sheer roar which is the last sung note of the opera. How could it be anything else? As one last loud T.U.D. underscores Joseph's sustained note of anguish, the story has played itself out; with the love destroyed, the revenge exacted, there is nothing left here for tonight's audience, already pulling their coats off the backs of their chairs to beat the rush to the lobby, because if there's one thing they can't stand, having already run a mad rush to the theater from work, it's getting trapped when they're on their way out. A lover, a family, a monster: they've all done their part in creating something not just interesting but *fascinating, mesmerizing,* to transcend all the stress about whether to change or where to have dinner or parking or whatever, and really *hear* the music. That's what opera's *for.* The opera—see the curtain come down—is over for *them,* and for the orchestra and all the people ready to mop up all this rain. But not for *me.* That's why I was screaming, because I knew it *wasn't* over, just as you, reading this, can feel the thick weight of unread book in your right hand even as the audience exits. There's *more.* Feeling the water seeping through my funeral clothes I knew *I* wasn't dead, that *some* story, if not this one, was still carrying me along like an engorged river. Rivers run someplace, as I would. Something more would happen to me, something more was waiting to happen to me now. Something more was already lurking in the angry depths of the river. Immerse yourself with me, as I struggle to see what's beyond the drenching rain and the thick fog of dry ice: *More? How can there be more? How can there be a second part?*

PART TWO

"Substitutions are possible for the <u>underlined</u> words in this subject area. For example: 'Migration paths of the <u>trumpet swan</u>' may be changed to some other bird or animal, provided the change is interesting and appropriate. (Remember, some animals and birds don't migrate.)"

—KATHRYN LAMM,
10,000 Ideas for Term Papers,
Projects and Reports

SO WHAT NEXT? *Exactly. Exactly* how I felt. A few nights in the hospital: the smudgy window of television, snipped off by the nurses when the news came on. Shock, and even in all that rain, dehydration: surprising to me but, somebody explained, not at all unusual in even the wettest of disasters. Survivors of shipwrecks, say. Adrift, at loose ends, and by court order locked out of the house, I wanted to skip this part. I dreamed of skipping this part. Inspired even by the agile commercials on late-night television, glimpsed through the prefab inertia of whatever dripped through my IVs, I could imagine skipping this part, the weightless freedom of each leg bending at the knee and skipping, skipping, skipping. Skipping this part. Skipping ahead even, but to where? There I woke up. Discharged like a halfhearted orgasm, I put on my shoes and signed papers saying I'd pay later. But what then? What next?

You'll never guess, and it was boring anyway, so I'll skip ahead here. It was years later, though not too many years. It was years enough that the hit song "Bing Bing Bing" had faded from the radio but worked its way into the lexicon. It was audial shorthand for sudden, electric comprehension: "I was just looking and looking at it," my boss would say, poring over the inventory list at Bindings "and then, suddenly—bing bing bing—I *got* it." It was enough years later that there was pretty much no hope of my ever getting the box of books from Mather College.

There was pretty much no hope. I went to California because it was on the opposite coast from my terrible summer. I settled in the cheapest town I could find, which also happened to be the ugliest, and it could have been called anything. This town loitered outside of San Francisco, but *way* outside, like there was a restraining order against it. It lurked in the featureless landscape of deep suburbia with perfect geometry: buildings with sharp, shaved corners, parking lots with parallel lines, architecture that tells a calm, symmetrical lie: *As you can see, the universe is perfect.*

Towns that tell you this lie can be called anything, and this one was called Pittsburg, Pittsburg, California—like Pittsburgh, Pennsylvania, but without an *h*. One letter and the whole thing is different: arid and open, dry without a hint of soot in the air. There was a flagpole in the downtown area, sagging in the no-wind which blew between the boxy drugstore and the shiny restaurant, one of a kit of restaurants shined up all over the country. At Christmastime, when I arrived, all the windows were caked with the same stale snowbank: that powdery stuff from a can, sprayed on the windows in vague, rolling hills, with a little tower of snowy circles for a snowman like the ones we'd all make at three in the morning, back at Mather, when the real stuff came down. This was California snow, available inside the drugstore next to the candy canes and all the other placid, grinning Gentile paraphernalia. There was a cardboard Santa head taped to the screen door of the ugly apartment I found, third from the left if you stood in the paved courtyard that used to be a motel parking lot until they converted it to apartments because nobody wanted to visit Pittsburg, California, or if they did they didn't stay in a hotel but just crashed out on the cousin's couch where they'd watch television after dinner came steaming out of the oven in heaping casserole dishes bought in the strip malls down the highway from my Santa face, which I kept there, the face of Santa, like a stubborn stain. I took a job at Bindings, a boxy building that sold books. I put the apartment's location on a change-of-address form, in case my box of books ever arrived, and went to work unpacking boxes of books in the back room where a tinny radio played unfashionably-old hit songs: "Crazy Love," "Tell Your Mother," "Bing Bing Bing." When the New Year hit, the pimply high-school students went back to high school and they promoted me to the floor, where I had to wear a tie, available next door at the store catering to tall men, coppery suits lined up along the walls, shiny and on sale and so big they looked like they were made for golems. It was a promotion; they covered an ERIKA nametag with forest-green tape and a clicking, handheld machine scragged out my name: J-O-S-E-P-space-H.

I thought it was a good idea. I thought I'd skipped ahead. My new town was so boxy I thought nothing would remind me of the curve of Cyn's hips against my hands as I drank from her. I thought the powdered fake snow on the shop windows would be as different from Pittsburgh's sooty brick buildings as black and white. I thought the bed would creak differently without her stroking me in it. I thought when I'd lean against the railing of my apartment complex, where in its previous incarnation who knows how many divorced salesmen poured scotch into the second courtesy glass (the first, gaping by the sink, rimmed with the snowy glaze of toothpaste) and gazed out past the thin, windless flagpole and the white and landscaped cylinder of the inexplicable Morrison Lab on the hill, I'd see nothing operatic. But the scarlet sunset looked like a painted backdrop. The Morrison Lab looked like the steel industry. And the back of the cardboard Santa, greeting me crookedly every morning as I left for work, looked like the pools of fluid Cyn would leave me with up in the sweltering attic bedroom before she'd go downstairs and do something I couldn't quite remember.

I felt my unhappiness close in on me like a fly-trapping plant. I'd leave Bindings mid-afternoon and find myself purposely brushing up against chubby moms, shopping bags tugging on one arm and sweatshirted kids on the other, craving just a taste of the motherly friction that used to be in my life. The sad songs on the radio were about me and newspaper articles foretold my doom—the *Pittsburg Bee* stung me full of information which would swell in my skull each night before I turned the radio off to dream of sex and clay. I read an article about a hostage crisis in the bank in the strip mall next door to mine: a woman was, the down-home prose of the *Bee* said, "minding her own business" when a man held a gun to her back and marched her out into "broad daylight." She walked by several acquaintances in the parking lot and nobody thought anything was wrong. He forced her to drive to "the house where she lived" and then, the

146

gun "still trained on her" (as she what? made coffee? tied herself to one of the matching chairs? tried to signal the mowing neighbor?), called the major news networks with "an outrageous list of demands." The police traced the call and the guy was arrested before everybody was home from soccer practice, but for the next few weeks I'd eye pairs of shoppers in the parking lot, wondering which one had the gun. When the drought broke in mid-January there was a story about a mother and father who had driven all the way from the hills into San Francisco for the opera. As Tosca's troubles multiplied, the thunderstorm made the parched earth into mud; a mudslide swarmed their house during the curtain call, smothering the two children—"a boy, eight, and a girl,"—and the teenage baby-sitter, who was the last to go: as the firemen dug and dug, they heard her screaming for an hour or so, and then nothing. I put the blankets over my head and knew there was something wrong with me.

But I didn't know I was in CRISIS until they put me in charge of New Age. It was actually more like Self-Help, but Bindings had learned somewhere that people didn't really want to help themselves, not in the suburbs anyway. I updated the stock and took away the slow sellers, made sure the Age got Newer and Newer with every shopping day. During my lunch break I'd sit in the back room and peruse the customer returns with my tie thrown behind my back like a swashbuckler's ascot to avoid stains. It was the one called *Breaking the SPELL* that did it for me. "SPELL" stood for "Sad People's Emotional Language Legacy," an acronym I accepted on pure faith. The first part of the book was about all the terrible things that happened to the author, but I skipped ahead. "So far, this has been a book about pain," the second part started, and I read right to the finish.

After work I'd drive to some undeveloped land and sit on my hood and read, sometimes out loud, little parcels of hardcover hope while the sun set on the scraggly fields awaiting perfect new buildings. "Regardless of how you feel about yourself, you are a strong, creative individual," the book told me. "You matter." I felt my body, so arid and loose, strengthen up, like I was cooking in a kiln. I matter. I *was* matter.

And matter in CRISIS. I turned the page and there it was, another acronym of truth. "Are you in CRISIS? There's an easy way to find out, and it's all hidden in the word CRISIS. Go through the word crisis with me, and decide if any of these things have too much control over your life. C—Compulsive behavior. Is compulsive behavior controlling your life?" I thought of my parking-lot rubs, my inability to throw away Santa's face. "R—rules. Are rules controlling your life?" If I was late three more times they'd take New Age away from me. "I— Idealization of family. Is idealization of family controlling your life?" Each night, I had only the most ideal glimpses of the Glasses: the curve of Mimi's breasts, the ripe flower of Cyn's sex contracting against her father's plump and accusatory fingers, the half-clenched, sweaty moans of Stephen's erection, and my own, each night, rattling the bed alone. "S—Shame. Is shame controlling your life?" And then, as the wan sun dribbled through my dirty bedroom window, the other glimpses would come: the block of clay, the frightened dog and the forbidden bend of the knee, which I would follow up the leg and beneath the hospital gown. My lust and shame would wrestle one another like siblings until I threw myself out of bed and into the shower to wash all this crisis off me, but the rush of the water would bring it all back, a flash flood: Mimi's mouth as Ben's robe opened around me, Stephen's bare chest, with the hair triangling down like a landing strip, and that scene, over and over, Act I Scene Two, the best sex we ever had, until my orgasm would flower around my spidery hand as I'd seen Stephen's, around Cyn's, and I'd stumble out of the steamy bathroom and realize, bing bing bing, I was late for work again. "I—Ideology. Is ideology controlling your life?" I was petrified of rabbis. "S—Social systems. Are social systems controlling your life?" All I had were social systems: converted motels, the painted stripes of parking spaces, boxes of inventory, radio hits, alphabetized overstock, parceled land already leased but not built on. I'd look out into the dark landscape and the constellations of warning lights they put on electric wires, so planes don't crash, so the perfection of the universe isn't disrupted here in the town named after the town that led me here, alone, in crisis. I'd mark my place with my fingers, lean back on my windshield and think: Help me.

Help was easy. "There aren't organized twelve-step programs for absolutely everything," the book said, "but the twelve steps are blueprints. Use them for an odyssey of recovery," an odyssey, I decided, which could counterpoint the *Iliad* I had already experienced. *Breaking the SPELL* laid out twelve neat steps like a strip mall: one-stop shopping, bing bing bing. I submitted to the twelve-step universe, perfectly devised, here in surburbia, also perfectly devised.

So far, this has been a book about pain. Now I will describe how I healed myself, how I broke my own SPELL and pulled myself out of CRISIS with the help of a twelve-step program. What next? I'd make next. When you're stuck in a story, a famous writer of detective fiction once said, have two guys come through the door with guns. And the funny thing is, that's exactly what happened.

Step 1

One morning, after knocking, two guys came through my door with guns. I looked through my little peephole and saw them: two suburban cops, wired with morning coffee from the new Queequeg Coffee Shop down the highway and the prospect of *action*. Outside of the sullen teenagers throwing beer bottles against the dumpsters behind the twelve-screen movie theater, there wasn't much going down, crimewise. It must have been cool to get the order to open the screen door, watch Santa's face swing by in a creaky, grinning arc and knock sharply.

"Joseph?" the officer asked, and then he said my last name, which has been changed to protect the innocent.

"Yes," I said. I had my pants on but not a shirt. They'd interrupted me as I stood in the shower, the water off but still dripping, as I'd been stroking myself remembering something I couldn't quite remember, and I'd thrown pants over my eager object on the way to the door. My heart was pounding from a denied orgasm, and from the arrival of two guys with guns. "Is something wrong?"

"You used to live in Pittsburgh, Pennsylvania, with the Glass family?"

"Well, I didn't live with them. For a summer. I stayed with them for a summer." My carpet was all crabgrass beneath my nervous feet. "What is it?"

The two cops looked at one another like they couldn't remember whose line it was. "There's been a death," the first one said, his hand travelling down to his waist toward his gun. My unfired equivalent throbbed briefly, and then I heard what he said and stepped back. I sat on the unmade bed. The cops stepped into my apartment and the one who hadn't talked yet slammed Santa behind him, a little too hard. They approached me warily and from different angles.

"Who—" I asked, and swallowed. "Who could be dead?"

The quiet one rolled his eyes. The talker looked at me like I knew the answer already. "Simon Glass," he said.

I'll pause for a minute while you dig out that old playbill, from that opera you attended a while ago, and check the character list.

The talking cop took my silence for shock, which maybe it was. He took out a small notepad, the kind you could get in pre-wrapped packets of notebooks two stores down from the job I was late for. "Now, your primary relationship was with Cynthia Glass?"

It took me a few seconds: primary, relationship, Cynthia. "Yes. She was my girlfriend."

"When did you break up?"

I blinked.

"*Hey,*" the quiet one suddenly snarled, and rapped on the wall of my apartment. "He asked you a question. *When did you break up with Ann?*"

"*Cyn,*" I said.

The talking one looked at us both, and then down at his notebook. "It's *Cynthia,*" he said tiredly, like *he'd* been the one whose tongue had made her cry out, up in an attic somewhere. "Simon's sister. Now, Joseph, when did you and Cynthia break up?"

"It's *Stephen*," I said. "*Stephen*. How did he—what happened?"

The quiet one pounded on the wall again. "*We'll* ask the questions, Stephen," he snapped, and it all became clear to me: It was *Good Cop, Bad Cop,* also the title of a thriller we were pushing this week at Bindings.

"You're not Joseph Last Name Changed to Protect the Innocent?" he asked.

"Yes I am," I said. "But Cyn's—*Cynthia's*—brother's name was Stephen."

Good Cop looked at the notebook. "Yes that's true," he said soberly. Bad Cop pounded the wall again, halfheartedly, and looked over at Good. Clearly they wished they could just start over, back at the Santa face.

"He's dead?" I asked.

"*We're* asking the questions here," Bad Cop said. "Now when did you break up with—"

"Cyn's dead," I said. My hand, spiderlike, clutched the unmade sheet. It was true.

"*When did you break up?*"

"Around the end of the summer," I said. "I guess. She was—she was *killed*. I don't want to talk about it. Now, if you will excuse me, I have to go to work." You don't have to read the thriller to know what happened next. What always happens when the suspect tries to brush off the police. Bad Cop shoved me by the shoulders, hard, and I was back down on the saggy mattress.

"*I don't know anything!*" I shouted. I looked at Good Cop for sympathy. "I'm just trying to—leave me alone, please. I just—I want to get away from that whole family."

"Which is why you moved here to Pittsburg?" Good Cop said skeptically.

I looked down at my bare feet. How in the world did I think I was going to work half-dressed? "It could have been called anything. It just *happened*," I said, "to be called Pittsburg."

"That just *happened*," Good Cop said, "to—"

"It's a different *spelling*. One letter and everything—"

"And just *happened* to be the place where Simon was working," Good Cop said. "I'm finding this hard to believe, Stephen."

"*Joseph,*" I said. "Stephen. What happened?"

"You're not making a lot of sense," Bad Cop said.

"I'm confused," I said. "I'm in recovery. I'm not even at Step One."

"Drugs?"

"The Glasses." The perfect grey of suburban morning was turning my bare feet paler and paler. I was late for work. "Can I get dressed?"

"Just keep your hands where we can see them," Bad Cop said. Cyn had said something like that to me once. In silence I unrolled socks, buttoned a shirt, tied a tie.

"Where do you work?" Good Cop asked, his eye on his notepad. Was he testing me? Was it already written down?

"Bindings," I said. "New Age." I took *Breaking the SPELL* from my bedstand and held it up for them. Good and Bad exchanged a look. They always do. "Where does *Stephen* work?" I asked. "What happened?"

By now I had my keys. Good Cop led the way, then me and then Bad Cop, with Santa bringing up the rear in a dull thud. My fingers were trembling around my keys, so much that I couldn't lock my door, and with a tired, superior glare, Bad Cop

153

took the keys from me and finished the job. I think I was being arrested, which was scary but brought a solid, clear calm. I could not go to work. I was sandwiched between two policemen; I could not escape. I knew I had the right to remain silent but I asked it again anyway. "Where does Stephen work?"

Good Cop looked at me like he wished I'd stop pretending to be so dumb, so powerless. But it wasn't an act: It was the first step. "Right in your backyard," he said, and pointed at the rising sun.

I took one step out to the railing. I looked out at the landscape and couldn't imagine what he was telling me. "What?" I pointed, too, but I couldn't see anything. *As you can see,* the parking lot said, the strip malls, the cylinder of the lab on top of the hill and the dry sun, rising over Pittsburg and making me late, *as you can see, the universe is perfect.* "What?"

With disgusted patience he grabbed my wrist and moved my arm over until I was pointing at the Morrison Lab, which had been there all along, like an alphabetized book. I had come three thousand miles to live in the shadow of the lab where Stephen worked, and I still couldn't find it until he helped me. It was the first step, all right: *I admitted I was powerless, and that my life had become unmanageable.*

"O.K.," I said hollowly, one hand clutching my book and the other still pointing at what had been there all along, and I went with them.

Step 2

"There are two things in the world," *Breaking the SPELL* says simply. "Nothing and semantics."

"I have to go to work," I said from my meek and sweaty place in the backseat of the cop car. It was filthy.

"You don't *have* to go anywhere," Bad Cop said, "until we say so." He had a point. I only had my book. Outside the strip malls descended, as if on freight elevators, as we took the mellow grade up to the Morrison Lab where Stephen worked before he died. The windows of the cop car were grimy and thick, giving Pittsburg a pale pollution, but even when we pulled up to the curb, already littered with cop cars, and Good Cop unlocked the door and primly beckoned me out, the sky still looked filthy.

The lobby of the Morrison Lab was evenly split between two costumes: white lab coats and police uniforms. Experts on what went on in the building, and experts on what had gone wrong in it: "Everyone," *Breaking the SPELL* encourages, "is an expert on *something*." Everyone was all bunched up in groups, muttering; the groups parted for Good Cop, Bad Cop and me like one of us was Moses. It seemed to take forty years to trundle down the arched hallways to the scene of the crime.

The lab was sputtered in brown. Surprisingly stagey equipment—colored liquids in shapely coed bottles, clear plastic tubing, metal boxes pimpled with dials and portholes for electric-green blips, Bunsen burners, mounds of computer printouts, like a mad-scientist opera set—was caked in something brown. The equations on the blackboards were splotched with it, in thick gobs of galaxy formations which extended up two walls. One of the other walls was draped in a big black plastic sheet, like a garbage bag, like everything was garbage. The floor was entirely brown. Even the cops were getting dirty, just from moving around in there, and a small circle of white lab coats were less white, and more worried, than those in the lobby. The only thing that wasn't slapped brown was a blank white sheet, draped over something in a corner, something tenting the sheet in four places. Something with four limbs.

"Recognize something?" Good Cop said, after I'd taken it all in. I turned to look at his face, slightly brown from the stained light fixtures.

"What?" I asked. "Ask the questions," *Breaking the SPELL* says, "and you might get the answers."

"He said," Bad Cop said, *"recognize something?"*

"Well, it looks like a lab."

Bad Cop spat, and it crackled on the drying brown floor. "You learn that at your fancypants school?"

I thought of Mather and couldn't think of a thing I'd learned there. "No," I said. "I just—I don't recognize anything. I've never been here."

Bad Cop stalked over to the sheet and pulled it back like we were going to bed. "What about *this?*" he shouted, and the worried lab coats looked up and glared at him. "Do you recognize *this*, by any chance?"

Stephen's mouth was gaping open at an unnatural angle, too wide, and off. Something had pulled his chin down like it was a stuck drawer. Inside it was filled with mud, filled to the teeth. There was a long cat-scratch down his right cheek, red in the brown minstrel show of his face, streaked with tears or water or something. His eyes were either closed or out—there was so much dirt in the sockets I couldn't see anything. His hands were half-clenched like knobby winter trees, one of them clasping nothing and the other pointing at nothing. For a second I couldn't figure out what was wrong with his arms, and then I knew: *everything*. They were folded and refolded like a map in the glove compartment, bent at places that weren't joints, accordioned in and out like someone had tried to force them to fit somewhere. His legs weren't bent anywhere but the knee, but the *wrong way*, either that or his whole torso had been wrung out like a rag, it was impossible to tell in all the mud which had hardened along his body in mid-tide. The brown wave tapered down his body like a landing strip, a blossom of crags under his broken neck down to a drained swamp where I assumed his sexual organs were still, somewhere. Stephen was naked except for a small tatter of white—the last of a lab coat, I assume—and the sheet which Bad Cop had flung back from him.

"I *assume*," he said, in best Bad Cop sarcasm, "that you'll recognize Simon Glass."

"*Stephen*," I whispered. Too dirty for even my dirty mind, and too splayed out for the geometrics of the suburbs where it lived, the sight pinned my head to the wall and stuffed it with clay, kept stuffing it even when it fell thrashing to the floor, broke my brain's arms in a dozen places and left its legs bent the wrong way, all wrong. Everything was all wrong. *Breaking the SPELL*, which I dropped in the mud as I stumbled backward, says this is a common feeling for people in recovery—"remember," it says, "everything is as likely to be right as it is to be wrong"—but they don't tell you how it feels. It feels awful. Good Cop caught my arm on my way back, and guided me to an immense lab table that rose like an altar from the floor. I couldn't sit on it but at least I could lean, my hand leaving a print in the mud tableclothed all over it. "It's *Stephen*," I said again. "What happened to him?"

The sheet went down. "Why don't *you* tell *us*?" Bad Cop said.

I swallowed, my throat empty and wet. "Do you think *I*—"

Good Cop leaned next to me. "We need your help," he said simply, gesturing around the room with an unstained hand. "We don't know what to make of this, and you're the closest thing we have right now to talking to Stephen."

I looked around the room again, the overturned equipment, the garbage bag. I swallowed. The mud, the sheet. "I'm not very close," I said.

"Close enough." Bad Cop walked over to me so I was between Good and Bad. "I understand the same exact thing happened to your girlfriend. *His* sister."

"What?"

"We've been on the phone with your rabbi," Good Cop said plainly.

What?

"What?" I said.

"Your—"

"I don't *have* a rabbi," I said.

Good Cop sighed and opened his notepad. "In Pittsburgh," he said. "*Pennsylvania* Pittsburgh. Rabbi Sour—Soar—Rabbi T-S-O-U-R-I-S."

"Tsouris," I said. One quick lesson. "He's not my rabbi."

Bad Cop looked like he wanted to *make* him be my rabbi. Good Cop looked like he didn't care *whose* rabbi he was. He glanced at his notepad again. "He told us what happened at the funeral."

"What happened to your *girlfriend*," Bad Cop sneered.

I started to put my face in my hands, except one of them was smeared with mud. *"Nobody,"* I said quietly, *"nobody* knows what happened at the funeral."

"Cynthia Glass was killed," Good Cop said quietly. "We know that."

"*And?*" I said.

"And Tsouris isn't entirely sure you didn't do it."

"That *I*—?"

"That you attacked her." Good Cop shrugged slightly. "Look, that's a closed book. It was raining, and nobody seems to have seen anything clearly. The Pittsburgh police said that Miss Glass was hit too hard for it to have been you. They told you that. You know that. Nobody's accusing you of anything."

"I have a theory, though," Bad Cop said in a kindly tone that was mean around the edges. "That hit-too-hard thing doesn't mean anything. People have superhuman strength in stressful situations. Strength they didn't know they had. Like that babysitter who dug herself out of the muddy house."

"What do you mean?"

"You must have read about it," Bad Cop said tiredly. "The big mudslide, while the parents were at the opera? The babysitter, a skinny little thing, dug herself out of a ton and a half of mud, all because of a panic reaction or something. She saved herself when nobody else could."

"So she's *alive?*" I said. All my dreams of that girl dying. Don't they fact-check the *Bee?*

"You could have killed her," Bad Cop said. "You probably did. I mean, now there's her brother, dead of the same thing, it looks like. And you just *happen* to live in town. Look, we're checking out your alibi now, but why don't you just give it up? There have only been two deaths like this in the universe, and you were poking around both of them!"

"What—" I said. "*What—*" My hand moved on the lab table

and brushed up against something hairy which turned out to be tinsel—some Christmas decoration lost in the fray. I couldn't choose a question. "What—what alibi? There's no—I haven't given you an *alibi*."

"Lauren did," Good Cop said. "Bindings." Sometime, while skipping ahead, I'd picked up a girlfriend along with my job: one-stop shopping. "Like my partner said, you're in the clear. We just want to ask you a few questions."

"*You* want to ask *me*—?"

"Down at the station," he said, and held out a hand to me like we were going to walk hand-in-hand, the end of a romance movie.

"I swear to you," I said, my mouth dry and crinkled, "I *swear* to you I had nothing to do with all this."

Bad Cop turned to me, furious. The white-coated mutterers stopped. "You just *happened* to move to his town," he said, "you just *happened* to live almost across the *street* from where he worked. He just *happens* to die in the *exact same circumstances* as the ones his *sister* just *happened* to die. And when we find you, you just *happen* to be holding a book written by his *fucking father*. Sure, you have *nothing* to do with it."

It was true. The book was muddied, like everything in the room, but I could see it on the back cover. "A former orthopedic surgeon, Dr. Glass now lives in the Pacific Northwest where he explores issues relating to both our personal and political psyches." And next to it, the muddied and smiling face of Ben Glass: the *fucking father*.

"God," I said.

"Only He can help you now," Bad Cop snarled in perfect character. "Why don't you tell me again that you have nothing to do with this, you *shit*? Why don't you tell me who else did? Why don't you tell me, if it wasn't you, what kind of monster could have done such a thing?

"What kind of *monster*?" I repeated, and to my raw and dim horror I heard I was laughing. "What kind of *monster*?" A cartoon pantheon marched in front of my eyes like a Halloween parade, all the monsters: "Wolfman?" I said, and howled like one. My eyes were tearing up, my shoulders shaking. "The Mummy?" I guessed again. "What kind of *monster? How about Frankenstein?*"

Bad Cop uttered one loud syllable and slapped me on the face just as my tongue was finding the *D* in "Dracula." My fangs snapped down and I felt my mouth burst into something wet like a red and copper orgasm. I uttered some syllable myself, and spat blood onto Ben's smile. *"What?"* I said, as Bad Cop stopped his second slap midflight. *"What?"*

"You're *under arrest!*" he said, all biblical thunder. I was still laughing when the sobs came. I had loved Cyn; *loved her*, and now everything was wrecked, raw, wrong. Where could I go?

"Let's go down to the station," Good Cop said, gently, and held out his hand to me. I felt my mind splinter at all wrong angles, like a stuck drawer, or a shattered jaw. What was happening here? Could I skip this part, too? What plot twists were encircling me, wringing me out like a rag? The sheet fell back on Stephen's corpse and I felt, all in a red rush, that I had done these things and then cast myself in an opera where everything was different. How could it be otherwise, with just me, a blot in this perfect universe, like a Christmas decoration up at the wrong time, and another muddy death? What else could have happened? When I opened my eyes Good Cop's hand was still waiting for me and I took it after all, grasping his fingers in mine and the book—the one from the bookstore near where Stephen worked, the one written by Stephen's father, this book which had been there all along, lurking on the horizon like a well-placed prop—in the other. I had nothing else. I let him take me back down the grungy hallways into the squinty day. I got back in the dirty car because there was nowhere else to go. I let the cops take me to the station like it'd been circled on the map all along. And it had. It was the second step: *I had come to believe that only a power greater than me could restore me to sanity.* I knew there were only two things in the world, and I was going with the book. If you didn't choose semantics there was only nothing. If you didn't choose semantics there was nothing left.

Step 3

They'd locked me, I think, in a room with a mirror I was pretty sure was one-way. I tried to frame myself in the glass, unconcerned and ready to help. Name: *Joseph Last Name Changed.* Age: Too old to be living in suburbia as a kid and too young to live there as an adult. Address: Stopped chewing on the pen as I wrote it in. Eyes: *brown,* and untrustworthy. Hair: just *brown.* Official Statement: state in your own words what happened, officially. This is for the official record. Already redundant, already, and I hadn't started.

The last time I had written an Official Statement it was for the Mather Undergraduate Application, earnest and extracurricular so I could get there and have sex without any parents walking in. I couldn't imagine what they wanted now. *I met Cynthia Glass in the fall of several years ago. We had a relation-*

ship for the duration of the school year. In June we drove to Pitts-
burgh—I went back and added in *Pennsylvania*—*where we were*
both to work at Camp Shalom, a Jewish day camp. We both lived
at her parents' house on Byron Circle. I had only been there a few
days when I began to suspect

What next? I paused and locked eyes with my reflection,
probably with a growling Bad Cop, too, sipping from a Styrofoam cup all frayed at the rim with his impatience. How
come I could imagine each tiny piece, sprinkled on a worn
wooden table like stage snow, and not finish the sentence in
front of me?

—that the family was having a lot of problems. I tried to tell
myself it was all in my imagination, and maybe it was. Then Mimi,
Cynthia's mother, got very sick, and that only added to the troubles
between everybody. Then she died. At her funeral,

At her funeral what? *Breaking the SPELL* had taught me that
regardless of how I felt about myself, I was a strong, creative
individual. But if the figure lumbering out of the riverbank was
my creativity, that meant that Stephen's gaping jaw, accordioned arms—*that* was my strength. What had happened at the
funeral? What was happening now?

"How we coming?" Good Cop said, opening the door and
leaning in. Wasn't locked.

I looked down at the Statement. Rows of blank lines lay there
like bleachers, waiting for me to finish. "I'm having difficulty."

Good Cop sat down beside me, plunking his Styrofoam cup
down next to the empty ashtray that would soon be brimming
with butts, lit by the interrogating bulb, if this had been written
by the man who invented two guys coming through the door
with guns. "Then why don't you just talk to me, instead of

writing all this out?" he asked. "Just tell me the story any way you feel like it."

"I don't," I said quietly, "feel like telling it at all."

He sighed, and his eyes flickered from me to the mirror, behind which I could picture Bad Cop draining his coffee in frustration: "*He* doesn't *feel* like telling it!"

"I know you don't," he said, "but you gotta understand, Joseph. Pittsburg's pretty quiet. We don't usually have murders here at all. Somebody holds up a gas station maybe, or kids and graffiti. Somebody gets drunk and kills their husband. I've never seen anything like this, though. A guy with his body all twisted and covered with mud in the middle of some science lab— nobody has. Nobody except, guess who, the police in the other Pittsburgh. And that turns out to be the *sister*. Now nobody saw what happened to your girlfriend except a rabbi who seems— well, a rabbi, and her father, who's holed up in the Eureka woods somewhere, we're trying to find out. And *you*. And look at you—you're living in the same town as the brother and you're reading the father's book, now you can understand that we need to ask you some questions."

"I know how it looks," I said, "but I—"

"And I know you have an alibi with the bookstore and everything, but from what we hear this Lauren girl is also your girlfriend, so it's not exactly an airtight alibi, all right? She might be covering for you."

"But I *swear* to you I—"

"—was doing inventory, I know, but *look*. I have to tell you that anything you say may be used in a court of law, you know, but you have to help me here. I look at you and I can't picture you barging into the Morrison Lab, late at night, with a ton of clay, and ripping that boy apart, even if your girlfriend would agree to swear, by penalty of perjury, that you were really doing inventory. It doesn't make sense. And a big college boy like you could get a lawyer who would make everybody *see* it doesn't make sense. That's why you're not in jail, and why you're technically free to leave whenever you want. But tell me what's— *what's going on. What is this?*"

"What did the rabbi say it was?"

"You don't want to know."

"A monster, right?" I said quietly. I looked down at the Official Statement and saw that it had blurred, the ink smearing beneath my palms. "Isn't that what he said?"

"He said he wasn't sure."

"But a monster, right?"

"He said he wasn't sure."

"Of course not," I said. "Of course not. You can't be *sure* about—"

"Why don't you tell me what happened that summer? From the beginning. Or however you want."

"*I met Cynthia Glass,*" I read, "*in the fall of—*"

"Just tell me about the *summer,*" he said, "when you were living there. What happened? I mean, she died, the mother, right, but what *happened?*"

"An opera," I said, "a melodrama." And now, I didn't add, it was a monster movie: *You gotta believe me, Sheriff! Big and clay and coming this way!* "The Glasses—they—everybody was sleeping together. I think. I'm pretty sure. I mean, it doesn't really matter, does it? Whether they were or I just *thought* they were—"

"It matters a *lot*," Good Cop said. "Where'd you get the idea it doesn't *matter*, for chrissakes?"

"A book," I said, and then I remembered. Sheepishly. "From the father. Dr. Glass. *Ben*."

"That book you're carrying around wherever you go?"

"It's *helping* me," I said. "I'm trying to—I'm in *recovery* from all these things that happened." I looked down at the Statement again; it was blurrier, but not, I realized, from sweat at all. I was crying all over it. "I consider myself sick. It's difficult for me to—"

"What do you mean, everybody was sleeping together? They were all having affairs?"

I took a breath and remembered the second step: I had to believe that a power greater than me could restore me to sanity. If I wanted a Styrofoam cup of coffee, I had to throw my change in the coffee can decorated with Bindings giftwrap stickers, contributing to the Employee Coffee Fund. But the government was paying for Good Cop's coffee. That was *power*. *Faith*. The second step. "With each *other*," I said. My reflection wiped its nose. "With each *other*."

I caught Good Cop mid-sip and he grimaced and swallowed, reluctantly. Mimi had done that when she stood up, retying her nightgown. "You mean—? You can't be—?" His reflection wiped its eyes. "No."

"It's *true*."

"*All of*—I can't believe you."

"*Yes*," I said, "*yes*. And then Mimi—that's the mom—was so upset about it that I think she, I don't know, dabbled in voodoo or something. Jewish voodoo—she built a—you're not going to believe this part, but she would sneak down to the basement and perform, I don't really—some kind of experiment, no, some kind of *ritual* I guess. I know it's hard to believe, but she was sneaking downstairs and—"

"She *couldn't,*" Good Cop said darkly, "even *bend her knees.* Listen to you. The rabbi *told* me, O.K.? She was *very sick.* She wasn't sneaking around doing whatever you think she was sneaking around doing."

"I *saw* her," I said. "I *saw* her bending her knees. I don't think—look, I *know* how it sounds—"

Good Cop glared at me, his reflection, I could see, shimmering in the one-way glass. "You're not making any sense."

"I'm not sure she's dead."

Not shimmering. He was trembling.

"They *all,*" I said, "slept together. I *know* this. And she made a monster and now it's killed Stephen. Probably me next, or maybe Ben."

"You *are* sick," he said. "Talking about a family that way. A family with so much—the rabbi told me *all* about it, all this tragedy—and then at the *funeral,* the daughter being—and now *look at you,* telling these sick stories. Who are you? What the hell are you doing?"

"I'm *trying,*" I said, but when I looked at my reflection I saw it was useless. I heard, suddenly, what it all sounded like, all this ranting and opera and voodoo. *Nothing.* All these half-remembered details forced into a myth, like a foot in a glass slipper—these were just nothing *and* semantics. My faith was crumbling like the rim of a cheap cup and I couldn't think of anything, anything to say. "What are you going to do with me?"

"*Nothing,*" Good Cop barked. "We *can't* do anything. Any lawyer could get you out of here in five minutes anyway, we don't have anything against you except you seem like you've lost your fucking mind." He stood up and put his hand *firmly* on the back of my neck, the way a lover might in order to kiss you harder or to keep your tongue in *that very spot,* because you were *so close.* A fucking mind indeed. But he was just escorting me out.

Bad Cop was sitting behind grimy glass in the lobby, giving me a manila envelope with my keys, my wallet and *Breaking the SPELL,* and a dirty look. To have been behind the mirror he would've had to sprint, unless there was a network of hallways I couldn't see, a whole way of getting around that was denied me. I'd believe that, too. Anything.

"We'll be keeping an eye on you," Good Cop said.

"Thank you," I said.

"Don't leave town," Bad Cop said, a stock exit line if there ever was one.

Out in the parking lot I realized blankly that the Cops had driven me there, leaving my car outside my apartment. I was only a few squares away but I didn't know how I'd get there. I believed that a power greater than me could restore me to sanity, still, but I wasn't sure it would get me a ride. Until I saw Lauren in the parking lot. Leaning against her car, shielding her eyes with those angular sunglasses only Gentiles can pull off. Without a word, her face unreadable behind the UV protection, she opened the passenger door and left it gaping as she strolled around to drive me home. We hadn't been going out very long, hadn't met her family yet even though they were just a couple of towns over. Lauren was Assistant Manager, which meant she didn't have to sign in and out when she took breaks. Her change stayed in the tidy pocket of her wallet because she was welcome to have a cup from the Manager's espresso machine in his office. She was, it occurred to me as I buckled up, a power greater than me. I let her drive me home any route she wanted, having reached the third step: *I made a decision to turn my will and life over to a higher power.*

"I don't," she said, breaking the silence, "like lying to the police," and I knew I had to answer her.

Step 4

My bed wasn't made and I was pretty sure that wouldn't turn out to be an opportunity to lie in it. Lauren put down her purse on the same little prefab table where she always put her purse down; behind it a subscription card from some magazine I'd swiped from Bindings leaned up against the wall like a white picket fence.

"Everyone at work is talking about it," she said, sitting down in one of the chairs still in tableau from Step 1.

"Am I going to get fired?" I asked.

"I don't know. I don't think so. I covered for you, but everybody knows about"—she gestured at the unmade bed—"us. Even the cops know."

"I'm sorry I couldn't be there today," I said.

"It's O.K. Slow day. Those new *Charlotte's Web Syndrome*s came in, but the world can wait until tomorrow for that."

"Right," I said. I sat down on the bed but it sagged beneath me, untrustworthy and loose, and I moved to the floor, dropping the manila envelope beside me. Lauren's eyes followed me like I was curtsying to her.

"What is going on?" she said, finally.

"I don't know," I said. "Well, I—I guess I *do* know. Sort of, anyway."

"The police asked where you were last night," she said. "I told them you were doing inventory at the store, because that's where you were *supposed* to be. I *wish* you would stop doing that, by the way. George—well, *everybody* thinks I let you get away with it because you're my—whatever-you-are."

"*Boyfriend.* What?"

"A *boyfriend,*" she said carefully, as if learning a new word, "wouldn't keep blowing off work when he knows that his *girlfriend* won't fire him. What do you *do,* when you disappear like that? Where do you go?"

"I don't know."

"Well, wherever you go, now you're in trouble with the police. And *I* am, because I lied. *Shit!* How'd you even—what in the world—some *murder,* is that right? At the Morrison Lab?"

"My"—can't say *girlfriend*—"brother."

She blinked, softened like a crumbling cake. "Your brother? Your brother has been killed? *Jesus,* Joseph!" She said it again. "*Jesus,* Joseph." All that was missing was Mary. "I didn't even know you *had* a brother."

I sighed. "He's not *my* brother," I said. "He's someone else's. He's the brother of—"

The cake reiced. "Joseph," she said, "what are you talking about?"

I felt myself sink in, drawing weight. "You matter," *Breaking the SPELL* said in what I now would hear as Ben's voice. I *was* matter. I felt my whole weight and volume sink into the rug, all angst and Archimedes's Principle. "It's a long story," I said.

"I took the day off." Behind her, the pale sun filtered through the screen and Santa's head, bending the light all wrong and mangled, the wrong way. The day was off, all right.

"I met Cyn Glass," I said, "in the fall of several years ago."

I met Lauren the day I got my job, and she was the one who recommended the converted motel to me when I mentioned I needed a place to live. She tried to draw a map on the back of a promotional flyer for a lowfat cookbook with recipes in it she actually cooked for me later, in her identical apartment eight doors down. The map came out all wrong and she decided to show me instead, giving me the job and letting me follow her down the highway past the cheap restaurants we'd later treat each other to. She parked gently and accurately, shrugging her car neatly between the lines so I could glide right in next to her, and I knew then, like the other girls in the other towns in the part I skipped over, that she'd let me into her body with the same tidy consideration. After two of the restaurants and three of the twelve screens at the multiplex down the way it was true. She had golden hair, long and dry like the hills of the drought, eyes so simple and clear they might have been biological models and breasts I would caress underneath her nametag when we'd take a break together. It shocked her. She was so noncommittal I couldn't tell if she was struck dumb by my voraciousness or if there was just nothing else to do in the suburbs. She said she loved me and bought me a sweater which I removed, telling her I loved her, in order to bring her to quiet orgasm with my tongue while the stir-fry overcooked. She placed her hand on the back of my neck, like a police escort, to keep me in the right place. I hoped she always would. She was a healthy choice, like the reduced-fat yogurt instead of the full creamy richness at Get

171

Your Licks. Lauren was promoted to assistant manager when I was promoted to the floor. Aside from the store we rarely saw each other more than twice a week, maintaining an equal fiction of busy lives even though I just moped at home with *Breaking the SPELL* and my own dirty mind, and she just printed mass mailings from her computer with all her high-school essays still saved on it. She was hoping to become a professional organizer. I was hoping to be professionally organized.

"That's," she said, "crazy. That's *crazy.*" If she smoked there would have been a pile of butts in something she'd use as an ashtray. "That's a crazy story."

"I know."

"*Crazy.*"

"I *kno*—"

"*No,*" she said, standing up, sitting down. "You *don't* know, Joseph. If you knew how crazy it was you wouldn't be here. If you knew how crazy it was you wouldn't have followed what's-his-name, Simon—"

"Stephen. I didn't follow him."

"—here. If you knew how crazy it was you wouldn't even be *telling*—I can't believe I told—I *lied* to the police, and you're—it's *crazy,* Joseph. *Crazy.*"

"I know."

"You *can't possibly*—"

I broke the seal on the manilla envelope and held up Ben's book. "Look, I *do* know, O.K.? I *know* it's crazy. I'm trying to get myself out of this. There aren't organized twelve-step programs for absolutely everything, but the twelve steps are blueprints—"

"You've *lost the blueprint,* Joseph. You—you need *help.*"

"I'm learning to help myself."

"You don't need help from a *book* by the *father* of the *girl-friend* you—*Jesus*, Joseph, *listen* to yourself. What is going through your head?"

"*Everything,*" I said tiredly, "is going through my head. I'm trying to do some rerouting."

Outside on the highway somebody honked their horn. I smiled; I couldn't help it. Lauren looked at me sternly for a second, and then joined me, in the smile and on the floor. It was the horn that did it, the perfect sound effect here in the suburbs: *As you can see, the universe is perfect. Don't lie about it.*

"I can't lie to you," I said, probably lying. "I just don't know what's going on. I'm scared, Lauren. I'm—"

She put a palm on my forehead, some gesture of benediction. My tears came like she flicked a switch. I tried to finish my sentence, a good little prisoner, but the walls came down and I sobbed in her arms. It was a good thing, to live out here in a land perfectly devised with a girl who'd take the day off to lie for you. But I couldn't do it. Something was tearing this life apart, bending it the wrong way, something made of clay which rose from the rivers of my mind only to sink back into them when I tried to catch up. I had to look for something submerged, like Archimedes, sitting in his bath and figuring out how everything worked. Lauren, however, didn't need help; she'd found something submerged as she held me, my groin firing up. Her other hand cupped me between my legs, peaking the khakis as my crying subsided.

"Ssh," she said, rubbing. "*Ssh.*" We fell together. I undressed her, the snaps and buckles and elastic all biting my hands which were shaking with the impatience of waiting in line for something. Her skin was sweaty and I could see, kissing her neck, where her makeup left off and the real thing began. Her sex rubbed up against my lips like a raccoon, like I was the trash she wanted to get into, but I didn't scare it away. Her mouth skipped that part, no matter how brazenly I hinted: brushing my erection against her chin, her cheek, holding her head in my hands like a globe and moving it toward my country of choice. But Lauren's mouth would not go south. In the prickle of the rug, with her hands moving like she was shaking a bottle of salad dressing, my tongue dreamt of another place.

We settled down. I felt Archimedes hover over me again as the undressed dread (T.U.D) rolled over me like bathwater. With Archimedes it worked wonders: he watched the water displaced by his own nakedness and the way of the world hit him: *Eureka!* I waited for something like that to come to me, and it did: *Eureka*. Like a *noir* voiceover it came: ". . . and her father, who's holed up in the Eureka woods somewhere . . ."

"Where's Eureka?" I asked Lauren.

"What?"

"Eureka. The town. I need to go there."

"Way up north," she said, and then, looking at me: "*Way, way* up north. Don't bother."

"I *have* to bother," I said, trying to keep it light.

She tried, too. "Just because it's the state motto doesn't mean—"

"I'm not going," I said, "for the state motto. I'm going for my own."

She sighed, would have lit a cigarette if she smoked. "I guess

I can let you have a few days. Everybody's already—forget about it. O.K., go. But let me help you plan what to pack." She smiled. This was what she wanted: to be a professional organizer, someone who comes in and makes lists for you. "How long do you want to go? The weekend? It's *cold* up there, you know."

"I'm leaving," I said, "entirely."

She blinked. "What?"

"It'll really be an organizing thing for you. A garage sale if you think anybody will buy anything. Otherwise I'll drop it off at—"

"*What?*"

"I can't stay here," I said. "I have to go to Eureka, and find—"

"Mr. *CRISIS*," she said. "You can't—don't be—*please,* Joseph. Don't *do* this thing."

"I can't stay here," I said.

"The police said you can't *leave.*"

"I—I *can't stay here!*"

"Because what?"

"Because—because—"

"Because of a *monster*? Is that what? *Listen* to yourself, Joseph. *Listen.* A *monster. Listen* to that. *Please, please* don't go get lost in the woods with some crank. Some father who did whoknows-what. Stay *here,* Joseph. I'll make sure you get help."

"I can't stay."

"Running away won't solve anything, Joseph. It never does."

"What if something's chasing you? *Then* it solves something, doesn't it?"

"Listen to yourself."

"I'm trying to, Lauren. I have to do this thing."

175

"You don't have to—you don't *have* to do anything, Joseph. Say *no* to this. Haven't you learned how to—don't you know that? You have to say *no* to this. Can't you say—"

"*No,*" I said. I felt a smile marionette itself on me. She smiled, too, but it didn't work; her face crumbled and cried. Her naked shoulders shook. I tried to hug her but she pulled away, covering her face, her breasts.

"Don't *do* this," she said beneath her hands. "Don't *do* this."

"Maybe if I do this—"

"*Don't.*"

"—I can come back." Even she knew this was a lie, even though, as she dressed and said she'd call me later, maybe she didn't think so yet. Ben Glass says it best: "We think much less than what we know. We know much less than what we love. We love much less than what there is. And to this precise extent, we are much less than what we are." Actually I have no idea what this means but I'm convinced he said it best, better than anything I said as Lauren picked up her purse from the table and opened the screen door. I saw her out, draped in a sheet from the unmade bed like a toga. Caesar thanking the Soothsayer for his time.

"I hope you *do* come back," she said, "when you've—when you've caught whatever you're chasing, Joseph."

"It's a golem," I said, "and it's chasing *me.*"

She blinked and the sunglasses went on. The car door slammed and I saw her pause before she started the engine. Was she going to come back and convince me? Outside the Morrison Lab caught the first few rays of the sunset in specific points Stephen probably could have mapped out on graph paper, three dots connected in some scientist way, like family secrets, or bodies in a crime spree. Lauren's hand was cupped to her mouth, crying maybe? Rehearsing one last word? But then she uncovered her face and I saw, even with the sun's reflection in my eyes, what she was doing. Lighting a cigarette.

All night long I debated whether or not to go, and all night long I packed. The packing was easy—thanks to Lauren and Bindings, I knew how to make lists and check them. What To Bring: not much, clothes, *Breaking the SPELL,* paper and pens, a Jewish prayer book if I had one, which I didn't. All my books were still in a box somewhere, being shipped, going off somewhere where they probably weren't wanted. What To Leave: my shabby furniture, the job, Santa and Lauren. The threats of stock-character policemen. These were easy inventories. But getting in the car and leaving was harder. In the morning the smog made everything look golemized, this perfect square universe, and it seemed Hansel-and-Gretel foolhardy to leave for the forest. *Breaking the SPELL* says the two basic questions are "Who am I?" and "How do I do it?" but in the grime of departure I had two other ones: "Would I be leading the monster?" and "Was I the monster?" Like everyone in recovery I didn't know if I was the victor or the victim. Only when I threw away the last sack of trash did I know I was doing the right thing: amongst the condoms I wouldn't need any more, the food I didn't cook and couldn't eat on the road, the J-O-S-E-P-space-H on the nametag, were my own lists, checked off each one: What To Leave, What To Bring. It was the fourth step, sneaking up on me like something in a dark alley: *I had made a searching and fearless inventory of myself.* I gassed up the car and headed north like it was just one more step away.

Step 5

Rather than following the highway through the sawdusty bulk of California's desert I skipped over to Route 1, driving along the coast with pop songs fading in and out of radio range. The road was excrutiatingly Californian: homemade salsa at the diners, espresso machines even at the grungiest gas stations and a quarterly catalog of meditation workshops stacked in thoughtful piles near the recycling bins. Amethyst Therapy, How to Communicate with the Other Side, Self-Actualization, the Gospel of Relaxation, the Gospel of Fun, the Gospel of Power, of Enjoyment; Bi-Gospel, Tri-Gospel, Pan-Gospel, closer and closer to Eureka while the Pacific stayed to my immediate left, blue and wrinkled just beyond my side-view mirror. Sometimes I'd stop and stretch my legs, taking deep salty breaths and looking at the couples walking hand-in-hand on the shore like the figures on condom boxes. But all the wet sand made me nervous and I never stopped for long. *Breaking the SPELL* calls it "E-motion: energy in motion" and I kept the e-motor running with espresso and snacks, passing up on the salsa and throwing the catalogs in the back with the napkins, unused and unread until I pulled into town.

People call Eureka "good-sized," but there's so much defensiveness in their voices you know before you take the exit that it's not true. There's nothing good about Eureka's size: too small to hide in and too big to be found. At the motel, I asked the desk clerk how many woods there were around. He blinked, took out a small map and pointed to all the tiny green trees somebody had inked in all over the place. I blinked, took the key and went to throw my bag down on the bed where I knew I wouldn't sleep a wink. I had dinner somewhere. I drove around town looking at the limp glitter of Christmas decorations grapevined around traffic lights which just blinked after a certain hour, even on a Friday night. Back in the room the TV had the Static Network on every channel, the fault of some satellite up in the chilly, busy sky. I lay on the bed and dreamt about mud.

In the morning I took off my shoes and my clothes, showered and went back to bed, waking up when the housekeeper knocked. I showered again, rubbed myself dry and then to orgasm with the skimpy towels. I sipped coffee and looked up "Glass, Ben" in a phone book caught in one of those beartraps, chained to a phone booth; there was one, but it was disconnected. No other information was available. I drove down a random road and stopped when I saw trees by the side of the road, wandered in about ten feet and wondered, *What am I doing?*

I pulled the car into a familiar-looking lot for a late lunch, realizing I'd left *SPELL* in the room so I'd have to read that catalog after all. I opened the menu and realized I was in the same place I'd been for dinner. I opened the catalog and saw that Ben Glass was leading a Creating a New Man Weekend Workshop at Campground 72, two exits up, take a left at the ramp, a right at the chain-link fence and look for the banner with the New Man logo, a fist rising out of starkly stencilled water, eighty dollars, space is limited.

I signalled for the check and then for the left-hand turn at the end of the ramp. The sunset was right in my eyes, making me miss the chain-link fence at first but even in the half-light there was no missing the banner: BEN GLASS: CREATING A NEW MAN WEEKEND WORKSHOP, strung up between two

179

trees like discarded clothing. I parked in a lot crammed with mid-life crisis cars, red and shiny and probably divorced. I'd thought I'd be nervous to walk underneath the banner but when I saw the enormous blue tent in the field, geometrically radiant and buzzing with loudspeaker talk, I strode between the trees like an admiral, like the battle was about to be wrapped up. I was energy in motion.

A flap opened like a fly and I walked into a tent which looked even bigger on the inside. A row of rented tables, stacked with paper plates and the tinny gurgle of brewing coffee, was along one of the walls, and inside everyone was dead: rows of bodies, bunched in twos and threes, covered the bulk of the floor. I made myself look again: they were sleeping bags, emptied of the participants who were gathered together at the far end, about thirty men sitting on the floor around a podium and a primitive sound system. The New Man was holding court.

"I'm talking," he boomed, "about Man-Making." As everyone nodded I tiptoed around the body bags. "Now, a lot of people say, 'Man-Making? I thought men already *had* it made.' " Nods and murmurs. You could feel earnestness billowing the tent like a powerful gas. "Most people in the world think that men are always perpetrators and never victims. A lot of experts say this. But it's my belief that *everyone's* an expert, so let me ask you— are you all perpetrators, or are you all victims?"

"*Victims!*" Some of them clapped.

"That's right, my brothers. My brothers in suffering and courage, you are *right. Victims.* And why? I'll tell you why. On the surface it might appear that we live in a system where men benefit and women are oppressed. But the reality is that nobody benefits from a sexist structure. When the world puts limits on individual diversity, everyone loses. Setting arbitrary distinctions—whether it's between the sexes, between the races, between the professions—inhibits the development of expression of individual talents. Then everyone loses. It's true for both sexes, men as well as women. Everyone falls victim to the arbitrary rigidities—could you sit down, please? Could everyone please remain in their seats? I need everybody sitting down, thank you." I squatted between two beards. One glared at me; the other did a "thumbs-up" sign. "Everyone, to continue, falls victim to the arbitrary rigidities which we have set up. But did you hear what I said? Which *we* have set up. *We* set them up, and we can bring them back down. We can change the stereotypes of the tough guy and the wimp. We can create instead a new man. I think we've done some remarkable work towards that goal today, and we'll continue to do that kind of work tomorrow. So let's eat, and talk, and share and we'll start up again in the morning." Some scattered applause dribbled into chatting. Ben smiled, and then clapped his hands into the microphone. It sounded like he was hitting somebody.

"Folks? Could we sit down again? There's one more thing I wanted to say. I vowed that I'd close tonight's lecture with this, and one of the traits of a New Man, I think, is that he should keep his word." Some clapping again. "I vowed that this would be the last sentence in my speech tonight: 'And this goes for all the women, too.' "

It was difficult to tell whether he got a standing ovation or if the men just stood up. Ben waved like it was an ovation anyway, and led the way out of the tent. He didn't meet my eyes when he passed me. Outside some invisible staff people had set up large grills and were throwing on big slabs of salmon. Two meek-looking men in glasses were removing plastic wrap from mixing bowls full of salad. The air filled with the sounds of crickets and pull-tabs. Ben graciously accepted the first salmon steak and sat down on a big log where a handful of the most beholden were waiting. I took a bottle of what I assumed was beer and turned out to be cider, and joined them.

"I don't remember this," a grey-haired man was saying as he tucked a napkin into his camouflage gear, "but I have been told that when I was four years old I drank detergent. Now I'm realizing that it was a suicide attempt."

Ben nodded gravely. "From early on, men don't get the care and the love they need. And what does that say about our world? From where I look, it's all the same thing. Either we care about things or we don't. This salmon is delicious, by the way. Who did the marinade?"

"I did," said the detergent-drinker, blushing.

"Great job," Ben said, clapping him on the shoulder and looking him in the eye. "You matter, Hal. You *matter.*"

"Al."

"*Al. All. All* of you matter. You know, I'm glad we're holding this workshop in a field, because we're standing at the edge of a whole new field, understand? A whole new field. A whole new *horizon.* Perfect for creating a New Man."

"A New Man," I said, "has already been created, Ben."

Everyone looked up, Ben last. He scanned my face like he couldn't place me. Then he could. His face fell. Then he blinked and composed himself for the others.

"Joseph."

"And it's coming this way," I said. I wasn't saying what I'd planned at all, the words coming out all wrong and raw.

"Joseph," he said again, with a wide smile. Then, to the faithful: "Will you all excuse us, please? This young man—this man, he's—he needs my help. *Alone.* Will you please excuse us?"

"I thought problems were solved quicker," Al said, "more quickly, when we all worked together."

"Not this time," Ben said. The others were already leaving.

"Like the Amish. Building together. Barn-building."

Ben widened his smile from maître d' to bouncer: *Get the hell out of here.* "Please, Hal."

"*Al*," he said, but scurried. We were alone. I thought with the disciples gone he'd drop the patriarch bit but when he turned to me I saw it still clinging to him. "Joseph."

"Ben," I said.

"It's been a long time."

"Yes," I said.

"How have you been?"

"*Fine*," I said. "I mean—look, Ben, I came here to tell you— you probably don't know—I'm sorry. I can't imagine what you must think—"

"What I think?" Ben said. "You should read my book, Joseph."

"I've been reading little else."

"Then you know," he said, "that we think much less than what we know. We know much less than what we—"

"Ben, somebody's after us."

"—love. What?"

"And I'm afraid it might be me."

"What?"

"What happened, Ben? What happened that summer?"

Ben nodded sagely and outstretched a hand until I had to sit next to him on the log. "I *knew* that's what was worrying you, Joseph. I *knew* you would come and find me." I had forgotten all this, his surefooted serenity, all wise and wrong. All those dinner-table speeches where he'd take a position and just *stay* there, like ugly condos. "As soon as I started lecturing all over the country, I *knew* that you and people like you would come to me for help. I'm honored to be able to give it."

"Ben—"

"Look at me. *Look. At. Me.* Do you need help or do you not?"

"Something happened that summer that I—"

"Why did you come here? You came here for help, am I right?"

Behind him the fist flapped in the evening breeze. "Yes," I said. "Yes."

Ben sighed expansively and put his plate down on the ground. "Have you ever looked through a thesaurus?"

Over by the grills a group of men laughed. Dirty jokes, maybe, or perhaps they'd worked through that. "What?"

"A thesaurus. One of those books with words that mean the same thing, have you looked through them?"

"*No.* Yes. I *guess* so, you know, at Mather."

"Do you remember what's under the word *manly?*"

"Ben," I said, "We can't—we don't have much time, and—"

He held a hand up, definite but calm. *"Do you remember what's under the word—"*

"*No,*" I said. "I *don't* remember what's under the word *manly.*"

"*Two-fisted,*" he said. "*He-mannish. Hairy-chested. Mighty. Red-blooded. Ready for anything.* What do you think of that?" What I thought was that *ready for anything* wasn't in any thesaurus, anywhere. "And where do you think you find words like *honorable,* or *decent*? *Delicate*? *Womanly,* that's where. Is that fair?" The last light was fading, the paper plate a grey glow on the ground, the coals of the grill making silhouettes of the men cleaning up. "I asked you a question."

"What?"

"Is that fair?"

"No," I said.

"*No,*" he said. "*Exactly* right, Joseph." I was embarrassed at my little surge of pride. "It's *not* fair. But that's the unfair *system* on which so many other things are built. Gender. Families. Professions. Religion—is that why you're here, because of the rabbi?"

"What?"

"I'm sorry. I thought you would have known. Rabbi Tsouris is dead."

"What?"

"Excuse me, Dr. Glass. We're done cleaning up here and we're going to go inside now." One of the men was holding a salad bowl like it was something sacramental.

"O.K., Bruce. Joseph and I need a few more minutes. I'll be in shortly."

"Will you make sure the coals are out?"

"*Yes,* Bruce. Thank you."

Bruce pattered off into the dark, closing the flap behind him. Now we were really alone, all the men chattering inside the tent, silhouetted against flashlights. I took a breath. "He died mysteriously, right, Ben? Something with mud, or drowning, and nobody knows what, right? *Right?*"

Ben blinked. "No. He—he shot himself, Joseph. He—"

"*What?*"

"It's true. He, well, obviously he was very unhappy, and I guess he thought it was time. They called me all the way out here. I was flattered that in Pittsburgh they've heard of my work. *God is now here,* his note said. Not that I approve of suicide, of course, but if he really thought that—"

"*What?*"

"He's *dead,* Joseph." His shadow shrugged: *Get used to it.* "I'm sorry to tell you like this. I thought you'd heard."

"When did it—"

"Just a few days ago."

I tried to count backwards to Good and Bad Cops, but it made my head ache, too much time lost in a driving blur. I couldn't remember when things had happened. "He *shot* himself?"

"Yes. What did you say—*mud?*"

"Yes, *mud.* Like Cyn. Like—"

"What?"

"Like your son."

"Stephen? I haven't talked to him in years. I never talk to him. Is he alive?" He smiled mildly, *Is he alive* some sort of joke, or some reference that wasn't reaching me.

"Um,"

"I never talk to him. We're taking some time away from one another, to better *focus.* At least, *I* am."

"He's dead."

Ben blinked. In the tent somebody was playing an acoustic guitar. "My son—"

"I'm sorry. I thought you would have—they said they were trying to reach you—"

"Stephen is—" Ben stood up, his face disappearing above me

in the dark. From nowhere he kept talking. "Are you—? Stephen?"

"I'm sorry," I said again. The men started a song as I heard Ben vomit onto the grass of the new field they were singing about. The stench flowed over to me in the pitch black, a dark and deep smell like he'd eaten not only the salmon but the salmon's whole life. It was a smell of dark water, of river and mud. It made me gag but I didn't move. Ben threw up again but I didn't budge from where I was. I felt something *shift* in me, like finding solid ground, like walking, at night, around someone else's house. Where is it, in the dark? Where am I? *There* it is. The steps. The fifth step: *Admit to yourself, to another human being and to a Higher Power the exact nature of your wrongs.*

"I'm sorry," I said again, into the black where another human being, and maybe even a Higher Power, waited for me. "I think it's—no, I won't lie. I *know* it's my fault." I heard Ben gasp, his feet lurching back and forth unsteadily. Though I couldn't see a thing I felt the solid presence of his body over me, anchoring me. "I don't know what happened, I can't exactly remember, but I know that it *did* happen. And I'm trying to seek help. Something about that summer changed me. I don't know what it was." I took a deep breath, and the dark smell filled my lungs. But I wouldn't stop. "Maybe it was the sort of love Cyn and I had. Or maybe the sort of family you all were, you know, so close. All that quality time. Maybe I was jealous or something. But I began to—I began to think that you were doing terrible things. I mean not *you*. *All* of you. It'll sound crazy to say this, but I really thought you were all sleeping together. I thought I could hear you all, late at night. I thought I *saw* something. But

I'm realizing now it must have been my imagination. Just my dirty mind, my horrible fantasies. I don't know how I ever believed you were all—*incestuous*." Ben gasped again, and then I heard a raw exhale, like he'd been hit in the chest. Like him I wanted to get it all out until there was nothing. "I'm sorry, because out of my guilt and shame over this I began to imagine something else. I began to imagine that your wife—that Mimi was going to get—that she was going to *avenge* what was going on—and that she was going to do it with—well, with something I clearly picked up from the operas she was doing. You remember the golem one, you know, the big clay figure? I heard Mimi talking that over with the rabbi and it got into my head that she was making one. I mean a *real* one, an actual monster to get revenge on her family."

From his gurgling I heard Ben laugh, a sound ripped from his throat, a sound more of pain than humor with a coppery, bodily scent to match. "I know it sounds absurd, but that's really what I thought." Everything was making sense to me now, like a series of steps: my fantasies of Cyn's family and Mimi's revenge, all cooked up in the grime of my mind, like the stench in front of me. "I can't remember what happened at the funeral, Ben, but I know it was *my* fault. For years I thought it was a golem—which is *crazy,* I know, but—that's what I thought. And now I know." Ben was crying now, the sounds strangling out of him in little gasps like a dying fish. I could hear his shoulders shaking, his brittle bones creaking over the sound of the men in the tent. "I don't know what happened—I guess maybe I cracked, with all the stress of Mimi—it's no excuse. But I think I attacked Cyn. And I think I attacked *Stephen.* I think you and the rabbi and who knows who else covered it up.

Maybe you didn't want me to go to jail. Maybe you didn't know what happened yourself. And I'm grateful. But it made *me* forget, too. Soon I didn't know what was going on, what was real and what wasn't. I'm *so* sorry—I can't *begin* to tell you how sorry I am, Ben. And I'll do whatever you say. Turn myself in, or, I don't know—I *don't know* what I can do. But it has to end here. It's *my* fault. It's the exact nature of my wrongs, Ben. And I hope you'll find it in you to forgive me."

It was quiet, except for the ruptured sound of the doctor's breath. For some reason even the crickets had stopped, and the men weren't singing. I don't know how long I'd been out there. I waited in the midst of that earthy scent for Ben to speak. And he tried to, I think. I hope. There was one more sound from Ben, a sort of low growl, and then a wet collapse, a damp ripping. Something splattered on my lap. For a few seconds I couldn't take it in, my fingers sliding through the mess of liquid, and a soft wet texture like fruit. An earthy putty, and then shards of something which felt like pottery. Like broken pottery, something which had cracked and then shattered, and I knew. The smell of clay. The raw gurgles. The dark shadow, the solid presence of a body, still over me. These were pieces of Ben's head in my lap, and we weren't alone. *I had admitted my wrongs to myself, to another human being* and to the Higher Power that was *now here.*

Step 6

It's amazing how quickly you can reach the next step, when your heart's really in it. I heard myself try to say something to the golem, a guttural syllable. I steadied myself on the log and felt a piece of Ben's hair beneath my palms. I rolled off, onto the wet ground, and tried to stand up. Inside the tent I could hear men whispering. Some of the lights were going off. In the morning they wouldn't need them, the sun rising up over another death of clay and violence, linked to his son, his daughter, by mystery and blood. Something which had happened when I was alone. Something without witnesses.

"*My* fault," I heard myself say to the golem. "*Me!*" I tried to stand up but something wet struck my knee and I fell back down. I felt it step towards me with sure, slow purpose, invisible in the night but unstoppable, like a dream you have and can't get out of your head. "*Me!*" I stretched out one hand and pulled at the grass, then the other, trying to drag myself away from this mess by my own volition, my own skill, if I could. I felt the air swish by me in an arc, arms swinging where they thought they could find me. It was best not to stand. I pulled myself along the earth, kicking my legs free of something which felt like a hand. I thought if I couldn't walk I could crawl, but that was no good either: something turned me over, logrolling my body like it had known how to do it since birth. "*Me!*" I was on my back now, with the Eureka skyline blocked by a dark form as familiar as my own shadow. My chest heaved with breath, slower and slower, steady now. The next step already, bing bing bing: *I was entirely ready to have the Higher Power remove all my defects of character.* Two hands, wet with clay and my victim's blood, closed in on my neck. I was ready for it to be over. I couldn't believe there could be any more.

Step 7

It was all a dream. I told myself I had dozed off, studying for my Kafka final at Mather: *As Joseph awoke one morning from*

190

uneasy dreams he found himself asleep in his car by the side of the
road, dazed and encrusted with mud like a gigantic squashed insect.

No. I washed up in a gas station bathroom and, looking in the stainless-steel plate serving as a mirror, threw up into the sink, rinsed my mouth from the faucet. The police—what time was it?—the police had undoubtedly been called by now and were finished interviewing all the liberated males. I could see them in my motel room, Eurekan variations on Good and Bad Cop, poking through my duffel with one of those metal sticks they use to pick up a gun, collecting hairs from the drain and putting *Breaking the SPELL* in a sealed plastic bag to keep the fingerprints on it. I'd pay for my next room with cash so I wouldn't blink on some computer screen. I could stay far away, cross the state line, drive through the wilderness, hole up somewhere until this whole thing blew over. It was my fault, I figured, ignoring Ben's exhortation to "escape self-judgment." If there were really a monster somebody would have seen it. If there were really a monster it would have killed me. At breakfast in a diner I squeezed my cantaloupe half until the rind broke and the meat of the fruit slopped into the bowl. I could do it. A skull was tougher, sure, but hadn't Bad Cop said you were supposed to have superhuman strength under duress? And if moving to a town to stalk my girlfriend's brother, fleeing the police and killing his father wasn't duress, what was? The waitress gave me a look when she took away the bowl and I vowed to wear sunglasses next time. I merged into whatever highway seemed most convenient, let the reflector-glows of exit arrows guide me wherever they wanted. In hotel rooms I propped myself up on the courtesy pillows and flicked through the TV, while I bent and straightened my knees. So maybe she *could* bend her knees, no matter how sick she was. It meant nothing. I was the wrongest person who had ever been: colossally wrong, my enormous misdeed finally freed from the basement of my mind to lumber across the countryside in plain view. By day I ate little, and froze with paranoia whenever a patrolman drove by, his face inscrutable as clay. By night I'd pull the cheap blankets over my body and try to think of what to do next, now that I'd already asked the Higher Power to remove all defects of character but it had just walked away. I wasn't dead. It wasn't a dream. I dragged the armchair over to the door, slipping it underneath the doorknob like in a TV show, and whether it was to keep something out or to keep me in was anybody's guess.

And then it came. Sometime during some night, some limb of mine had flicked the car radio to maximum volume, so the next bleary morning when I put the key in the ignition the voice spoke to me like God: "Lost?" the radio boomed, over a wind-and-sea sound effect. "Confused and adrift? Today's young people can find the job market a hard place to navigate. Higher Power Employment Agency can be your lighthouse." Now a fog-horn, a tugboat. Some sound-effects technician loved the metaphor. "Come in for a free evaluation and information session about our counselling and placement services. Let Higher Power"—here the seagulls, the creaking of ropes—"guide you safely to your future career." I pulled over to much impatient honking, riffling through the ashtray for pay phone money. I needed counselling and placement, and free was what I could afford. An English major for three years at a prestigious university and I'd been felled by a spelling mistake. It was H-I-R-E. Hire Power Employment Agency.

"A lot of people make that mistake," Marc said cheerfully,

showing me into a tiny office dominated by a photograph of the open sea. *Expect the Unexpected,* the caption said, inexplicably; was there a giant squid lying in wait under the surface? "These people tell me, 'It took me forever to find you in the phone book.' " His voice rose unpleasantly as he imitated *these people.* He was in his mid-forties with a terrifyingly fit body and wire-frame glasses. Marc was calling me Joe. I wasn't calling him anything. I took a seat with quiet and simple faith and a Styrofoam cup of warm and weak coffee. I was comfortable.

"Comfortable?" he asked.

"Yes," I said. I'd sworn to myself to tell the truth.

"Soooo," he said, heartily and at length. He opened up a file which contained a form I had filled out in a waiting room full of photographs and captions. "Mather College," he said, approvingly.

"Yes."

"But you didn't graduate."

"No. Or, not yet."

He smiled in a way I could see he imagined as winning. I tried my hardest to be won. "That's my boy. So why'd you leave?"

"Incest."

"Just weren't interested, huh? Well, it's good you figured that out. You don't want to be in college if you aren't focused on it. Interest is important, Joe. Interest is important. So what have you been doing since then?"

"I worked at a summer camp in Pittsburgh," I said. "A day camp. And then—well, skipping ahead, then I worked at a bookstore in Pitts—here in California. Through New Year's. Didn't I write this down?"

"Yeah, but I like to get a feel for things in person."

"Me, too," I said, looking down at my hands. *Keep your hands where I can see them.*

"So that's where your résumé ends," Marc said. "What have you been doing since then?"

I looked at the sea, at Marc, at the sea. "Not much," I admitted. "I've been sort of—driving."

"What, pizza delivery or something? That's nothing to be ashamed of." His voice said: *Of course it is.*

"No, just driving. You know, um." I looked at the sea again and decided to go for the adventurer approach. "Just exploring. I wanted to see a little bit of this country of ours. The good old U.S. of A."

"A little bit?" His eyebrows raised. "For five months?"

"I was sort of adrift."

"And where's your family?"

"Smothered."

"I'm sorry. Where's your *mother?*"

I blinked, shifted in my chair. I started to say *elsewhere.* I looked at Marc and the sea again. I didn't say anything. This wasn't going well.

"I'm sorry," Marc said, insincerely. "You don't have to tell me if you don't want to. But I have to tell you, Joe, this five-month gap is *not* going to look good to prospective employers. If you had a diploma, *maybe,* but this Jack what's-his-face, *Kerouac* thing is *not* going to fly."

"I *know* it doesn't look good, but I was hoping," I said humbly. "I was hoping that you could help me make up for all that time." The seventh step: *I had humbly asked a Hire Power to remove my shortcomings.*

"I don't think we can help you," he said briskly. "Quite frankly, Joe, we're looking for people who are *ready* to face the challenges put in front of them. Not people who are looking for escape. You seem to me, if you don't mind me saying so, stuck in 'the past.' " He put two pairs of bunny ears around all my suffering. "We want people who are heading toward 'the future.' I don't think we can help you."

Marc stood up. His head floated in the lens-captured sea. I tried to think of something I could say that could stop him in his tracks, like a spell. "I don't *think*," he said again—

I put my faith in words I didn't understand. "We *think*," I said, "much less than what we know."

Marc blinked. "We *know*," he said carefully, "much less than what we love."

"We love much less than what there is."

I had him. "And to this precise extent," he said, pausing to sit back down. We said the rest together: "We are much less than what we are."

Marc reached over his desk with both hands, knocking over the little sign which said MARC. He took my hands in his. "No *wonder* you're at sixes and sevens," he said. "You should have *told* me you were a New Man. Don't be ashamed of that. Ben Glass's death has hit a lot of us *very hard,* Joe. No *wonder* you're lost. Well, for a brother in courage and suffering I think we can find something."

He opened a file cabinet which as far I was concerned was stuffed with faith and love, and pulled out a full-color brochure. "How would you feel about leaving the country?"

"Saved," I said.

He chuckled. "The pay's not much, and I don't think you can

call the work challenging, but for someone a little at odds it might suit you. Have you heard of The Vast Resort?"

"No."

"Terrific place," he said, opening the brochure. Inside the folds some very tiny women were swimming. "The biggest self-contained luxury resort region in the Western Hemisphere. They're looking for some temporary assistance in the service department. Folding up lounge chairs or something. Maybe a towel boy. I could make a phone call. What do you say?"

I looked at all the bright, bright blue they were selling: sky and swimming pools and beach umbrellas with the V in *Vast* scrawled across them in white. "I say *yes*. Where is this place?"

"Some island somewhere," he said, gesturing like it might be in the potted plant in the corner. "Check in with me in a couple hours and I'll give you the verdict."

"Thanks," I said.

"Thank *you*," he said. "Thanks for reminding me what I should be doing for my fellow man, especially now that Ben's gone."

"Yes," I said, uprighting the MARC sign.

"Thanks," he said, noticing. We stood up together. "Because a lot of people think that men are always perpetrators."

"And never victims," I said, nodding.

"*Right*," he said, and patted me on the shoulder. We were walking back out to the waiting room where I stopped and read the posters lining the walls: "*Speak, hands for me!*"—*William Shakespeare, Macbeth*, over a field of flowers. "*Beauty is truth, truth beauty.*"—*Robert Frost*, Ode on a Grecian Urn, as a sun set over a forest. "*There is no benefit in the gifts of a bad man.*"—*Euripides, Medea*, below a kitten napping in a basket, and this last one invigorated me most. I remembered what the rabbi, poor man, had said: "At the end, they ask her, Medea, what is left? Everything is destroyed, everything is gone. And you know what Medea says? She says, 'What is left? There is me.' *There's* a woman for you." I strode out of Hire Power knowing that I needn't be at sixes and sevens, now that I had reached and passed them and was heading toward Step 8. " 'What do you mean what's left? Everything is left. *I* am left.' " I turned left out of the parking lot and put the radio on, peering out the grimy windows hoping to spot a mall. I'd spend the last of my money on clothes for hot weather. A Vast Resort was ahead of me and I wanted to be ready.

Step 8

The morning sun was shining like the best cellophane money could buy. You could see every wrinkle in the sheets of the bed, captured like a topographical map. I looked out the shiny, shiny window and saw for the first time a sun that looked just like a child's drawing of a sun, each bright ray careening like a market-researched exclamation point in a brochure. It was *fantastic!* I *loved* it! I'd never seen sunshine like that, never been able to clean something as thoroughly as the pool's faux-marble steps. They were cleaned so often that when they were my assignment there was scarcely any dirt to be found, just a slight lace of beige I could just pluck from the stairs with a Vast Resort rag bleached to toothpaste-white. I'd never seen a pool that circulated with a carefully-constructed tide, controlled by a machine locked inside a shack hidden behind palm trees. This universe—I'm not lying here—was *perfect!*

"How does that work, anyway?" I asked Allyson. She was

curled around the mattress like a bracket, looking for something under the bed. If we were children it would have been monsters, but we were all grown up and it was a book.

"How does what work?"

"The tide machine in the pool."

She blinked at me absently for a moment, placing the tide machine, the pool, probably me. "They built a mechnical moon," she said slowly, "which they control via satellite, to orbit around The Vast Resort for the convenience of our guests. I don't *know,* Joe! Who am I, Einstein?"

Allyson wasn't Einstein, but that was her last name so it was a joke. The moon thing, too; Allyson was pretty funny. And, funny-pretty: long, long arms and fingernails! Fireworks of blond hair! Freckles! Breasts so sharp they were like pieces of paper folded in half, two of them! She was some gorgeous joke book I got to read in bed. She was very tall but when you looked at her, in the shorts and sweatshirt they made you wear, you couldn't tell *where;* I tried to find out by kissing my way down her body but she didn't like oral sex. She'd never had an orgasm, or sushi. She liked things cooked. She'd pulled my head away, and up, until I was facing her face and we'd made love with me on top, the way she preferred, taking the condom off herself when we were done, tying it into a knot and tossing it behind her, without looking, into the shiny white basket I would later empty into a shiny white dumpster.

Love, that book with the drippy soundtrack says, is never having to say you're sorry, and we never did. We never were. They kept us pretty busy at the Vast, as the staff called it in casual conversations over the absurdly colorful fruit salad they'd serve us each morning at the Breakfast Meeting. Allyson had worked there for three years, an Entertainment Coordinator, so she stood up front with sheafs of schedules bulging under the clip-grip of her clipboard. She spilled my coffee when she gave me my copy. She didn't apologize, but smiled and said something about the table being shaky. After the meeting we huddled beneath it and looked at the legs. We kissed there and elsewhere. Our lunch hours were our own. She'd make cheap Entertainment Coordinator jokes, and, when I was promoted past the faux-marble to become her assistant, cheap debriefing jokes.

"Aren't you supposed to be briefing me?" I asked.

"*De*-briefing," she said, looking up from her book to slap my thigh. "And I did already." See?

"Really," I said. "I'm supposed to know what's going on, Al. If Mike finds out that all we're doing is fucking—"

"*Joe,*" she said. Despite the jokes she hated language like that. Allyson had the cleanest mouth I'd ever encountered. No oral sex will do that, I guess. "Watch your—"

"I was going to say fucking *around.*"

"*—language! Joe!*"

"I'm—" I would have said sorry if we said such things. "I just—I just want to do a good job."

"You *are,*" she said, puzzled. "You're doing a *great* job. Why do you think you got to be my assistant after just a few weeks?"

"I thought," I said, gesturing to the bed.

"*No,*" she said. "Don't *think.* You're doing an *excellent* job, Joseph. That's why Mike and I wanted you to work with *people* more, instead of, I don't know, the garbage cans and the buffet table and everything. I think you can be a real asset at Vast."

I felt myself blush. Mike was the boss, the real boss. "Thanks."

"Don't mention it."

"Can I mention the briefing, then?"

"Let me just finish this chapter," she said, glancing at the Vast clock that perched on the wall in everyone's room like a wide, white eye. "We still have a few."

Minutes, she meant. I stared out at the tide. Allyson was reading the latest by an author she loved, a woman who had written about vampires and sold millions, written about other things and sold hundreds and then returned to vampires with a vengeance, a series about vampires, vampires everywhere, everybody sucking everybody else dry. Bindings had a cardboard figure of the author, dressed as a vampire. I wasn't reading anything. I was spending my time trying to make a list. Living on an island somewhere didn't mean I was leaving behind the twelve steps, which were now as obvious and squeaky-clean as faux-marble.

To hit Eight I had to make a list of people I believed I had harmed. The trouble was, I knew that Step Nine was making amends to them, and so far everyone on my list was dead. The faux-marble steps weren't just decorative; they *went* somewhere, leading from the pool to the bar which was decorated with palm trees, half real, half fake. All day long, I watched my guests use those steps to get what they wanted. Even now, the early risers were dangling their feet in the shallow end, sipping fresh juice poured by Marco, who tended a bar at the top of the steps like a faux-marble prize. As Allyson finished her chapter they trickled in: the couple enjoying the first honeymoon of their second marriage, the fat man with the girl everyone hoped was his daughter, the three single women who knew each other from work, the old guy who looked like my family doctor and his silent sunglassed wife propping her book against her bent knees, the mom and her three daughters spending alimony like water, the retired couple who heaped extra entrees onto plates and brought them back to their room because of some Holocaust thing they had. I'd watched them all over the past few days, at a distance. These people were *doing* things on those faux-marble steps: getting tipsy when sober, refreshed when parched, rinsed when hot, always wetter and wetter. Those steps *accomplished* something; my own steps, I vowed, wouldn't dead-end, either. But what to put on the list?

"O.K.," Allyson said, tossing the book under the bed.

"How're the vampires?"

"Hungry," she said, baring her teeth and looking at where they'd do the most damage, before changing her mind and getting out her clipboard. "Tonight's the costume party and everybody is going to ask you for costume help at the last minute. To cut down on the costume rush, Mike suggests that we see if anybody looks bored today. Then we can suggest getting to work on their outfits. So keep an eye out. The Pearsons bring theirs, of course—they always wear these fancy cowboy things— but most people are going to need all the crepe paper we can spare."

"Who are the Pearsons?"

"The, you know, *older* couple. You don't know everyone's names yet? It's already Day Five."

"I don't know *anyone's* names," I said. "How could I?"

"The *list,*" she said, pinching open the clipboard. "Here's a spare copy. I gave you the list at the first Breakfast Meeting."

She put a piece of paper into my hands and sighed. Outside the palm trees rustled, even the fake ones, like her sigh had travelled all the way to the tourists.

It was a windy day.

"I guess I never got it. Maybe"—here I lowered the sheet a little bit—"you spilled coffee on it."

She tried to look cross and finally smiled. "Maybe I did. In any case, you'd better go over this. You're supposed to call the guests by name, you know. Here, it's alphabetical. The Andersons are that couple, you know, with the fat guy."

"She's his daughter?"

"Oh. I never thought of that. I assumed she was his wife."

"She looks *thirteen*."

"Mrs. Bitburg has three daughters: Jenny, Elizabeth and Wendy, oldest to youngest. You can remember who's who by *Jew*. Jenny, Elizabeth, Wendy. Got it?"

"Jew. Got it."

"Are *you* Jewish, Joe?"

"I used to be."

She smiled. "*Jesus* used to be Jewish. Margot and Lou Giltmore, they're honeymooning. Remember we brought them free champagne the first night?"

"Yes, and I know who Sarah Hackett is, because she made a pass at me."

"Really? The redhead, the one who's—?"

"*Fat*."

"*Joe!*"

"Yes."

"What did she do?"

"She asked me up to her room."

"You know that's not allowed."

"What am I supposed to do? Report her?"

"No, for *you* to—you know, for you to—"

"*Fraternize?*"

"You're smart. Yeah. It's even supposed to be against the rules for, you know, *this,* so watch your—self. Who else have we got? The honeymooning Kleins. Susan Runnon, with the, you know—"

"*Breasts.*"

"Yeah, Joe. Thanks. The other woman is Kristin Timball, and then there's this last couple with a name you will not believe, it's like the book, this is funny—"

And it *was* funny, the wind rising like that and opening the door on an illicit couple like it had done so many times before, curling up the staircase like smoke and hovering over the worn carpet in the staff quarters building until it found the right room. That would only happen, you might think, in a perfect universe, but here on the shiny island it could happen all the time, even when the door was latched, even when the boss was walking by. Allyson togaed the sheet around herself and went to close the door, but Mike was already in the doorway like an armed guard. A guy with a gun. A guy who didn't get the joke. "*Al?*"

"Mike," she said, calmly.

He took another step in. "*Joe?* What are you—the two of you—?"

"*Mike,*" Allyson said, "*Excuse* us, please. Could you close the door?"

He stepped further into the room and closed the door so there were three of us. Two illegal lovers and the whistle-blower. "This is—*Al*, I'm *surprised* at you! *Shocked!* This is—"

"*Mike*—"

"—against *the rules!* Against *regulation!* You're not supposed to, you're not—it's against the rules to—"

"*Mike*—"

"You're not supposed to be doing this," he said, quieter. Allyson gathered the sheet around herself with one hand and put the other one on his shoulder. He shrugged it away. "I *mean* it, Al. It's in the *rules*, for chrissakes." Allyson didn't say anything. "Your primary responsibility—your *sole* responsibility—is to our *guests*. You guys are on duty *twenty-four hours a week*. I *mean* it. A *day*. You *know* what I mean. Deep down you *know*, I *know* you do, and then—*this? This* is *disgraceful*. Al—Joe— you have wronged not our *staff*, but our *guests!* Every last guest depends on you, and *this* is what you do! Joe, you are no longer Al's assistant. Al, you are no longer—*Joe's* boss. You have wronged them, really. I want you to think about that. And get out of here, Joe. These aren't even your *quarters*. This isn't even"—the wind blew the door open again, and Mike slammed it shut, then looked at it and opened it so he could leave—"this isn't even your *room*." *Slam*, but then the door stuck on something. *Slam* again.

"Joe?" Allyson asked me. Only when she put her hand on my shoulder did I see how badly I was shaking. "*Joe?* It's O.K., Joe. We—he'll cool down. You'll see. He's just upset because—"

"He's *right*. We've done those people *wrong*."

"Don't be silly. He and I used to—"

"He's *right*. He's *right*."

204

"He and I used to go *out,* Joe. He's just *jealous.* Can't you tell? He wasn't upset at what he saw, at all. He's just *jealous.* Jealousy will do that to you. Why is this upsetting you so much, Joe?"

I didn't know. My spine, inside, was twitching all wrong, bending backwards like a wire hanger. I was shivering, and my head was ringing with a full-orchestra blare, some operatic soundtrack shaking me cold. The flashes of skin from Allyson's bare shoulders, and my own, were sticking in my eyes but all blurry and underwater. The slide show in my brain was switching from the Glasses to the cops, to the men in the tent and everyone at the bookstore, quick costume changes and curtain calls. The history of doors opening was drowning me. I guess jealousy will do that to you. But even at the bottom of the pool you can see the faux-marble steps, shiny and clean and rising towards the prize. "I was abused. I'm—the door opening like that made me remember, upset me. I'm sorry."

Allyson's eyes widened and she came to me. In some untroubled corner of my mind I could tell this was going to keep me laid. "You don't have to *apologize,*" she said, sheet slipping. "That's *terrible,* Joe. Do you feel like talking about it?"

"Not really," I said. "It's just—when a door opens suddenly like that, or when I see something muddy, anything with a family—"

"It was your *family?* Oh my God."

"It was the *whole* family," I said. "I'm sorry—"

"*No, no.* Don't apologize. I can imagine how upsetting this can be. Joe, I hope you've sought help."

I smiled thinly. "I'm around the eighth step now."

She put both hands on my shoulders so the sheet slipped all the way to her waist. Her breasts were sticking out like they were reaching for my shoulders, too. "I'm very proud of you. I *mean* it. You're surviving so well. This kind of thing can destroy so many people."

I saw the wreckage at the lab. "It *has*."

"That's what I mean. I've read about this, Joe. When your family abuses you it's like—I don't know, but anything can happen, you know? *Anything*."

I took a deep breath. "A monster."

"It *is* like a monster," she said, curling beneath the bed again for the vampire book. "Why do you think people write things like this? I bet it's a what's-it-called, an allegory. It's allegorical. I bet you anything she was abused or something and it felt like a monster was after her. So she wrote about it—"

"But *I'm* the monster," I said. "I think I am, anyway."

"Oh, honey," she said. "*You're* not the monster. You've got the allegorical thing all wrong."

"It's hard to tell," I said.

She hugged me, her breasts like tines against my chest. "I know it is," she whispered. "That's why I'm so proud of you. It's hard to tell, and you told me." She smiled down at my erection and patted it briefly, like a pet that had fetched the wrong thing. "Now we *really* have to get back to work, Joe. Listen, I'll talk to Mike, if that's O.K. with you. I'm sure you can be my assistant again. Can I tell him—?"

"Yes."

"And we're done with"—she ducked beneath the bed again and found my piece of paper. With a start I realized I had been given a gift. Hire Power hadn't let me down; the boss they found for me had given me the eighth step. I'd been trying to make a list all the time and it turned out it was a handout from the

Entertainment Coordinator. Mike had said it: I had wronged all the guests here at The Vast Resort, and here was a list of them, alphabetized and everything like some index of a perfect universe. "We're done with this, right? You know who everyone is?" I took it from her and gazed at it. The Andersons. Mrs. Bitburg and the *Jew* daughters. Giltmores. The horny Hackett. Everyone I'd wronged, all down the alphabet from A to—"Oh, wait. I didn't get to the punch line. Look at the last entry—it's just like that book. Frank and Mimi Zhivago. And he's a *doctor*. Get it? *Dr. Zhivago?*"

It was true. In the cellophane sunshine there was no way you could miss it, the names in neat black ink at the bottom of the page. Zhivago, Dr. Frank. Zhivago, Mimi. I had the allegorical thing all wrong. Cyn, Stephen, Ben: It wasn't *like* they'd been killed by a monster; they had been. I wasn't the monster, not at all; the *monster* was. It wasn't *as if* Mimi, back in the fourth act, had gotten up out of bed and shaken hands with Zhivago over a scene well played; she *had*. Then they'd gone to a resort.

"Yes," I said, back from flashback. "Yes," I said, holding the eighth step in my hands like a life preserver. "Yes." I looked out the window and saw him at once, getting out of the pool and walking on the faux marble. He didn't look like the family doctor, not at all. He *was* the family doctor, and once you knew that, you could trace his path to the silent sunglassed woman propping her book against her bent knees. Once you knew that, it was as easy as climbing stairs, as easy as getting dressed and walking right up to her yourself. "Yes, I get it."

Step 9

My twin reflections blinked at me, one head each in Mimi's sunglasses, drained of color so my faces looked like masks, as I stood over her and waited. Frank Zhivago was over at the half-real palms, getting drinks and chatting with Marco over the roar of the juicer. I just waited for her to feel the chill my shadow was casting over her tan body, and look up.

"Yes?" she said politely, and then looked again. The shades came off; I was unmasked. For a second, Mimi looked startled, but then just disappointed: Oh, it's *you*. Her eyes, her face looked the same as I remembered, except tan. I scanned down her body, glistening in the heat like it had been scorched. Everything looked the same, more or less, or not the same but easily fixable, in my mind: slightly larger breasts, hair back, a sharper chin than the face in nightmares. Of course she looked the same. It hadn't been that long. Yet somehow *I* was disappointed, too, as if I'd expected something else, which I guess was true. When someone's dead you expect you'll never see them again.

"I never thought I'd see *you* again," she said. The juicer stopped. "How are you?"

Years of social systems—the final S in CRISIS—almost made me say "fine." I swallowed but I couldn't think of a word. "Um—"

"Would you like to sit down?" Mimi moved her legs and I found myself sinking to the deck chair like we were sharing a bed. I heard a sharp crackle and I thought maybe my bones were breaking, but it was just my fist, clenching around the list, damp with sweat, of people I had wronged. Now I was supposed to make direct amends. "You're looking good, Joseph," she said, almost conversationally. "You look, um, *good*. Healthy."

"So do you," I said, automatically, and then found a foothold. "Considering."

She blinked and slipped her sunglasses back on. She shifted her legs up towards her, her limbs moving fluid as tide. She extended a curled hand and I thought for a minute she was going to grasp my shoulder, but she was just taking juice. "Thanks," she said to her husband, who was lowering himself into the neighboring chair and opening a spy novel. "Frank, I'm going to go off for a minute with him. We have to—"

Frank Zhivago looked up in mid-sip, his eyes pausing on me briefly. I looked familiar. Oh yes, I worked here at the Vast. "Work on costumes," I said to him, holding up the list, and then frowning and uncrumbling it professionally. "Tonight's the costume party, you know."

"I know," Frank said, and started reading.

"Back in a few minutes," Mimi said. She stood up and wrapped the towel around her shoulders, not because it was cold but, I guess, because it was indecent. I was guessing at everything. We walked through a gap in the trees to a field which later would be "festooned," as Mike had put it, with Japanese lanterns, the better to make last-minute costumes work. Beyond the field was the beach with sand so white it looked vacuumed. A ways down on the shore was what looked like a tiny tan globe, probably the gut of the fat man, Anderson, while his let's-hope-daughter waded topless in the foam like a Venus somebody was trying to throw back. It was as good a setting as any.

"It's so pretty here," Mimi said. "Everything looks *perfect*. How long have you been working here?"

"Not long," I said.

"It's nice," she said, looking around. Out past the exquisite ocean was a thin green line of ink, another island maybe, or the tip of continent we were closest to. "Peaceful. I suppose you're surprised I'm here."

"I'm—I'm surprised you're *anywhere*. You're *dead*, Mimi."

"No," she said simply.

"Yes," I said. "*Yes*. I *know*. I *see* you. But I can't believe—"

"Your own eyes?"

"*—what you put me through*," I insisted. "What—what happened?"

She shrugged, paused, shrugged again. "I don't have to tell you, Joseph."

"But I have to know," I said. "I've been up nights—every night—you won't believe the things I—you owe me an explanation! You owe me—"

"*Nothing*," she said, her face finally clouding over. This at least was something, something else besides descriptions of the scenery. At least she was angry. "I don't owe you anything, Joseph. Not a *thing*. After what I've been through?"

"After what *you've*—?"

"Not a *thing*. Why don't you think about what you owe *me?*" She kicked at the grass and then looked at me firmly. "Think about somebody *else* for a change."

"Just tell me why you left!"

"You *know* why," she said. "You don't have to hear it again."

"I *don't* know! I've been—all this time I've been trying to figure it out! No one can tell me but *you*, Mimi, and *now*, when I've found you, you won't—"

"Because my husband was fucking my daughter, is that what you want to hear?"

210

"*Yes!*" I said, instantly. Exultation and shame slapped me at once, like a flipped coin landing right on its ridge. The world seemed greener, all of it: the grass was brighter and the trees looked better, but the sea had become sickly, the sky all jaundiced and the Anderson girl, turning around to face the shore, exposed alien breasts, miscolored and wrong in the light. "*Yes.*"

"It's what you *always* wanted to hear," she said. "You wouldn't leave it alone."

"I didn't—I never knew if it was true."

"*True?*" she said, sharply. "What did *true* matter to you? What could it matter? You just wanted us to see it! You just wanted—"

"I didn't *know,*" I said. "Everything was—"

"You just wanted to wreck everything," she said quietly. "You think I didn't know? You think you needed to wake me up, late at night in my own house, to show me things I didn't know? You think, after a couple of months up in the attic, you had *news?*"

"I didn't *know.* I didn't—"

"*Selfish,*" she snarled at me. "So *selfish.* You think you were the only one in this family? I planned for *years.*" She began to pace the lawn like something, someone caged. "Saving money. Getting everything set. Getting all *ready.* And you had to—"

"I didn't *know.* I thought I was going crazy."

"You thought *you* were going crazy? What about—"

"I *knew,*" I said, smiling despite everything, "that *you* were going crazy."

"I was *planning,*" she said. "You can't just *disappear* from someone like Ben. The way he—the way he works? He'll *find* you. I was planning to take everyone with me, my daughter, my *son*—"

"Let's talk about your son," I said. "Your—"

"—and then I *couldn't*. You spoiled everything. All that shouting in the hospital, sneaking around at night—"

"Your son you—*fucked*," I said. "We can talk about him."

She looked down. "I *know*," she said. "It was working on *all of us,* don't you understand? Stephen and I were being torn apart by him. He brought so many terrible things into our house. He was *teaching* them—Stephen was *learning* all those terrible things. He started in on Cynthia, too—my *daughter,* Joseph, my *daughter*—so, I—I—*what could I do?*"

"I can think of about a million things," I said, "that you could have done, besides seducing your *son* and faking your own—"

"And *you,*" she said, sneering. "Don't forget about *that. You* and I—"

"It's *different!*" I said. "It's—you're *wrong!* You—you weren't my *family,* for God's sake."

"My point exactly," she said. "We weren't *yours.* We *aren't* yours. You could have left any time, just walked out—"

"So could you."

"*No,*" she said. "*No.* You don't *know,* Joseph. You didn't *know.* You walk in for a few weeks and think you can open everyone's eyes. But you don't know."

"There's nothing," I said, "*nothing* you could tell me that would make this all make sense. No matter what I didn't know. There's nothing you could tell me—"

"And there's nothing I *will,*" she said. "I'm not here to give you answers, Joseph. What could you hear, what could I tell you, that would make sense of this? Of *any* family? I can't tell you anything. I'm trying to get on with my life."

"This is *absurd*," I said. "This is *unbelievable*."

"It's *all* unbelievable," she said. "You could have walked down Byron Circle, Joseph, to *any* house, and knocked on the door and found something ugly you could expose if you wanted to. And I wish you *had. Any* other girl, *any* other family."

"And found *this*?" I cried. "Incest and a secret escape plan and—*no*. Not like this. *Not like*—"

"There's *no* family," she said, "like any other one."

The Anderson girl skipped over to her father and kissed him full on the mouth. His hands went to her green breasts and I hoped that she was his wife after all. "O.K.," I said. "O.K."

"You should have let us be. *Everything* would have been better."

"It—it bothered me—*haunted*—"

"You think *I* wasn't haunted? You think, every day, wandering around with Frank, trying to *relax*, trying to *recuperate*, it doesn't haunt me still? Did you ever, *ever* think of us, Joseph? Think about what *we* wanted, instead of what was bothering *you*? We're *real people*, Joseph. A *family* even, despite everything. This wasn't some opera put on for your own fascination, some drama to thrill you. Did that ever occur to you?"

"No," I said. "It *never* occured to me. Why didn't you tell me?"

"I didn't owe you an explanation," she said. And it was true. I looked down at the perfect lawn, my own feet in Vast uniform sandals, the wet and crumbled list on the ground. *Attempt to make direct amends to the people you have wronged,* the ninth step began. It was too late to leave the house at Byron Circle, but I could leave this lawn.

"I'm sorry." Mimi didn't say anything. The Andersons stopped kissing and lay side-by-side, taking in the sun. "I'm *sorry*."

"Your apology," she said finally, "is not accepted."

"Please."

"No," she said. Her voice was firm now, all mom-like and intractable. "There's no forgiveness here, Joseph, for you or anybody else. I don't think there can be. I'm trying to lead a better life now than the one I was forced into, but I can't erase what's happened. I guess if I can run into you when I'm on a tiny island in the middle of nowhere, someday I'll run into Ben, and Stephen. I'll run into Cynthia. They'll all try to apologize, all of them. But it won't—"

"They won't apologize," I said. "They're *dead*."

Mimi closed her eyes for a second, and I could see her face collapse within, even as her tan skin stayed taut. Just for a moment, one relieving moment, I saw her crumble before the mask went back on. "He killed them, didn't he?"

"Yes."

"Ben—?"

"That *thing* you made," I said.

"What?"

"You *know*," I said. "You don't have to hear it again."

"I *don't* know."

"The thing in the basement," I said. "The *golem,* O.K.? The golem *you* made, Mimi, to attack—"

"That was for the *opera*," she said flatly. I was confusing her. I saw that I had gotten it all wrong again; it was clear as day.

214

The light everywhere was curdling from green to brown, darkening everything. "What are you talking—"

"You didn't make a golem?" I said slowly.

"What? It was a *prop*, Joseph. But what—"

"*You didn't*—you didn't try to make one for *real?*"

"I don't—I might—I don't know, Joseph, I was very upset towards the end. I thought maybe religion—I thought that that charlatan of a rabbi could help me, heaven knows why I thought that—"

"You never—"

"He was always looking down my blouse, but I was *desperate*, I thought maybe I could pull myself through all this with, I don't know—"

"But you *never*—"

"I don't know, Joseph, *yes, maybe, maybe* I talked to him about making a golem, but I was *hysterical*. I don't want to talk about this! I had to work on that thing like everything was normal when I was about to leave, and you, *you* were—"

"*You never*—"

"I *don't know! Yes!* I think that night in the basement I screamed about the golem rising up and killing everybody who harmed me, doing whatever magic spell the rabbi taught me, but he was *nothing!* It was *nothing!* You can't just wear white and walk around a clay body and have everything turn out O.K.! I said to rise up and get revenge but it didn't work, nobody was *listening!*" By now she was crying, her bathing suit heaving like an exercise class. "God wasn't *listening* to me, Joseph!"

"*Somebody* was," I said. "*Somebody* carried out your instructions to the letter."

"*I don't want to talk about this!*" she screamed. "*I don't want to*—I'm trying to move beyond—*I don't want to*—"

"Fine," I said. I tried to turn away from her but couldn't move. The light was growing darker, darker, brown everywhere as dark as earth, as clear as mud. "Don't talk about it—"

"*What happened to my children? What happened to my babies?*"

"You don't want to know."

"*What happened? Tell me what happened!*" Her hands grabbed my shoulders, both of her hands, both of my shoulders, and I came to life. I felt a cold strength surge inside me and I pushed her to the ground, *hard.* She uttered a rough sound as she fell, the sheer physical surprise of pain. When she reached the lawn I could scarcely see her, so muddy was my vision, but I saw the places on her body where my hands had pushed, two darkening bruises of handprints like my palms had been smeared with something, or created, years ago, out of clay. But then I stopped. *Attempt to make direct amends to the people you have wronged,* the ninth step said, *except when to do so would injure them or others.* I made myself step back from her, my knees stiff, my hands clenched.

"He killed them," she said, panting. The towel had collapsed around her, a bedsheet, a costume, a body bag. "He killed them, didn't he? *Tell* me."

"If *you* don't owe *me* an explanation," I said.

Mimi crawled toward me. "*Just tell me if he killed them.*"

I tried to step away but I'd have to step forever. I saw she'd crawl everywhere to find me. I'd had a moment to leave, years ago, but it had passed somewhere in the blur of everything we'd done. "Yes," I said, letting the slipperiness of a pronoun slide whatever pieces she needed into place. What did it matter, anyway? It was all like that: *his* fault, *her* fault, what *he* did, what *she* did, what *I* did. What did *true* matter to me? What could it matter? "Yes. He killed them," I said.

Mimi shook her head like she was trying to get something off her. "No," she whispered. "No."

"I tried to stop him," I said. "I'm still trying."

Step 10

Step 10: *Continue to take personal inventory—*

"You're packing?" Allyson said.

"Yep." I looked at my duffel bag, gaping open like a hungry mouth. What to feed it? Jeans, shoes, toothbrush—I needed to make a list.

"Don't you think it's wrong to just walk out like this on a commitment you've made?"

—and when wrong, promptly admit it. "Yes, I do."

"Joe—"

"I have to go, Allyson. You and I have something—the possibility of something special, *really. Really* special. But—"

"I meant the job."

"But—"

"The *job,* here at Vast. You're supposed to be my assistant, the Entertainment Assistant—"

"Al, I *can't*—"

"—and you're ducking out right before the big party, the night I count on you *most.*"

"Let's just say I don't think I can assist anyone in being entertained tonight, Al."

"*Joe*—"

"I thought *you* might understand," I said. "After I—it was

217

difficult to tell you about it, Al, but I *did*. I thought you'd understand."

"But *why* are you leaving, Joe? You owe me an expl—"

"I *don't owe you anything!*" A pair of empty shoes stomped into the duffel. "I—look, with what happened to me—*with me*—"

"I *know* what happened to you, Joe," she said. She sat beside the duffel; the mattress sagged like something giving up. "And you're getting help, which is *good*. But at a time like this you need your friends around you. You need people to—"

"If I don't leave," I said, "I'm afraid I'll hurt you."

She took my hand. "I think I can make that decision for myself."

I felt my hand curl around hers, harder, harder. I remembered some nature photograph, some silent and powerful snake, some defenseless little creature. *"If I don't leave,"* I said, *"I'm afraid I'll hurt you."*

Al stepped back, snakebit. "You don't mean," she started carefully.

"Yes."

"Joe, if you're really in danger of *hurting* someone, even yourself, I can't in good conscience let you go."

"—to a costume party," I finished for her.

"Anywhere," she said. "Not in good—"

"You're the only one here with good conscience, Al."

"What *happened,* Joe? We were discussing the list of guests and you got up and walked out like you were hypnotized. Then you spent all afternoon working on Mrs. Zhivago's costume, and—"

"Mrs. *Zhivago!*" I shouted. "Mrs. *Zhivago!* Why don't you check on this Mrs. *Zhivago?* Go on, check the Vast records, see if you can dig up her *past!*"

"Don't be—that's *ridiculous!*" she said. "Check the records? We're a *resort,* not some computer spy ring. What is this, some cheap thriller?"

"Yes, unfortunately," I said. "It is."

"What *happened?*" she asked.

"Figure it out yourself." I rolled socks into a tight sphere. "*Einstein.*"

The joke wasn't funny any more. "What *happened,* Joe? Did she—did she say something—that *guest*—"

"She's—part of the family," I said.

"Part of the family that *you*—"

"Yes."

"How can that be? She doesn't look a thing like—"

"It wasn't my family."

She stood up and looked at me. I couldn't; I looked out the window instead. From my window, on the opposite side of the building, you couldn't see the pool, but the *real* tide, with a moon lurking above it, a moon that could be mechanical except the joke wasn't funny any more. If Mimi wasn't dead everything in this perfect universe could have been devised. "Not your—"

"No."

"What do you mean? You *lied* to me about—about—"

"Yes. Well, not really—*yes.*"

"So *nothing* like that happened to you?"

"No."

Her face hardened, and set. I looked out at the moon, the

water below it reflecting light which had left long ago. Nothing would budge. Everything was set in stone. "Why? You made that up—just to get laid, or what?"

"You'd already laid me," I said.

"I don't understand a word you're saying."

"*I have to go,*" I said. "Do you understand *that? All* of you try to help me—you, and Lauren, what's-his-name, the guy from Hire Power—"

"What? Who?"

"—but you *can't.* I'm—*beyond* help. *Far* beyond." I looked out at the moon, a perfect postcard circle. "I'm so far from help that the light from help would take a million years to reach me."

She snorted, then smiled despite herself. "You're—"

"—*crazy,*" I finished for her.

"You *are,*" she insisted. "What am I going to do with you?"

"Let me go."

"Well, not tonight," she said. "You can't—"

"Abandon my job, I know, I know. You don't get it."

"No. You can't *leave,*" she said. "Not unless somebody's private jet is picking you up. We're on an *island,* remember? Out in the middle of wherever."

"There must be a boat for, I don't know, emergencies."

"You're not an emergency," she said, picking up her clipboard from my bedstand. There was a wadded piece of tissue there next to the clock, having mopped up from the last bit of sex we'd had. I couldn't tell if she'd looked at it, too, if she knew what it was. It was hard to tell what anybody was seeing any more. Al looked at me, opened the door and padded down the hallway carpet which was as brown and dark as mud. "You're just a jerk," she called.

I looked down at my limp duffel and realized I couldn't take it anywhere. "Shit," I said to it. "Shit shit shit." I listened to everything forbidden come out of my mouth: "Shit shit fuck shit fuck goddamn fucking fucker. *Shit!*"

Like a ghost Al's voice floated down the hall to me. "You kiss your mother with that mouth, Joe?"

Outside they were switching the lanterns on and a masked, six-piece band was tuning up. Out in the half-light the party would start up with or without me. "Not *my* mother," I said.

Step 11

The band was playing something that told the Japanese-lit guests to take two steps forward, two steps back, but watching from my room I was stepping back further than that. Dance with me, like a partner: back through all the steps I've shown you to the muddled tragedy that brought them on. It's often hard to describe the plot of a book to others, even when it's still going on; you remember the parts you like but those aren't all the parts that happened. And your own family is the book you can't put down. When you live there it's an opera, the scenes you remember: violence, peeping through doors, arguments, meals, everything loud, loud, loud. For years your ears are still ringing. Then you review it again and you realize there must have been quiet parts, too—every opera has them—but where did they go? Like all master criminals they're untraceable. You remember a little wooden box, elaborate and you're pretty sure Indonesian, but there's something else on the coffee table now and your mother doesn't know what you're talking about. Your father lent you a robe, but it's not the one in photographs and, now that you think about it, it might have been your robe all along. You remember huddling in the hospital, all of you together in numb grief, but if you were all together who was in the hospital bed? You can remember their pale and bare legs, the wheezing of the machinery, but the rest slipped past the sightlines while you were watching someone in the orchestra. You were wrong, maybe; *somebody* was. When did the dog die? Where's your favorite little plate? What lie was believed long after the liar forgot all about it? If you didn't remember to make the bed, why are the blankets pulled taut, the sex stains hidden under throw pillows bought at a store that went under years ago? When did he tell you she called, where did those tiny plants go, the ones you grew in Styrofoam cups, when did that cut heal? When did that song slip out of heavy rotation on the radio, into the slang and then into a resort band's repertoire? Bing, bing, bing, everything is re-edited; you know you heard it in the overture but you still didn't expect it in the finale.

The golem is a figure in Jewish myth—sort of a Jewish lie, sort of a Jewish truth. It appears to wreak havoc but really, it'll do anything you say. You don't have to tell it twice. If it tries to speak for itself, the Word of God tumbles out and the golem turns back into clay. It's a monster, sort of, but who isn't a monster occasionally, particularly among family? It moves quickly and quietly, creepily, anywhere you want it to: out of its room, along the edge of the pool leaving muddy footprints somebody will have to clean up, towards the Japanese lanterns it can bring down with one swing of its arm. It moves closer, closer. You don't have to tell it twice.

Marco was ladling out punch into plastic cups with the concentration of a surgeon. I grabbed two and downed them, ignoring his frown. Al was calling something to the drummer over the amplified cha-cha. The lanterns made everybody look pink: the Pearson cowboys, the honeymooning Giltmores dressed in their wedding outfits, the J-E-W daughters all dressed as ballerinas, with a witch for a mom, two other witches who knew each other from work, Mr. Anderson wearing a tin-foil crown and his wife in a Vast gift store tiara, Dr. Zhivago in a cowboy hat he undoubtedly borrowed from the Pearsons, and Mimi, where was—

"Joe?"

I turned around to find Sarah Hackett, alight with punch and having asked me to her room a while back. She was dressed as an opera Viking, her red hair covered by a horned helmet and two long yellow yarn braids, her fat body panelled in tin foil and construction paper. Behind her the king and queen were starting a conga line. "Hi, Sarah."

"Great band, huh? They're going to let me do a number later."

"Well, I don't want to miss that."

"Why aren't you in costume?"

"I was so busy helping everybody *else*," I said, "that I never—"

"I have plenty of costume stuff in my room," she said. "Let's—"

"No," I said. "I have to stay here, Sarah."

"*Really,*" she said. "I gave Mrs. Bitburg all her witch stuff. All the witches are my work."

Just beyond the row of lanterns, towards the sea, I thought I saw a flash of white, like a sheet, a robe. "You must be very proud."

She giggled, then frowned. "Are you making fun of me?"

"I don't have time," I said. I walked around the snaking line of tourists. Al and her clipboard glared at me.

"I thought you had to stay here," Sarah called.

"Have to run," I said. I reached the pink perimeter and saw her clearly: Mimi, walking along the shore towards the Vast canoes, lined up like tools for surgery. It was true: I had to run.

I caught up with her at the foamy edge. She turned to face me before I grabbed her arm.

"Let go."

"Mimi—"

"Let *go!*"

I let go.

"Thank you. Now *leave.*"

"Why? What are you doing here?"

She turned to me, eyes incredulous, incredible. "What am I— I'm walking along the beach, Joseph. It's been a very upsetting day for me, thank you very much."

"For me, too."

The surf ran long, encircling our feet. I felt a soggy chill crawl up me. "That's not my problem, Joseph."

"I don't think we should be alone."

She laughed rough, one syllable: *"Ha!* Then leave."

"I don't think *you* should be alone."

"What business is it of yours?"

"You're the only one left, Mimi."

She looked at me, her face clouding over as the moon did. "What is that supposed to mean?"

That's when the hands pulled us under.

I surfaced choking, kicking at the mud beneath me before I

realized I was lying down in a half-inch of water. "It's O.K.!" I shouted to Mimi, grabbing her arm. "It's O.K.! It was just the surf! Just the surf!"

Mimi stood up, shaking me free. She was soaking. "I *know!*" she shouted. "I *know* it was—what *else* could it be?" She shook herself long and hard, like a large dog. "What are you talking about? Did you—" She stopped and looked out toward the party, covering her mouth. Her eyes grew wider, frightened. I scrambled to my feet and followed her gaze to the long, tall figure, silouetted by the lanterns and striding toward us. "You *led* him here, didn't you?" she said. "You led Ben here to—"

"Ben's dead," I said. Behind me was only the Vast sea, dark and unreadable. There was nowhere to hide. The figure lumbered closer.

Mimi wiped the hair out of her eyes. "Then who—what—?"

Not tall enough, moving too quickly and—if that weren't enough—wearing a cowboy hat, Dr. Zhivago stepped into view. "Mimi?" he asked, taking in the scene: his wife, a young resort employee, alone in the dark and soaking wet. I read once that you can read the end of your relationships in their beginnings; did Zhivago lie awake nights, wondering when his wife would fake her own death to elope with somebody else? "What is happening here?"

"Nothing, Frank," she said. "Nothing." But he stepped closer and *saw;* a miracle he hadn't seen it before, really.

"*You,*" he said, his voice thick with punch and recognition. "*You're—you're—*"

That's when the hand grabbed my shoulder. I turned around: *Al.* One more false alarm and I'd have a heart attack.

225

"You're what's-his-name!" he shouted.

Al blinked, then extended her hand. "Al Einstein."

"Not *you*," he said. "*Him.* He's—"

"Joe," Al said.

"*Joseph,*" I said. "Last Name Changed."

Al looked at the Zhivagos, all clipboard-professional. "Let me apologize for Joseph," she said. "He's been dismissed from The Vast Resort and is leaving first thing tomorrow."

"I wasn't *dismissed,*" I said. "I *quit.*"

"Why don't I take you both back to the party," Al said, "where you can enjoy a complimentary cocktail." She tried to take each of their arms like she wasn't allowed to cross the street. Mimi allowed. Zhivago resisted.

"But what is he *doing here?*" he said. "How did you *find*—"

"He's a *former employee,*" Al said, "who is *leaving first thing*—"

"He's been following us," Mimi said, quietly. "He won't leave us alone."

"I'm sorry about that," Al said quickly. "Look, why don't we go back to the—"

"Why not?" Zhivago said, turning to me. He looked tired; everything did. "Why won't you, Joseph? Just let us live our lives. They're none of your business. Just leave." And then *he* left, or started to, Al and Mimi in tow. After two steps they stopped and looked at me, all of them, as if I should have vanished already. I turned around and looked out to the Vast ocean, thinking they were right, but it turned out *I* was. It turned out, rising from the ocean so large and dark that it stood out even in the moon-covered night, that I was right, and that the one that wouldn't leave us alone, the one lumbering slowly, so huge, with sure and wet purpose toward the shore, wasn't me.

"What is that?" Al said, the only one who didn't know, the only one who had no reason to lie about it. *"What is that?"*

You don't have to move so quickly, not if you're so huge. A few strides will get you there. *"What is that?"* Al screamed again, and the golem swung at me. I ducked in time to escape impact but not the earthy scent, the *swoosh* of air, the cold, cold prick of a few stray drops clinging to those enormous arms. It was real, the scent, the sound, the feel. It had always *been* real, this golem. Mimi had created it, down in the basement, just like I'd always said, and it had followed everyone, hunted them down, strangled them or smothered them or whatever it was that golems did, to get revenge, to obey the wishes of its creator. Mimi wanted it to kill everyone who had harmed her, and here it was: Cyn, Stephen, Ben and now me. Now me, now here. The golem was *now here.* This was real as real could be, as real as this gets.

I ran thickly, my pants soaked with surf. I ran right into the others and we stumbled together, clogged, through the sand toward the party, like some bedraggled caboose to the conga line. I kept looking back at the golem, advancing with silent calm. It walked so easily, acquiring menace with every step. Its stride was muddy, and effortless, almost *elegant* in its surety.

"And now, ladies and gentlemen, as a special treat we have a little preview of the talent show. Performing with our own Vast Orchestra, Ms. Sarah Hackett—" Mike just frowned when the four of us tore into the party. We must have looked like mere rule-breakers. "What—" he started to say, and then he looked past us and saw. The band, already poised, froze further as the guests turned around to see who the party crashers were. One of the witches screamed, but most everybody was silent, caught mid-sip, mid-saxaphone, mid-finger food, mid-vocal debut. The Anderson royals started to smile, knowing of course what it was: some prank, some costume party finale. Even Mike's scream sounded canned, a high feminine scream he might have performed every session, just when the party might be dying and the people were ready for something new. But it wasn't.

The four of us ran toward the guests as the golem reached the middle of the dance floor, and now, bathed in the pink light of the lanterns, everyone could see it was real. A full ten feet of clay, wet but solid, was swiveling slowly toward me, and you could see it wasn't anybody in an outfit, not moving like that, not built like that. Not with a thin slit of unmoving mouth, or with those deep-set eyes, larvae-white and without pupils, blank in their sockets. Not with those enormous arms, raised overhead and toppling the lanterns from their wires. Some of the debris fell onto the table, which folded in on its spindly legs and tipped the punch bowl, a cascade of sugary blood on the floor. Now everyone was screaming. Panicked but frozen, we were screaming and huddling together, and the golem swung an arm and caught the oldest ballerina, sending her careening to the ground, rolling away, her limbs in fourth position, fifth position, unconscious. Nobody had ever been thrown like that, not by a person. This was something bigger, scarier, a monster, a force beyond our control, a Higher Power.

Towering over us, the golem swung at other people who were in the way, the cowboys tossed together, Zhivago punched to the ground, Al hurled amidst a flurry of clipboard paper. And then it reached me—the eleventh step. I closed my eyes tight, *seeking through prayer and meditation to improve my conscious contact with the Higher Power as I understood it*—I felt the damp hands clenched on the scruff of my neck—*praying only for knowledge of the Higher Power's will for me and the power to carry it out. "What do you want? What do you want from me? What do you want from me?"*

The hands went gentle, briefly, and in the pause I opened my eyes. I was slid to the side; I heard Mimi and Mike whimper behind me. The golem's head was tilted toward me, a polite angle, almost deferential, quizzical. *"What do you want from me?"* I screamed again, and the slit of a mouth opened, slowly, the square jaw dropping like an unstuck drawer.

The golem leaned in close and the Word of God tumbled out: *"Nothing,"* he said. He leaned even further, further than you'd think a figure that size could lean, curving past me, over me, moving over me like something being poured from one place to another, dissolving onto Mimi in a wet and crumbly mess. It was magically instant, the golem curling over to suffocate Mimi in a last gesture before disintegration, all over in seconds, and all over *Mimi.* It wanted *Mimi.* The monster didn't want me any more than I wanted the monster. One word and it was over, the weight pouring over her before anyone could move. Mrs. Glass gave one half-scream, and then the mud was upon her and she was mute and finished forever.

Step 12

The golem was done just as everyone else came to life: the groaning cowboys; Al, a sheet of paper in her hair; Marco emerging from underneath the table; the ballerina wailing; Mike wailing; everyone wailing. Dr. Zhivago crawled to the mass of clay and punched at it, his mouth open and mute, but you could hear from the sound of his blows there wasn't any digging her out. The clay was hardened already, ceramic. Somebody dropped their trombone. The mother witch took off her hat, crying; the wig was attached and the whole thing fluttered to the ground. Sarah Hackett stared numbly at the clay, still clutching the microphone. The fat lady never got to sing.

Because it wasn't over, of course. Still isn't. It never is. Within hours some bemused local cops arrived on a tiny little boat but what could we tell them? There were so many versions of the story that eventually the two of them stopped even pretending to take notes. Dr. Zhivago couldn't speak, or wouldn't, just stayed wrapped in a blanket by the palm trees. The clay was absolutely impenetrable to the shovels we had lying around the Vast gardening shed, but after a few days the cops lost interest in digging through it anyway because they couldn't find any record that Frank Zhivago even *had* a wife. I'm sure the mound of clay is still there, even though the brochures I receive— through some perverse twist I'm still on their mailing list, no matter how many times I call—there aren't any photographs of it. But that's hardly surprising. You take a bunch of pictures, but you only put the best ones in. Tiny women swimming. A deserted beach, the canoes lined up like surgical tools. Buffet. The Andersons demanded a refund and got one.

Stories like this happen all the time, and you read about them, but they just slip by in little strips of paragraph at the side of the bottom of the back page of the newspaper. Some town in South America reports a giant snake, swallowing children whole and cows; neither the snake nor the story appear again. They dig up an ancient, undisturbed tomb, and find stereo equipment in it, as inappropriate as a baby in a basket washing up outside the Pharoah's palace. You blink and wait for the next story. A strange weather something is killing all the fish in a lake somewhere. Somebody died, far away, we don't know why. A bored and ambitious reporter might link up the deaths someday, one in Pittsburgh, one in Pittsburg, one up in Oregon and one on an island, but the editor won't O.K. the travel money to go check it out. Somebody might decide to write the biography of a big-shot in the men's movement, and the Andersons will get that knock on the door they've been half-waiting for since that vacation they took a long time ago. But they'll be wrong about where the resort was, and what year they went; the rest will sound untrustworthy, too. And it *is* untrust-worthy; *why*, a reader would say, *if it was so scary and everything, did Joseph manage to sleep with Allyson three more times before he left?*

I don't know why. One day your family is spinning around your head, blurring everything your eyes take in; the next day it's all at rest and you just want to get laid, eat dinner, quit your job, get on with it. It turns out that your life is made of specifics, no matter what you learn at college about Tolstoy: Each family is different, whether happy or unhappy. Their influence melts into you like ghosts, untraceable, imaginary. You can formulate something out of it, if you must; you can force things into a structure like librettists do, telescoping months of action into a four-act-farce, or like therapists do, stuffing all you think into twelve little steps like folded clothes in a duffel. Call it the Old Testament and scribble it on lambskin. But why? The truth just flows under you like a river. You can float on it but you don't know where it's going. The investigation was over and I was free to leave.

They almost took my duffel back off the boat as it idled; I

had loaded my stuff and myself onto it as the Vast boatmen unloaded supplies for the next round of guests and for a second my baggage got confused with somebody else's. If I hadn't noticed in time they would have left me with a large post office box, covered with stamps and the inkings of rerouting. The post office box had travelled everywhere, this baggage, looking for the right spot. If I wanted to fit everything in neatly I would say it was my box of books, finally; they'd caught up with me and I could write my paper, finish my education. But I just looked at Al, standing next to the box, as the boat started up. She wanted me to stay but we'd constructed some sort of truce. Even though she was mad at me, and scarcely said a word, she hugged me briefly and stood there watching as the boat pulled away.

If you need link it all up, you bored and ambitious reader, open the box, there on the shore. If you need it to end like a book let it be the books. It's the books, then, there on the shore, just missing me like people who fall in love at the wrong time, in novels, and have to part from each other at a train station, an airport, a rickety wooden pier. You can imagine me where you want. I felt like my story wasn't over, but you can pretend the twelfth step was already upon me, you can pretend *I had a spiritual awakening as a result of these steps, and have vowed to carry this message to other addicts and practice these principles in all my affairs.* I felt like the river was still uncharted, an unruly Nile, running all over the place the way water just will, but you can sit on its banks and read any story you devise.